The Moment We Began

Books By Sarra Cannon

Young Adult

Peachville High Demons series:

Beautiful Demons
Inner Demons
Bitter Demons
Shadow Demons
Rival Demons
Demons Forever

A Demon's Wrath Part I

Eternal Sorrows series:

Death's Awakening

New Adult

Fairhope series:

The Trouble With Goodbye
The Moment We Began
A Season For Hope

The Moment We Began

Sarra Cannon

THE MOMENT WE BEGAN

Find Sarra Cannon on the web!
www.sarracannon.com

Cover design by Sarah Hansen at Okay Creations
Editing Services provided by Dragonfly Editing

ISBN: 978-1-62421-018-1

To Tonya

You've always been like a sister to me.

I honestly don't know what I'd do without you.

Chapter One

I pour another shot and throw it back, my fingers trembling as I wipe my mouth with the back of my hand. The tequila burns my throat and I squeeze my eyes shut.

I lean against the edge of the sink, my head down as I breathe in and out, trying to steady my heart.

I don't know why I'm surprised. He always does this. Every time I think Mason and I have a real moment—something that gives me hope for a future with him—he does something to prove he's not interested in monogamy.

Why would today be any different?

I look up. My eyes are full of fear. Hurt. Anger. My forehead is wrinkled with worry. Not exactly my best look. I need to get it together. Sure, I've loved this guy pretty much all my life, but I've seen him with other girls a hundred times. They never stick around for long. I'm the only one he keeps coming back to.

I push the air from my lungs, then turn the bottle over again. This is the last of it. No more excuses for hanging out in my stateroom, avoiding the inevitable. I pick the crystal shot glass off the counter, hold it in my hand for a long moment, psyching myself up. With a quick jerk, I down the shot and slam the glass against the granite.

My head swims.

My heart aches.

I want him with everything that I am, but the harder I try to hold on to him, the more violently he pulls away.

I'm so tired of watching him parade these bimbos around like trophies. I'm tired of the anger that consumes me every time he puts his lips on someone else's. And it's always someone else. Someone new.

I don't want to be mad anymore. I don't want to have to pretend I'm not wanting him every single second of every day. I don't want to have to laugh at his stupid jokes and pretend I'm happy when he's with someone else.

I just want to be the one he's kissing.

I close my eyes and think about last night. My fingers run across the softness of my lips, remembering how it felt to be in his arms with his lips on mine. They're still sore this afternoon from kissing him for so long. I kept telling him to shave, but he never did, and I didn't really care. He looks so sexy with that little bit of stubble growing after a couple of days.

I'm smiling at the memories, but the second I think about the blonde he's got upstairs on the sun deck right now, my stomach twists with disappointment and regret.

When he walked onto the yacht, his arm around her, his eyes searched mine for a long moment. I felt it straight down in the core of my heart. He wanted me to understand that he doesn't belong to me. He's free.

Message received, Mason Trent. Loud and fucking clear.

I turn the bottle of tequila over again, but only a few drops fall into my glass. I toss it into the trash can.

I wonder how drunk I'd need to be to stop caring about the girl in his arms.

I wonder if I'm there yet.

Someone knocks on the door to my room, and I study myself in the mirror. I run two fingers under my eyes, sweeping away any stray eyeliner left from when I'd been crying. My eyes are a little red, but I can easily blame the alcohol.

I expect it to be Bailey or Summer or Krystal. Someone coming to get me to tell me to get my ass back to the party.

But when I open the door, my breath catches in my throat and the world around me spins in circles.

"Mason," I whisper.

Chapter Two

Mason's eyes drink me in. He takes his time, his eyes traveling from my newly painted toes upward to the tiny red bikini that barely covers my breasts.

The look is hungry and it awakens an ache deep within me.

"What are you doing down here?" I ask. I want to be unaffected by him, but he caught me by surprise and it takes me a few seconds to recover. "Is someone else babysitting your date for you?"

He swallows, then meets my eyes. He doesn't react at all to my comment about his date. "I came down here for you."

His words take my breath away, and for just the tiniest heartbeat, I think he means he's come to tell me he made a mistake and that he wants to be with me.

But then he follows up with, "Preston asked me to come find you. He wants to know if there's any more champagne.

Trina wants me to make her a mimosa."

I push the hope back down like I've done too many times to count. "Trina?"

He shrugs. "The girl I came with," he says, like it's not a big deal. Like he wasn't just with me in this room—this bed —a few hours ago. "She said she's dying for a mimosa, but Preston can't find the champagne. He thought you might know where there was more."

I straighten my shoulders. "No, sorry," I say. "I think that must have been the last of it."

I'm lying, of course. I know where there's an entire case of champagne in the store room, but I'll be damned if I'm lifting a finger to make Trina more comfortable on my boat.

"That's too bad," Mason says, but he doesn't really look upset. His gaze keeps dipping to my breasts and when he meets my eyes again, I know he wants me.

What I don't know is why he denies it every chance he gets.

For the past year, Mason and I have been playing this game. Push and pull. Love and lose. We'll spend a passionate night in each other's arms, but in the morning, he's always gone. His body says there's something more between us. I see it in his eyes, too. But in a crowd, I'm never the one on his arm. Out there, I'm just a friend.

And that's exactly how he likes it. He wants to have it

all. He tells me he doesn't want to be tied down to any one girl, and how am I supposed to object? If I do, he's not going to change his mind. He's just going to stop being with me.

I can't let that happen. I need him like I need air to breathe.

So if this is how I get him, I have to learn to live with that.

There's a part of me that hates myself for allowing him to hurt me over and over again. I want to be the kind of girl who stands up for herself and takes the high road, but when he looks at me like that with those green eyes, his dark blond hair slightly longer than normal and messy on top, I can't deny him.

He's my addiction.

The one drug I can't ever get enough of.

"Aren't you going back up?" I ask.

He's wearing nothing but a pair of black swim trunks, and I have to stop myself from running my hand across his tanned, muscular chest. He's been working out more than ever and it shows. His abs are perfectly cut and my eyes follow the trail of fine blond hair as it leads toward his waistband and beyond.

"Yeah, I need to get back up there." He says the words, but his feet don't move.

He's several inches taller than me, and I have to lift my

chin to meet his eyes. When I do, his lips part slightly and his breathing speeds up.

I know I should tell him he's an asshole. I should send him away and tell him I never want to see him again. That he's a jerk for bringing a date to a party after what happened between us last night. After he held me in his arms for hours and talked about everything from music to movies to fantasies about the future.

But I can't. I'm powerless when it comes to Mason. I want him any way I can get him.

Even if it means my heart will break a thousand times. I know when he kisses me again, he'll put it back together.

I step forward and place my hand on his chest, just over his heart. It's racing just as fast as mine.

"Kiss me," I say, and he obeys.

He leans down, his lips meeting mine in a fiery kiss. He pushes me back and steps into the room. The door shuts behind him and he lifts me up, pulling me close against him. My legs wrap around his body and he turns, backing me against the door as he crushes his mouth against mine.

I whimper, a throbbing need gathering inside me.

The alcohol and passion mix and I let go of all reason and logic. I don't care about the party upstairs or the girl he brought. I don't care about the fact that he'd rather keep this a secret than tell anyone he's been with me. All I care about in this moment is possessing him.

I move my hands over his body, exploring him as if it's the first time. Or the last.

He moans and kisses me harder, our mouths opening and closing, tasting each other with a furious need. He's holding me up with one arm, but the other hand cups my breast, then travels down and hooks on the string of my bikini bottom. With a swift motion, he unties it on one side, then pushes it aside just enough to give him access.

I lean my head back as his fingers plunge inside me.

He kisses my neck, then bites as he moves his fingers in and out.

"I want you," I say, my voice a gravelly whisper.

I press one hand flat against his chest, following the rock-hard muscles down to his waistband. I tug his swimsuit down, then wrap my hand around his fullness.

He pulls his head back and his eyes meet mine. They are stormy, filled with a dark passion. He's at war within himself, I think, wanting me but not wanting me to have this power.

I make the choice easy for him, lifting my body and positioning him at the edge of my wetness. All he has to do is move his hips forward, but he hesitates for the briefest moment as our warm breath mingles in the space between.

I want to scream at him. I want to know why he's

holding back. What I've done wrong. What I could possibly do to make him fully surrender himself to me.

Instead, I hold his gaze, waiting for him to make the move. To let me know that despite his pulling away, he can't resist me any more than I can resist him.

He enters me all at once, taking my breath away. My nails dig into his back and I move my hips forward. He thrusts hard, slamming my back against the door. My heart beats wildly against my chest and I pull my legs tighter around him, wanting him deeper, harder.

And when he comes, I cry out, clinging to him with my entire body.

Never wanting to let him go, but knowing he won't stay.

Chapter Three

"Will you stay here with me tonight?" I ask Mason as we're heading back up to the sun deck.

He pauses on the stairs, then turns back to me. "You know I can't, Pen," he says.

I want to be able to let it go at that and act happy, but I can't. After a year of being with him in secret, I'm ready for more. But I have no idea how to get it.

I put my hand on his and he pulls away.

"So you just fuck me when it's convenient for you and who cares what I want, right?" I absolutely didn't mean to say that out loud, but it comes pouring out anyway. I blame the alcohol.

"That's not fair," he says.

"Fair?" I feel the anger brewing inside, and I can't control it. I already know I'm in the danger zone, but I can't stop myself. "So what is fair? You think that being with me one night and then bringing someone else onto my boat just a few hours later is being fair to me? Or are we only talking about you, here?"

He glances up the stairs, then walks me back down to the main deck. I can hear voices coming from the direction of the galley, but we're in a small hallway and no one can see us. Just the way he likes it.

"I never promised you more than this," he says. "I have always been open and honest with you about what I wanted, haven't I?"

"Yes," I say. "You've made it crystal clear that you don't want anything beyond a physical relationship with me."

He closes his eyes and runs a hand across his forehead. "You make it sound so cheap," he says. "We both know there's more to what we have than just a physical relationship."

"Then what's the problem?" I ask. I put my arms around his waist, but he pulls me off and steps away.

"The problem is exactly how much more you want," he says, shaking his head. "I love you as a friend, Pen, I really do. I like hanging out, and you know I love the physical part, too, but I'm not looking for a girlfriend. I need to have my freedom right now."

"So many girls, so little time," I say. "I completely understand."

The Moment We Began

He narrows his eyes. "Look, if you aren't happy with this, maybe we need to just stop seeing each other for a while."

A lump forms in my throat, but I push back any threat of tears.

"Is that what you want?"

"I want you to stop asking me for more than this," he says. "I told you a year ago this was the most I could offer. If it's not enough for you, then maybe we should stop."

My memory flashes back to a little over a year ago when we slept together for the first time. It was here on my family's yacht after a party one night. Mason and Preston had decided to stay afterward with me and Bailey. Bailey ended up going home after a couple of hours and Preston passed out in his stateroom on the lower deck.

Mason and I stayed up most of the night watching movies and talking. We'd been flirting more and more over the past several months, but I knew it meant more to me than it did to him. We were playing cards and drinking. It didn't take long before any inhibitions were gone, and the next thing I knew, we were kissing.

He told me up front that he wasn't the kind of guy who falls in love. I told him I was okay with that.

Two days later, he showed up at the beach with another girl on his arm. That's when I realized for the first time that I was in love with someone who would never love me back.

"Maybe we should," I say, and I can't believe the words have left my mouth. Panic shoots through my veins like lightning. I want to take it back, but it's too late.

"Fine," he says. The only sign he gives that he's not fine is a tightening of his jaw.

My heart falls to the pit of my stomach. Can he really let me go that fast? Just like that?

"Great," I say, my voice trembling. I feel the sting of tears, but refuse to let him see that I'm upset. I take a deep breath in and force a smile. "There are a few guys I can think of who will be glad to take your place."

I breeze past him and smile for real when his hands tighten into fists. He doesn't follow me right away, and I don't dare look back.

When I get up to the sun deck, the party is raging. The music is loud and fast and a lot of people are dancing, their bodies grinding under the canopy. Several people are gathered in the hot tub and around the deck. Preston is behind the bar mixing drinks for a crowd of mostly women.

I want to keep walking until my body falls down deep into the water, disappearing beneath the surface, and floating down into the darkest depths. I want to end this pain in my heart.

But instead, I smile and greet my friends and play the

part of a proper hostess.

I slip behind the bar and give my twin brother a hug and a kiss on the cheek.

Preston laughs. "What was that for?"

I shrug. "Just wanted to let you know I love you," I say. "Thanks for mixing drinks."

"Did you find the champagne?" he asks.

I lower my eyes and raise an eyebrow. "For Trina? Do we really want to waste our good champagne on yet another of Mason's temporary amusements?"

Preston makes a face at me. "You've got to learn to let that go," he says. He's clueless about what's really been going on between me and Mason. My brother believes I have some schoolgirl crush on the guy and that it's nothing serious. "What about Braxton?"

I shake my head. "Who?"

"Braxton. The guy mom was trying to set you up with," he says. "He's Danielle Sullivan's youngest son. I guess he's transferring to Fairhope Coastal this upcoming semester."

I stick my tongue out. I need another of my mother's setups like I need another hole in my head. She keeps trying to send me on blind dates with her friends' sons, and every time I say yes, I end up spending the evening at the country club with another boring guy in a suit and tie who wants to talk about my trust fund.

Preston rolls his eyes. "You never know," he says. "This could be the one. You've got to start going out some, Penny. You're too young to be heartbroken over some jerk who can't see how great you are."

I laugh. "He's your best friend. Are you really supposed to call him a jerk?"

"When it comes to you, yes," he says. "Do you want something to drink? I'm going to make a few more, then go see if I can find a date of my own for next weekend."

I stare down at the bar. I most definitely want something to drink. Something strong.

I pick up the bottle of tequila he has set to the side and his eyes widen.

"Oh, no you don't," he says, taking the bottle from me. "You remember what happened last time you drank tequila? You went totally off the rails. I think you should stick to something tame. Like rum or wine."

I snatch the bottle back from him and search for a shot glass.

"I don't remember," I say.

I pour myself a shot, down it, then pour another.

"Not remembering is the whole point."

Chapter Four

I wake up hot.

The sun is beating down on my back and sweat trickles along the side of my face. I open my eyes, then close them against the bright light of the morning sun. Or at least I think it's morning.

I sit up and there's a sucking sound as I peel my skin off the couch.

My head throbs and my throat is so dry, I can hardly swallow.

I'm still out on the sun deck of the Opportunity, my parents' yacht. The place is trashed. Plastic cups litter the deck. A half-eaten pizza is smashed against the wooden deck. Wet towels are strewn across everything. Trash cans overflow with beer bottles and paper plates.

I stand and walk down the steps to the salon. I open the mini-fridge looking for water, but it's empty. I go down to the main deck and grab one from the fridge in the galley, downing half of it without taking a breath.

I can barely remember what happened last night. I remember drinking. I remember dancing on top of the table with Krystal. I cringe as I think I might remember taking my bathing suit off in the hot tub. I have no idea how the night ended or how everyone got home, but I do remember seeing Mason leave with the blond he'd brought along.

Just thinking of them together makes me want to run to the bathroom. My stomach turns over and I sit down and put my head between my legs until it passes.

When I come back up, I see the digital clock above the TV and my heart skips.

Shit.

It's Sunday.

My parents are going to kill me.

Sunday morning brunch is our family tradition. Rain or shine, we are all supposed to show up for brunch on Sundays at eleven.

I've been late three weeks in a row, and I'm going to be late again.

I run to my stateroom and search my bag for a change of clothes. I jump in the shower and quickly wash the stink of tequila off my body, then brush my teeth and try to make myself presentable. Bloodshot eyes stare back at me in the mirror. I scrabble in my bag for the eye drops and blink as I drop them into my eyes.

My dark brown hair is wet from the shower, so I pull it up into a French twist, securing it with a pearl clip. I dust my cheeks with some light pink blush, sweep some brown eyeliner around my eyes, and pray it's enough to keep me from looking too hung-over.

I toss my red bikini into my bag and throw on a simple black tank top and my cutoffs. I know mom prefers for us to dress up for brunch, but this is all I brought with me on the ship and there's no time to sneak up to my room before they start.

If they haven't started eating already.

I hurry off the ship and toss my bag into my Audi, then floor it all the way home.

It's eleven-thirty by the time I pull through the security gate and into the driveway of my parents' house. I rush into the dining room, but no one is there. I finally find them by the pool out back, their plates full of fresh fruit and omelets.

Mom stands when I appear. She hugs me tight. "You're late," she says. "I was worried you weren't going to make it."

"Sorry," I say, not bothering to remove my sunglasses. Since we're outside, maybe I can get away with leaving them on.

"How many weeks in a row is that?" Dad asks. He doesn't get up so I cross over to him and give him a kiss on the cheek.

"A couple," I say. "But I'm here."

I sit across from Preston. He looks almost as hung-over as I am. Our eyes meet over the table, like we're partners in crime. A smile pulls at the corners of his mouth as he takes a large bite of his eggs.

"I think it's more than a couple," Dad says. "I'm really disappointed in you, Penelope. You were always the responsible one, and now I feel more and more like you're being careless. What were you two doing up so late? Preston said you stayed on the boat again."

I nod and say thanks to Flora as she brings a plate for me. The omelet is cooked exactly the way I like it—with goat cheese, strawberries and spinach. "Can I get some coffee, too, please?"

"Yes, Miss Penny," she says.

"I did," I say. "I didn't want to bother driving home when I was so tired."

This is a lie, of course. And not a very creative one.

"I hope you left it in good shape," he says. "I invited some of our friends to take a cruise this afternoon down to Sea Island so they could take a look at the development of the new hotel."

The Moment We Began

I nearly drop my fork. I look up at Preston and he makes a face.

What am I supposed to tell him? That the place is completely trashed? He'll kill me.

"What time is that?" I ask, trying to keep the panic out of my voice.

"Probably around three," he says. "It depends on when the Benson's can get down here."

Flora brings my coffee and I load it up with cream and sugar, then drink it down like it was water.

"I need to run to the restroom," I say. "Please excuse me."

I take my purse with me and slip into the downstairs bathroom. I search my phone for someone who might come in on a Sunday for a little extra cash. If Dad's friends are coming in three hours, I might need two or three people cleaning to make it look decent.

I make a few calls and finally, after offering a stupid amount of money, someone takes the job.

I head back out to the pool and Preston's eyes meet mine. I nod and his shoulders relax. Our parents don't seem to notice any of this.

"How was your week, Penny?" Mom asks. It's the same question she asks me every Sunday morning. "Are you excited about school starting back in a few weeks?"

Words cannot express how very not excited I am about school starting back. I'll be a junior this year at Fairhope Coastal University, and the only thing that excites me about that is only having two years left instead three.

"Of course," I say, because you're supposed to tell your parents you're excited about school. "And my week was great, but next week is going to be better. Leigh Anne's coming back tomorrow."

"How are things going for her with the lawsuit?" Dad asks.

A few weeks ago, my best friend Leigh Anne came forward with the fact that she was raped while at college up in Boston. What's worse, the guy who raped her is a famous movie star named Burke Redfield. The media had a field day with the case when it was first brought up, but after several more victims stepped forward, the evidence against him was undeniable.

"Really positive, I think," I say. I've been doing my best to keep up with what's been going on while she's been in Boston the past few weeks. "The big news now is that the university finally voted to suspend Burke pending the trial."

"That's definitely a step in the right direction," my father says. He tried to help Leigh Anne cover it all up for the sake of protecting her family's image, but I think he was really proud of her when she stepped forward anyway, and told the truth. I don't think he's ever been that proud of me before.

Flora refills my coffee, then offers pancakes.

"I'll take a couple," Preston says.

"Me too," Dad says. "Penny? You want some. They're your favorite."

I wrinkle my nose. "I can't eat that stuff anymore, Dad."

My mouth waters at the thought. Pancakes sound a hell of a lot more appetizing right now than eggs, but I can't afford it. It took me forever to get this weight off, and there's no way I want to go back to being fat.

Dad laughs and shakes his head. "You look beautiful no matter what, sweetheart. You shouldn't worry so much about having one or two pancakes here and there."

"You have to say that because I'm your daughter."

"I still mean it," he says, then winks at me.

I push my food around my plate as they talk about work and the plans for an upcoming charity ball to raise money for one of Mom's pet charities. I try to pay attention, but my thoughts keep coming back to Mason. How could we have shared such a passionate moment and then five minutes later, called things off entirely?

I feel sick just thinking about it. It would be a lot easier if I just didn't have to see him again for a while, but he's my brother's best friend. He's in my life, no matter what, so I know I won't be able to avoid him. Not without avoiding my brother and all our friends, and there's no way that's going to happen.

We're supposed to have a get-together at Leigh Anne's boyfriend's bar on Friday night. Knox wants to throw her a welcome-home party. He said she's been lonely in Boston and that it's been a really emotional time for her. He plans to close the bar early so that we can have a private party to welcome her home. She's a real town hero these days, and even though I want nothing more than to celebrate with her and tell her how happy I am to have her home, there's also a part of me that's jealous of her and what she's found with Knox.

He's perfect and sweet and you can see by the way he looks at her that he's head-over-heels in love. He'd do anything for her.

I wish more than anything that I could find a guy who looks at me that way.

For as long as I can remember, I've wanted that guy to be Mason. How many times does he have to hurt me for me to realize it's never going to be him?

"Penny?"

I look up. I have no idea what they've been talking about. "Yes?"

"What are your thoughts, sweetheart?"

24

The Moment We Began

"On what?"

Mom breathes in, then lets it out in a long sigh. It's her best disappointed sigh, and it isn't lost on me. "For the charity ball? Should we go with a black and white theme again this year? Or is that overdone?"

"I think it's classy," I say, because I know that's what she wants me to say. The truth is this town could use a little color. Everything stays the same around here, year after year. "What's overdone is the charities you keep patronizing. Why don't we start a fund for the children's hospital? Or the homeless shelter here in Fairhope?"

"Penny, we've been over this a thousand times," she says. "If we start giving money to every person in this town with their hand out, we'll have everyone knocking on our door."

I press my lips together and close my eyes. How can she be so blind to the problems right here in our own town? "These people don't have their hand out because they're greedy, Mom. There are a lot of children in Fairhope who don't eat three meals a day. Or even two. Wouldn't you rather give directly to the local organizations where we can really make a difference, than these big foundations that spend money on office space in New York and trips to the Caribbean."

"Drop it, Penny," Dad warns.

"I was simply asking for your opinion on the theme of the party," Mom says. "Not the charity. I'm just wondering if we should spice it up a little this year. Maybe it's time for a change."

I bite my lip, then take another sip of my coffee. Maybe it really is time for a change.

The only thing I'm more tired of than trying to convince Mom to change her mind about supporting local charities is the constant pain I feel when I think about Mason Trent. If I can't change one, maybe I can change the other.

"Mom?"

"Yes, dear?"

"You know that guy you were trying to set me up with," I say. "What was his name? Brandon?"

"Braxton," she says. Her eyes light up and she sits up a little straighter. "Did you want to meet him?"

"Can you see if he's free Friday night?" I ask, thinking of the get-together for Leigh Anne at the bar.

This time Mason won't be the only one bringing a date. I want to show him exactly what he's missing by letting me go.

Chapter Five

Preston stops me on my way up to my room.

"How are you feeling?" he asks. "Do you even remember what happened last night?"

A sick feeling rolls around in my stomach with the eggs. "Not all of it," I say. I turn and keep going up the stairs toward my room. "Why?"

Preston follows me, taking the stairs two at a time. "Penny, you were out of control. The whole party got out of control."

I keep walking, not really knowing what he's expecting me to say. I'm sorry? I can't remember a damn thing?

"Hey, you need to be careful," he says, grabbing my arm. "I'm assuming you found someone to come clean up the boat, but what happens next time when Dad actually shows up to take his friends out in the morning and you're lying there passed out and the place is a complete mess?"

I pull my arm away from him. He has no idea what I've been going through lately. And I'm not in the mood for a lecture. "I wasn't the only one out there partying yesterday," I say. "You invited just as many people as I did, and you were the one pouring alcohol down everyone's throat, so don't lecture me about being careful."

I turn and push the door to my room open.

My room is more like a suite of rooms, really. It's like having my own apartment inside the main house. My parents built this for my sixteenth birthday. It involved tearing down a few walls and re-imagining the whole space, but I love having a large suite all to myself. And right now, I don't really want Preston in it if he's going to make me feel bad about last night.

We walk through the foyer and into the living room. I set my bag down on the table and slide my sunglasses up on top of my head.

"Our parties on the boat never used to get that wild," he says. "It got way out of control. I finally had to ask for Knox and Jeremy and a couple of other guys to help out with getting everyone off the yacht and home safely. You can't blame me for that. I wasn't the one who brought out six extra bottles of tequila and started inviting people to do body shots."

The Moment We Began

I bite my lip and turn away. Did I do that?

I honestly have zero memory of getting more alcohol out of the store room. If Dad finds out, he's going to be pissed. He usually keeps that stuff under strict lock and key and we know not to mess with it if we're having people over.

Preston walks around so he can see my face. "Penny, you know I love you more than anything in the world, but this shit has to stop," he says. "I don't know what's gotten into you, but it's like every weekend you're so drunk you barely remember your own name."

I cross my arms and shake my head. "You're exaggerating," I say. "It hasn't been that bad. This is the first time I've had anything to drink since Leigh Anne left. That was weeks ago."

"Yes, but before that you had several nights when you were out of control," he says. "It's like all of a sudden this summer, you're the ultimate party girl."

Is he really giving me crap about partying too much? "This, coming from the guy whose apartment was crowded with party after party your entire sophomore year in college?"

"Look, I'm not saying we can't have parties and have a good time. I'm just saying to tone it down a little bit. Be more careful," he says. "I'm worried about you."

I look up toward the ceiling and put one hand on my hip. "Well, I appreciate the concern, but I'm doing fine. I just want to have some fun, that's all."

I'm lying to him, though. And maybe a little to myself. If he knew how messed up I felt over Mason, he'd understand. Sometimes I just need to get him out of my head and have fun for a little while.

If I stayed sober at all these parties, I'd have ended up stabbing one of his fake girlfriends by now.

"Fine," I say when he makes no move to walk away. "I'll cool it down for a while. I'm going out with this guy, Braxton, probably next weekend. We'll go to dinner then go to Knox's bar for a while. It'll be very calm and tame and I promise I'll be on my best behavior. Besides, it's only a few weeks until school starts back and I have to start getting up early for class again."

Preston comes over and wraps me into a bear hug. "Okay," he says. "I just want you to know I'm looking out for you."

"Thanks," I say, hugging him back. "But I really can take care of myself. I promise."

He leaves and I take my bag into the bedroom and turn out all the lights. I close the blinds and slip off my shoes, then lay flat on my bed in the cool darkness.

I know it was a close call with Dad today. He's already

upset with me for showing up late to family breakfasts, and I'm sure it wasn't hard to tell I was hung-over this morning. But it all worked out in the end and the boat will be clean for him and his friends. No big deal.

Preston's just overreacting about nothing. I'm doing fine. I just wanted to have some fun, that's all.

And body shots sound fun.

I only wish I could remember it.

My head is still pounding, so I take a couple of aspirin and lie back down, grabbing my cell phone out of my purse on my way back to the bed. I crawl under the cool, silky covers and dial Mason's number.

His voice mail picks up after a couple of rings and my heart sinks. A couple of rings means he saw my name and declined the call. I hang up without leaving a message, then toss my phone aside and close my eyes.

By the time I wake up, the sun has already gone down and the night, like my heart, has resolved itself for darkness.

Chapter Six

At noon the following day, I step inside the neonatal care unit of the Fairhope Children's Hospital.

Nurse Valerie's eyes light up. "Penny. I'm so happy to see you today," she says.

"Got any babies I can snuggle for a little while?" I ask, washing my hands.

She smiles. "Always."

I walk into the nursery with her and she carefully lifts a small baby boy from his crib. He's swaddled tight in a soft linen blanket. I sit down in one of the rocking chairs and she hands him to me.

"He's so tiny," I say. His skin is so pink and wrinkly. "When was he born?"

"About a week ago," she says. "We missed you last week."

I frown. "I know. I had to go to Atlanta for a couple of

days with Mom," I say. "What's wrong with this little guy?"

I unwrap his swaddle and draw him close to my body, warming him. It's part of the Kangaroo care here. There are almost always babies here who need someone to rock them and hold them. There's proof that babies grow stronger when they're held more, but sometimes their mothers aren't always able to be here.

I volunteer as often as I can, but it's never enough.

"He was born about three weeks premature," she says. "His name is Isaac."

"Hello, Isaac," I say, staring down into his sweet little face.

"He's a strong boy, though. The doctors say he's going to be just fine."

I look around the unit and see an even smaller baby inside an incubator. "And him?"

Nurse Valerie's mouth twists down. "He's not doing as well," she says. "He has a heart condition. He's fighting for his life every second of every day."

I swallow, a lump forming in my throat. "Isn't there something they can do?"

"Surgery," she says. "But it's expensive and his parents don't have the insurance coverage or the money to pay for it."

"How much?" I ask.

The Moment We Began

This is exactly the kind of thing my mother forbids me to do. It's not that she's completely heartless. She does a lot for charity and I'm sure the money does a lot of good somewhere. I just think we should be doing a lot of good here, in our own community.

"Five thousand dollars," she says. There's hope in her eyes when she looks at me.

I know she would never come right out and ask me for money, but how could I turn away from this sweet baby and not help?

"I'll see what I can do," I say. "When do you need it?"

"As soon as you can," she says. "The earliest the surgeon could do it would be next week. If we don't get it scheduled, though, it might get pushed out even farther, and I'm just not sure he'll hang on that long."

"See if you can get him on the schedule," I say. "I'll get you the money by Monday."

Her eyes tear up and she sets a soft hand on my shoulder. "You are a saint, Miss Penny."

I shake my head. "I am a sinner," I say. "Trust me."

She smiles and wipes at the corners of her eyes.

An hour later, I'm walking back into my parents' house when my phone buzzes in my purse.

I'm home! Heading to Brantley's.

I shriek and run back out to my car. Leigh Anne's home!

Brantley's is the local steakhouse where Leigh Anne works. I'm dying to see her. We've talked on the phone a few times since she left for Boston, but she hasn't had a lot of extra time to chat.

"Where are you running off to?" Preston asks. He's coming home just as I am about to leave. His car is parked next to mine in the garage and he's standing with one arm propped against the frame.

"Leigh Anne's home," I say.

A brief shadow crosses his face. It's so slight, no one in the world but me would probably have noticed it. But I noticed.

I pause, keys in hand. "I'm sorry. I wasn't thinking."

He shakes his head, acting tough. "Don't worry about it," he says. "I'm glad she's home. Tell her I'm hoping to stop by on Friday if I can."

"I'll let her know."

I give him another sympathetic look. I can tell he's bothered just by the thought of her. He really did love Leigh Anne, but he was the one who screwed it up back in high school when he cheated with one of our best friends. I understand what it feels like to be heartbroken, though. Even if it's your own fault, that doesn't make it hurt any less.

"Are you going to be hanging out here for a while?" I

ask. "Or are you heading back to your apartment this afternoon?"

I still live at home, but Preston has his own place.

He shrugs. "Not sure. I thought I might hang out in the game room for a while. There's absolutely nothing else going on today."

"Okay, well if you're still here when I get back, maybe we can watch a movie or something," I say. "Just the two of us."

He gives me a look, and I know he sees right through me. "I don't need your pity," he says. "I'm happy for her. Really."

"Fine," I say, eyebrows raised and head turned to the side. "Don't watch a movie with your twin sister who loves you more than life itself. I don't care."

Preston laughs and rolls his eyes. "Just go," he says. "You're making it worse."

I laugh and get in my Audi. It only takes me a few minutes to get to Brantley's. It's possible I was speeding most of the way there, but this car has a mind of its own sometimes. If I go slowly, it taunts me. Luckily, I have yet to get pulled over. Dad would kill me.

I park and run inside, cringing slightly at my reflection in the glass doors as I pass through the entrance. I look like a bum in shorts and a tank top, but I didn't want to waste time changing.

Luckily, the restaurant is dead except for a cluster of servers at the bar. I rush up and practically tackle Leigh Anne, who is sitting in the center of the cluster.

"Oh, my God, I'm so glad you're home."

She hugs me back and a few of the people who were standing around walk back toward the kitchen.

I finally pull away and take a seat at the barstool next to hers. "When did you get in? Just now?"

"Yes," she says. "Jenna threatened death if I didn't stop by here first."

"I heard that," Jenna shouts from the door of the kitchen.

"Well, you did," Leigh Anne shouts back.

I look over and see Jenna carrying a tray of food out toward the main dining room. She's got the sleeves of her white shirt rolled up and most of her arms are covered in tattoos. Her white-blonde hair is parted in the middle and braided on both sides.

I've only hung out with her a few times, but she seems really fun. I invited her to a couple of parties on the yacht and at Preston's apartment while Leigh Anne was out of town, but she never showed.

"What's her story?" I ask Leigh Anne. "She never comes to any of my parties."

The Moment We Began

Leigh Anne shrugs and turns back to her drink. "I'm honestly not sure," she says. "She hasn't told me much about her past except that she transferred here from some school in Macon."

I turn to the guy at the bar. Colton. He's a cutie with his shaggy brown hair and piercing blue eyes. "You hang out with her a lot, right?"

He looks up from the set of glasses he's cleaning. His mouth drops open, like I've just caught him doing something naughty. "Sure," he says. "We're friends."

He stumbles over the word friends, then looks longingly toward the dining room. My stomach feels heavy when I see that look. I know that look, because it's exactly the way I look at Mason. Colton must have it bad for Jenna, but from the sadness in his eyes, I'm not sure she feels the same way.

I want to tell him I feel his pain, but I barely know this guy. And I certainly don't want to confess to a stranger that I'm in love with a guy who doesn't love me back. Not exactly a good conversation starter.

"Has she mentioned to you that I invited her to a few parties lately?" I ask.

He shakes his head. "Not that I remember, why?"

I sit back and pout. "People don't usually turn down invites to my parties. I wonder why she didn't come?"

Leigh Anne takes another sip of her sweet tea. "Maybe

she was working those days."

"Maybe," I say, watching as Jenna comes back toward us. She winks as she disappears into the kitchen. "Maybe she doesn't like me."

"Not possible," Leigh Anne says.

I smile and shake my head. "Thanks, but you're crazy," I say. "I bet there are a lot of people in this town who don't like me. They still usually come to my parties, though."

"Speaking of parties, Knox told me a bunch of us are getting together Friday," Leigh Anne says. "Are you coming?"

"Of course," I say, turning back to her. "And I'm bringing a date."

She raises an eyebrow. "Oh? Anyone I know?"

"Nope." I lean over and grab a menu from behind the bar. "Just another one of my mom's fix-ups."

Leigh Anne laughs. "Hopefully this guy will be better than the last one," she says. "That guy was weird."

I twist my nose up. "Don't remind me," I say. "I might have gotten over the fact that he was only five-foot-five if he hadn't spent the entire evening bragging about his extensive coin collection. He even asked me if I was going to inherit any coins along with my trust fund. Seriously? I felt like he was only on a date with me to scope out the potential for good loot."

40

The Moment We Began

Leigh Anne is laughing uncontrollably. "I honestly don't know how you managed to finish dinner," she says. "How could your mom have thought you would actually like that guy?"

"Because his parents are the right kind of people," I say. "That was literally the only thing she knew about him before she set us up."

"She's ridiculous. I can't believe you're actually letting her set you up again."

Colton scoots a Dr. Pepper toward me, and I'm impressed he remembered that's what I drink without me even having to ask. I tell him thanks, then turn back to Leigh Anne after he walks away. "I'm desperate," I say quietly, taking a sip from my straw. "I can't handle another night where Mason has a hot date and I'm all alone."

I swallow and stare down at my hands. I'm not telling her the whole truth. She has no idea Mason and I have been sleeping together for the past year, and I have no idea what she'd say if I told her.

Okay, well, I have a little bit of an idea.

She'd probably tell me I'm stupid for letting him treat me like this. That I'm only setting myself up for heartache. That if he can't commit to a real relationship with me, he doesn't deserve to have sex with me either. But I already hear those things in my head. I don't need someone else

41

confirming it or making me feel worse about it.

Leigh Anne's the queen of doing the right thing, lately, which only makes me feel like crap for doing all the wrong things.

She leans toward me until our shoulders are touching. "He's an asshole," she says.

I nod, but something deep inside my heart protests. Yes, he acts like a dick sometimes, but there's more to him than most people get to see. When he isn't around a crowd or trying to push me away, he's really kind of amazing. Funny, sweet, understanding. There are moments when I think he gets me more than anyone else in the world. Even more than my own twin brother.

But every time I catch a glimpse of how good we could be together, he slams a door in my face.

"Are you okay?" Leigh Anne asks.

I look up, realizing I've been staring into the bubbles of my drink for the last few minutes. I didn't even realize her food had come. "I'm fine." I force a smile. I feel like a selfish jerk for talking nonstop about my own problems when she's been through so much lately. "Tell me all about you and Knox and the cute babies you plan to make someday."

She laughs and hits my shoulder, but when I look over, her eyes are shiny and happy.

And for some reason, I suddenly feel very much alone.

Chapter Seven

"This is the one," Leigh Anne says.

She takes a black dress from my closet and holds it up against my body. I don't even recognize this dress. I take it from her and see the tags are still attached. I shudder. This has to be one of the many dresses my mother bought me back when I was twenty or thirty pounds heavier. She would hang them up in my room and when I'd insist it wouldn't fit she'd always act surprised, like she had no idea I couldn't fit into a size five.

I've never worn a single one of those dresses. I used to stare at them and binge on chocolate.

"You don't think it's too dressy?" I don't want to tell her why I hate this dress.

Leigh Anne shakes her head and stands back. "I think it's perfect," she says. "Try it on."

I stare at the dress. What the hell?

There's only so long a girl can hold onto pain before it becomes so heavy she can barely stand up anymore. Tonight is for trying new things and letting go of the pain of the past. I shrug and slide my current dress down. Underneath, I'm wearing the sexiest underwear I own. A very dark pink lace bra and panties I bought in Paris last year. Thigh highs with a garter. I'm going all out. If Braxton gets far enough to see it, he'll be the first since Mason.

Then again, what are the odds he will get that far? I've only had sex with two guys besides Mason, and neither one was very impressive. Mostly, I was just trying it out to see if sleeping with them would make me forget that the guy I really wanted didn't want me.

It didn't.

And once I finally did get a taste of the one I wanted, I knew I was ruined for every other guy on the face of the earth.

The thought of never being with Mason again makes me want to forget this whole night and crawl back under the covers.

Instead, I pull the black dress over my body. It's snug and there's no zipper, but the soft fabric has a little stretch to it. Leigh Anne rushes over to help me pull it into place.

"Wow," she says, her eyes wide.

The Moment We Began

I turn to look in the mirror and have to agree. It's gorgeous. It fits me perfectly.

Turns out not bingeing on chocolate might have actually been worth it for a change. Maybe.

"Braxton is going to flip out," Leigh Anne says.

I groan. "How will I know if he's really flipping out over me, or if he's just flipping out over the thought of my parents' money?"

Leigh Anne sits down on the bed. "Is that really what you think about every guy you go out with?"

"What? That he's probably after my money?"

"No," she says. "That he'll like your money more than he likes you?"

I bite my lower lip and turn to the mirror again. I lift up on tiptoes, trying to picture which shoes will look best with this dress and trying to ignore what she's saying.

"Even if you were poor, you'd still be just as beautiful," she says.

"Would I?" I pull the tag off the dress and hand it to her. "If I were poor, I wouldn't be wearing a $1200 dress that's been sitting in my closet for four years."

I don't mention how much the underwear cost.

Leigh Anne crumples the tag. "The dress is great, but it's the girl wearing the dress that's special. You need to learn to see that for yourself or you're never going to be happy."

I shake my head. There's no use arguing with her. She just doesn't understand. No one knows what it feels like to be Tripp Wright's only daughter. I can't really complain to anyone about it, because all they see is the money and how fortunate I am to have all these things. If I complain, I look like an ungrateful bitch who doesn't realize there are starving children in Africa or something.

Still, I know better than anyone that a lot of my relationships are based on money. If I lost everything tomorrow, I bet there are a lot of people I'd never hear from again.

I come to sit down beside her on the bed. "Enough about me, I can't believe I haven't had a chance to talk to you about the trial. I didn't want to bring it up at the restaurant with everyone standing around. What's been going on? How was your trip to Boston?"

I couldn't believe it when I first found out about what happened to her in Boston. At first, it really hurt my feelings that she hadn't told me earlier, but I was so proud of her when she stepped forward and told the truth. Life has been tough for her since then, but I have seen so much more of my old friend again lately, and I think that means she's healing. I don't think it's ever the kind of thing you get over completely, but it's good to see her laughing again.

The Moment We Began

Knox is a big part of that. Who knew he was such a sweet guy? I always thought he was just a loner, or a loser. Goes to show you really can't judge someone until you've walked in their shoes.

"It's been really hard," Leigh Anne says. "I was really happy so many other girls stepped forward to tell the truth, but just going through the whole re-telling of it so many times has been exhausting. I think I've told the story at least twenty different times now to different lawyers. I just want to be able to move on."

I put my hand on hers. I have no idea what to say to her. I know nothing will take it all away or make it any easier. "It won't last forever," I say, but I know I sound stupid. "And once it's over, he won't be able to hurt anyone like that again."

She gives me a small smile and squeezes my hand. "I know. It's just going to be a while before it's all over," she says. "At least the media never really covered Knox's past like we thought they would. It could have been such a nightmare."

"The whole time he lived here, everyone whispered all these stories about how he killed someone or beat the shit out of someone and spent years in jail, but no one had any idea what kind of crazy shit he'd been through," I say. "I still can't believe it, to be honest. It sounds like something out of a movie."

Knox's father, a very rich and influential man in Chicago had called the police one night and had Knox arrested for beating his step-mother. Knox went to juvenile detention for two years for that, but it turned out he was never the one who hit her. It had been his dad all along. Apparently, his step-mom eventually got fed up with it and shot the asshole one day when he got home from work.

That woman's my fucking hero. I wish I had the balls to go shoot the guy who raped my friend.

"Why do you think the press left it alone?" I ask her.

She shrugs. "Knox thinks it's because so many of us came forward," she says. "If it had been just me, the media might have crucified me, saying I had a history of making bad choices, but with so many victims coming forward, I think it became pretty obvious that Burke really is a rapist asshole. Suddenly the coverage switched to our side and they started pulling all of his skeletons out of the closet."

I snort. "Thank God for the fickle whims of the American Media."

She laughs. "You're telling me," she says. "Anyway, most of the other victims have given their affidavits and a new set of charges have been filed. Now we're just waiting for a court date. The attorney thinks it could be as soon as December."

The Moment We Began

"That's not too bad," I say. "Did you decide for sure what you're doing about school starting back?"

She'd been trying to decide between going back to school in Boston or enrolling here at Fairhope Coastal.

"Knox said he'll come with me if I decide to move back to Boston," she says. "But I haven't really decided what I want to do. Up there, the trial will be my life, you know? Plus, Burke still lives there, even if he's not allowed to go to classes. The last thing I want is to be running into him every day."

"I still cannot believe six women from the school accused him of rape and it took the administration this long to suspend him. What kind of bullshit is that?"

"I know, it's disgusting," she says. "They kept saying he hadn't been convicted of anything."

"Yet."

She smiles. "Yet. Anyway, this conversation is a downer," she says. "Let's talk about your date with Braxton tonight. What shoes are you going to wear?"

I look at her and smile, wanting to tell her just how impressed and how proud I am of her. How much I wish I could be like her. Instead, I just wrap her up in a huge hug and pull her toward the closet to help me pick out shoes.

Chapter Eight

Braxton pulls up to the gate at exactly seven on the dot.

He's driving a black Escalade with tinted windows, so I can't get a good look at him through the security cameras.

Mom is pretending not to be interested, but she's walked by me about six times in the last ten minutes. When she walks by this time, I turn toward her and smooth my hands down the front of my dress.

"How do I look?" I'm wondering if she'll even recognize this dress.

She stops and raises a hand to her mouth, studying me. "You look gorgeous as always, sweetheart," she says. "You really need a bracelet or a watch or something, though. Your wrists look so bare."

She unhooks the clasp on the ten carat diamond tennis bracelet she's wearing.

My mouth drops open. She's never let me wear her

jewelry before. "I can't," I say. "What if I lose it or something?"

"Don't," she says, a smile growing on her face as she secures it around my wrist.

I twist my arm, watching the diamonds sparkle in the light. It's breathtaking, but it's heavy and it scares the shit out of me. I really don't want this responsibility.

If I take it off, though, she'll be upset.

"Just give this guy a chance, okay?" Her voice is soft and serious and when I look up at her, her eyes are fixed to my face. "That's all I'm asking."

My stomach fills with a nervous wave of energy. Is it so obvious that I'm closed off to every guy who isn't Mason?

The doorbell rings and I take a deep breath. I really hope this guy isn't a troll. Or a coin collector.

Our butler, Jameson, opens the door and I turn as Braxton walks inside.

Definitely not a troll.

He's tall and handsome with broad shoulders. He's dressed in a pair of jeans with a crisp white shirt and a tailored black blazer. He smiles as I walk toward him.

"Penny?" he says as I give him a quick hug. "It's so great to meet you. You're even more beautiful than the pictures your mom sent."

I glance back at my mom. "Thanks." She just smiles, but

The Moment We Began

I make a mental note to drill her later about which pictures she's sending to people without my permission.

"Braxton, this is my mom, Lucy."

She steps forward and he reaches for her hand.

"It's a pleasure to finally meet you," he says. "My parents say such great things about you and your husband."

She practically swoons at him. "You are too sweet," she says. "I'm so glad we could finally get you and Penelope together."

I cringe when she uses my full name.

"We'd better get going," I say, slipping my arm inside Braxton's. "We have reservations."

"I actually canceled the reservations you made," he says, surprising me. "I hope you don't mind, but I wanted to take you someplace a little different tonight."

Mom raises an eyebrow and gives me a look that says this one's different. I have to restrain myself from kicking her, inching toward the front door instead.

"Sounds fun," I say, praying he's not going to try to make me eat sushi or something. "Goodnight, Mom."

"Goodnight, sweetheart," she says. She's practically giggling, she's so excited. "Call me if you're planning to stay out too late."

I don't respond to that, but I know the implication is that maybe, for the first time since she started trying to set me up with one of her friend's kids, she finally hit the jackpot. Maybe this is the one who will finally break through to me.

I feel everything inside me rebelling against the idea as we walk toward his car together.

Yes, he's good looking and rich and probably perfect for me on the outside, but there's something about him that's too perfect. Too rehearsed. Definitely too good to be true.

Besides, my heart has belonged to someone else for so long, I can't even imagine falling in love with another guy. No matter how great he is.

He opens the door for me and as I climb inside and wait for him to step around to the driver's side, I think about how crazy I am to be thinking about Mason right now. He flat-out told me he didn't want to be with me. That he didn't love me. Why am I still holding on? If he really, truly doesn't want me, there's nothing I can do about it. Am I going to spend the rest of my life heartbroken and alone?

God, I hope not.

As Braxton slips behind the wheel and drives off toward some mystery destination, I wonder if it's even possible for me to open my heart to someone new.

Chapter Nine

"Where are we going?" I ask as Braxton pulls onto the main highway.

He flashes a smile. "You'll see," he says. "I figure if you're anything like me, you're sick of these kinds of blind dates. And even sicker of always going to the same boring place for dinner each time."

I study him, but don't admit that he's right.

"Your mom sets you up on blind dates a lot?"

He sits back against the seat, one hand high on the steering wheel. "All the time," he says. "After the last one, I told her I was done for good."

I can't decide if he's playing me or not, but I'm definitely intrigued, so I ask the question he so obviously wants me to ask.

"If you're done, then why did you come tonight?"

He looks over at me and his eyes flick from my knees

up to my face. "Because you're not like those other girls."

"How do you know?"

"I saw your picture remember?" he says. "How could I possibly say no? I figure worst case scenario, I get to have dinner with a beautiful woman. Best case, we actually hit it off."

I know this is the part where I'm supposed to swoon, but I can't help feeling he set that whole thing up just so he could impress me with how sweet and romantic he is.

When he pulls into a little Italian restaurant near the beach, I don't bother telling him I've been here before. He seems really proud of himself for coming up with a way to stand out from the crowd of other blind dates.

"I found this place a couple of years ago," he says. "It's one of the best kept secrets along this part of the coast. If you like Italian food, you're going to love it."

I guess he does get points for taking me off the beaten path, but I can't help wondering how many other girls he's brought here. Or how many times he's used the line about having dinner with a beautiful woman.

"I adore Italian food," I say.

Inside, it's dark and romantic. A pretty girl with long, dark hair takes us to a secluded booth near the back of the restaurant. Either we look like the kind of couple who wants to be alone, or he called ahead to make sure his favorite table was available.

We settle in and I know it won't be long before he starts trying to impress me with his knowledge of fine wines.

It's something all the rich guys like him do. Like they were given a dating instruction booklet when they were kids called 'How To Bag A Rich Girl'.

It takes precisely thirty seconds.

"We'll take a bottle of the Stag's Leap Cabernet Sauvignon," he tells the waiter. He doesn't even look the guy in the eyes when he orders. "When I was touring the vineyards in Napa last fall, I fell in love with their cab. At first, you taste the berries, but it finishes with a slight hint of vanilla."

He doesn't bother asking me if I like red wine, which I don't.

He also orders an appetizer without asking for my opinion.

I'm not wearing a watch, but I'm guessing we've only been on this date for about fifteen minutes and I've already got him pegged. Sure, he's more handsome than the average guy, but other than his looks, I've been out with this exact guy before.

Guys like this start out very charming. He says all the right things. Wears all the right clothes. Makes all the right moves. But eventually, he'll make it clear the only thing he really cares about is himself. I already know that every time he asks me a question that appears to be about me, he'll quickly turn the conversation back to him. He'll continue to do exactly everything he wants to do tonight without asking what I want, but then try to pass it off like he's being the ultimate gentleman.

He'll expect me to be very impressed by him by the time we leave the restaurant, and when I'm not, he'll either turn into a mega-jerk or he'll try harder by announcing that he wants to take me to some other mystery place that will turn out to be some excessively romantic hillside where he'll try to get in my pants.

I usually play along with these guys and stroke their egos long enough to make it through dinner and the drive home, but I'm not in the mood for listening to him talk about himself all night. Maybe it will be more fun to not play along. I'm curious what he'll do when I refuse to fit into his perfect plan for the night.

When the server brings the wine and a basket of bread, I place my hand over my wine glass and shake my head. "I actually don't like red wine," I say. "Can you bring me a vodka and cranberry?"

"Of course," the server says. He pours Braxton's glass, then sets the bottle on the table and leaves.

"I'm sorry." He tugs at the sleeve on his blazer. "If I'd

known you didn't like red wine, I wouldn't have gotten a whole bottle."

"If you had asked, I probably would have told you," I say.

He laughs a little, but doesn't know how to take it. I can tell I've put him off balance.

He clears his throat and reaches for the bread, offering me a piece first.

"Thank you," I say. "I love the bread here."

He lowers the basket on the table, his expression pinched. "You've been here before?"

I look around. "A few times," I say. "Never on a blind date, though. I usually just have guys take me to the country club. I'm comfortable there and everyone knows me, so I feel safe."

"Would you rather have gone there instead?"

"No, this is really nice," I say. "You surprised me bringing me here. It's a nice change."

He smiles, but it's forced. I've taken the upper hand here and he doesn't like it one bit.

The waiter brings my drink and takes our order. He doesn't order for me, which is a relief. While we wait, Braxton asks me basic questions about my life and just as expected, ends up mostly talking about himself.

"What's your major?" he asks.

"Political science," I say. "Mostly concentrating on pre-law courses."

It's the perfect chance for him to ask me where I want to go to law school or why I want to be a lawyer, but he doesn't.

"I'm a senior at Emery this year," he says. "I'm starting back in a couple of weeks. I'm pre-med, hoping to get into Fairhope Coastal for med school."

I almost laugh. A doctor and a lawyer. Looks great on paper, but if we got married, we'd probably never see each other.

Not that I can really see myself as a lawyer. My mom has had her heart set on it since I was little. I think she has this idea that since she got pregnant half-way through law school and never finished, I can pick up where she left off. It was easier to just do what she wanted than argue about it, but when it comes time to start applying for law schools, I'm going to have to put my foot down. No way am I putting up with another three years of this crap after undergrad, much less the rest of my life.

After our food arrives, Braxton continues to talk about his career aspirations and what it's like living in Atlanta. By the time I'm done eating, I've heard about his perfect GPA, the various awards he's won over the past few years, and how he's sure he'll have no trouble with med-school after acing his MCATs.

Meanwhile, I've had three drinks and am happy to just let him blab on and on.

At least he's pretty to look at.

When there's finally a break in his endless love song to himself, I speak up. "Do you want to go to this bar in Fairhope with me?" I ask. "A group of people are throwing a little welcome home party for this friend of mine, and I told them I'd swing by."

He hesitates. I'm on the edge of my seat waiting to see which way he'll swing. Mega-jerk or over-the-top romantic.

"I was kind of hoping we could keep it just the two of us tonight," he says. He leans forward, his arms resting on the table between us. "I know this really gorgeous spot just down the beach from here. I'd love nothing more than to grab a blanket and walk on the beach with you tonight. I think there's really something special about you, Penny."

Over-the-top it is, then. I like that better than the alternative, but I'm disappointed I was so right about this guy.

"Aww, thanks," I say, patting his hand twice, then standing up. "That's really sweet, but I should get home soon. I promised my friends I'd come out there, and it's really important to me."

He scrambles to his feet. "Oh, well, I don't want to take

you home," he says. "If you really want to go to this party, let's do it."

"Yeah?" I'm surprised he's still trying.

"Yeah," he says. "It'll be enough just to be with you."

I smile, but suddenly have the overwhelming urge to cry. I would give anything to hear words like that from Mason, but from this guy, they mean nothing.

Still, I wonder if I'm being too hard on him.

I shrug my shoulders and start walking toward the door. He takes a few long steps to catch up with me, opening the door just before I get to it.

"Wait," he says. "Is that a yes?"

I turn to him. "Tell me something, Braxton."

"Okay," he says, shifting his weight.

"Why did you really want to go out with me tonight?"

His gaze darts toward the shore, but it's too dark for us to see the water from here.

"I thought you were gorgeous in your pictures," he says. "I really wanted to meet you."

"Bullshit," I say, my lips buzzing slightly from the alcohol. I'm not drunk, but I'm on my way there if I can get to another glass before the buzz wears off. "You probably see pretty girls all the time up in Atlanta. I bet you have them knocking down your door. So why me? Why does a handsome guy like you go on a blind date?"

The Moment We Began

He puts his hands on his waist, pushing his blazer back. "I've heard really great things about you from my mom," he says. "I'm not seeing anyone in particular right now, so when she mentioned a possible date, I was excited to meet you. It's not every day I get to go out with a beautiful, intelligent woman like you."

I smile and shake my head. He's not actually going to be honest with me right now, and I guess I wasn't really expecting him to be.

"Come on," I say, reaching for his hand. "Let's go have some real fun."

He takes my hand and we walk together to his car.

"Are you always this blunt on a first date?" he asks.

"No," I answer truthfully. The only guy I've ever just been able to be myself with is Mason, but he's never actually taken me on a date. "But I've always wanted to be."

Chapter Ten

Leigh Anne shouts and waves me over toward the bar.

It's crowded in here still, but we're early. Knox isn't closing the bar until ten, so most of our other friends aren't here yet.

She stands and gives me a huge hug. "I'm so glad you made it," she says. She buries her face in my hair and whispers, "He's cute."

"Cute and perfect," I whisper back. "And completely wrong for me."

She makes a face.

"What can I get you guys to drink?" Knox asks from behind the bar.

There's country music playing through the speakers. He's decorated the place with balloons and a big welcome home sign. There are two dozen red tulips sitting on the bar in front of Leigh Anne with a little note sticking out that says

'I love you'.

I swallow down a bit of jealousy and turn to my date. "Braxton? What are you drinking? And no more bullshit red wine tonight. We're drinking real drinks from here on out."

"I'll take an IPA," he says. "What do you guys have here that's good?"

I shrug. I guess beer is better than nothing. He and Knox start talking pale ale and Leigh Anne pulls me onto the bar stool next to hers.

"Jenna and Colton and some of the other servers should be here soon," she says. "Summer's here, but she went to the bathroom. Is Preston coming?"

"I'm not sure," I say, thinking back to the sadness I'd seen in his eyes. "He said he'd try to stop by."

Braxton finally picks his beer and then, surprisingly, asks what he can get for me.

"Jack and ginger," I say.

Leigh Anne's eyebrows go up and I smile. I'm determined to have a good time tonight. I'm so over being depressed about Mason all the time. Why can't I get him out of my head? He has me so turned around, I can't even get through a single night without thinking about him.

But if he doesn't want me, then fuck him. His loss.

Of course, I've given myself this little pep-talk several times over the course of being in love with Mason Trent. It usually only works until the next time I see him, when my knees buckle again and my heart breaks as it hits the floor.

Well, dammit, not this time.

If he's really done, then so am I. And if moving on means dating guys like Braxton for a while, then so be it. I don't have to marry the guy, right? Maybe I've been going about this night all wrong. Instead of trying to calculate our compatibility and see him as a potential boyfriend, I should just be trying to enjoy myself and go with the flow.

Knox sets my drink down, and I lean over the bar.

"Can I get two shots of tequila, too?"

Knox looks at Leigh Anne and she holds her hands up. "Don't look at me," she says. "She's a grown woman. She can handle it."

Knox pours the two tequila shots and I slide one across the wood toward Braxton, throwing him a challenging look.

I expect him to push it away or tell me he doesn't plan on staying long. Instead, he lifts the shot glass up in a kind of toast, then throws it back without so much as a wince. I'm impressed. I grab his hand, then pour salt between his thumb and index finger. He raises his eyebrows at me, but doesn't pull away. I lean forward and seductively lick his hand, then down the shot. Braxton picks up a lime and I eat it right out of his hand, my lips grazing his fingers. He bites his lower lip and I realize that narcissist or not, he's hot and he's interested in me. I suck the juice from the lime, then toss it on the counter.

With the alcohol buzzing in my system, I throw my arms around his neck and kiss him, hard and strong. A couple of people around us whistle and clap and my lips smile against his.

"Want another?"

He kisses me again and I close my eyes, then tap the bar and hold up two fingers.

Chapter Eleven

By the time Knox shuts the bar down, I'm well on my way to wasted.

Braxton only did the one shot with me and has been nursing his beer for the past half hour.

Now that the bar is officially closed, Leigh Anne is ready to start drinking. "Until I'm twenty-one, I just don't want to get Knox into any trouble," she says.

I love Leigh Anne with all my heart, but I wish I could find a few flaws in her every once in a while. If nothing else, it would make me feel better about being such a mess lately.

"Do a shot with me," I say, laying my head on her shoulder.

"Okay, but not tequila," she says. She leans over the bar to get a closer look at the bottles. "Can you make me something that's going to taste good on the way down?"

Knox leans toward her and gives her a long kiss.

"Whatever you want, my love. Tonight's your night."

I grab Braxton and kiss him again, but it's empty and meaningless. A poor substitute for what Leigh Anne has. I feel like a cheap knock-off, and I hate myself for it.

The door to the bar opens and Leigh Anne clears her throat and gives me a subtle tap on the arm.

I break away from Braxton's kiss and turn to see who has come through the door.

Mason stands alone just inside the entrance. He's staring at me with a mixed expression I'm way too drunk to decipher, and I realize I couldn't have timed it more perfectly if I'd tried.

He had to have seen me kissing Braxton, and he doesn't look happy about it. At all.

Preston comes through the door and nearly runs right into him. Mason seems to wake up. He stuffs his car keys in his pocket, then shakes his head and tears his eyes away from me, but I'm glad that for once, he actually showed some kind of reaction. I'm glad it bothered him. It's about time he got a taste of his own medicine.

I never expected him to be alone tonight, but I'm glad he is. Now, it's his turn to sit back and try to pretend he doesn't care that I'm with someone else tonight and he can't have me. I don't even turn to say hi to him. I work to focus all of my attention on my date, but my body is hyper-aware of Mason's presence now. My skin flushes with warmth and I have to sit down.

Braxton sits on the stool opposite me and starts telling some story about a vacation he took to Germany earlier in the summer with some of his buddies. I think it has something to do with the beer he's drinking, but I can't concentrate. The room is spinning now, and I feel sick to my stomach. In some dark corner of my mind, I'm aware of the fact that I'm out of control. I know I'm doing a horrible thing by leading this guy on just for the sake of having a fun night and making Mason jealous.

But I can't stop myself. This night is like a rollercoaster. It started out bumpy, but once I got over that first hill and decided to make the most of it, I've been in a free fall toward disaster.

I grip my most recent drink in my hand, focusing on the feel of the cold glass against my skin.

"Have you ever been to Munich?"

I blink, forcing my attention back to Braxton. "What?"

"Munich?" he asks, putting his hand on my knee and moving it up and down my leg. "Oktoberfest. I go every fall. You should come with me this year. I'm renting a house with a few buddies of mine, but I'll have my own room."

It takes me a second to realize he's actually talking about a future with me. Or at least sex. Flying across the deep blue sea and staying in his room with him.

I have no idea what to say to that. I guess there's a possibility I misjudged him or that if I give him a real chance, he'll surprise me more and more. But the truth is I can't see a future with this guy. I just wanted to kiss him for a while. Is that so wrong?

"What do you say?" he asks. "Do you think you would want to go?"

I look down at my shoes, and that's when I realize there's an extra pair of feet standing to my right. I look up and see Mason standing beside us.

"Hi," I say. I'm clutching the cold glass even tighter now, begging my stomach to stop turning.

"Hey," he says. "I didn't realize you were bringing a date tonight."

"Mason, meet Braxton, the genius med student," I say, waving my hand between them. "Braxton, meet Mason, the guy who keeps breaking my heart."

Oh shit.

I don't know why I said that, but the second the words came out of me, I wanted to stuff them back inside.

"What?" Braxton asks. He takes his hand from my leg.

The music is still playing, but I feel like it's one of those moments where everything else should have gone silent. Like in an old western when the big bad guy walks into the room and everyone stops to look.

Mason closes his hand around my upper arm and my body pulses at his touch. "Can I talk to you in private for a minute, please?"

I want to say no, but I can never say no to him. He lets go of my arm and takes a step back, and all I want is to feel his touch on my skin again.

"I'll be back," I tell Braxton.

"You sure you're okay?" he asks, standing. He places himself a little between me and Mason, as if he's protecting me. "We can just go somewhere else if you don't want to talk to this guy."

"Stay the hell out of this," Mason says. "I've known Penny a lot longer than you have, so don't offer to sweep her away like you're some kind of knight in shining armor here to save the day. I just want to talk to her."

"You're right," Braxton says. He steps even more between us. He's a little bit taller than Mason, but there's no doubt Mason's stronger. "I don't know your history, but until you walked in the door, Penny and I were having a great time tonight. I don't want you ruining that or upsetting her."

"You need to take a step back before you get your ass beat," Mason says. He clenches his fists and the muscles in his arms ripple.

I come around Braxton and stand between them. "Just give us a minute."

I grab Mason's hand and pull him toward the front door. He doesn't take his eyes off Braxton until the door closes and we're standing outside alone. I've seen Mason fight before, and I know it would not have ended well for Braxton tonight.

"What is your problem?" I say. The alcohol is making my thoughts fuzzy. I put my hand on Mason's chest and push him back.

He comes right back at me, but doesn't touch me. He just gets close enough that I can smell the heady scent of his cologne. I've buried my head in that scent so many times, it sends an electric shiver down my spine.

"My problem? You're the one who's draped all over some stranger one minute, then telling everyone I broke your heart the next," he says. "Why would you say that?"

"Because it's true," I say. "And you know it."

"Doesn't mean I want all our friends to know it," he says. "We agreed to keep those things between us."

"No, you insisted we keep everything a secret," I shout. "That was never my idea. That was never what I wanted."

"How was I supposed to know that?" Mason lifts his hand in the air. "Until last week on the boat, I had no idea you felt that way about me. And I was honest with you from the start, Penny. I'm not the kind of guy—"

"Not the kind of guy who falls in love," I say, finishing his sentence for him. "You've made that abundantly clear."

"Then you have no right to go around telling people I broke your heart," he says. "I warned you not to give me your heart in the first place."

"By then it was too late," I shout. "I loved you long before that first night on the boat."

Tears of anger and frustration roll down my face. I didn't expect to end up out here arguing with him tonight. I wanted to look happy and carefree. I wanted him to know I was over him. Instead, I've just managed to make an even bigger fool of myself.

He steps toward me and puts one hand on my cheek, then tilts my face up toward his.

"I didn't know," he says.

I stare up into his eyes. "Yes, you did."

Chapter Twelve

Mason leans toward me and I'm helpless to do anything but lift up to meet him.

His warm lips cover mine and I am gone.

This is nothing like Braxton's kiss. No, this kiss is an explosion. A symphony. A match that ignites an even stronger fire within.

I lift my arms around his neck and press against him. The world around me spins and pitches, but as long as he's kissing me, I have an anchor.

He walks me backward until the back of my legs bump against the front of his car. He leans me back against it, the hood bending a little underneath me as he presses his weight against my body. I wrap a leg around him, pull him closer. I lift my hips and he grows hard against me.

He groans and leans his head back. I kiss his neck and run my hands along his arms, his back, his stomach.

He pulls away, then reaches down and grabs both my hands in his and lifts them over my head, pressing them against the hood of the car. I stare up at him, my breath coming in short gasps. My chest rises and falls rapidly and the place where I feel him against me pulses with need.

"Don't stop," I whisper.

He shakes his head. "I don't know why I can't just walk away from you," he says.

I clasp his hands tighter. "Maybe it's because you're supposed to be walking toward me," I say.

He searches my eyes and for a moment, I think he's going to kiss me again. To let in the possibility of love between us.

But whatever keeps pulling him away from me grabs hold and yanks him backward. He releases my hands and punches the hood of the car.

I feel him slipping away as he stands.

"I can't be with you, Penny," he says. "I don't know how to make you understand that."

I don't know why I do it, but with a quick movement of my wrist, I dip my hand into his pocket and pull out his car keys. I'm so angry and hurt. So tired of this game.

Before he can grab me, I have the car door open. I slip inside and slam the door closed. Mason lunges toward me, yanking at the handle on the door just as I press the button to lock the doors.

He's too late.

I slide the key into the ignition and rev the engine.

He's never let me drive his car before, but just like mine, this car wants to go fast.

"Penny, stop," he shouts. He bangs on the window with both hands, but I barely glance up.

My heart is racing. I'm in no condition to drive, but I'm also in no condition to stop myself. I put the car in gear and press hard on the gas. The tires squeal and the car bursts forward. I go straight over the curb, the car bouncing and lurching to the side.

I hit the brakes and stare ahead, lining the wheel up with the lines on the road.

Adrenaline surges through me and I press my foot down on the gas again, accelerating fast on the straightaway, then braking and turning the wheel hard to the right. I turn onto Broad Street and punch it again.

It's the third turn that gets me. I don't slow down enough and pull the wheel too far. Too fast.

My heart skips as I feel the tires slide across the road, then catch, then let go.

I scream as the car rolls over. My head slams into the seat, then jerks toward the window.

Then the world goes black.

Chapter Thirteen

Lights flash and people shout.

My eyes flutter open. A piercing pain explodes near my temple, and I moan and try to lift my hand. But I can't move my arms.

Panic shoots through me and when my eyes focus on what's happening around me, I see that my arms are strapped down on a gurney, a needle stuck through my arm.

I let my head fall back and my eyes close again. Nausea rolls over me, sending me twisting and tumbling through the darkness in my head. Sounds are muffled and when I swallow, my throat is dry as a bone. I'm lifted, then jerked forward.

Behind me, I think I hear Mason's voice, but maybe I'm dreaming.

Maybe I'm dying.

My eyes open again, and I see tight white walls and a

man in uniform peering over me. He shines a light into my eyes, then shouts something to a person behind me.

Doors slam shut and a siren wails as the ambulance begins to move.

Someone takes my hand, and I look over to see the wide, worried eyes of my twin brother.

"Preston," I say, but my voice is raspy and harsh. An involuntary sob escapes from my mouth and my breath hitches. Tears well up in my eyes and roll down the side of my face and into my hair.

He leans forward. "You're going to be okay," he says. "I'm here, Penny. It's going to be all right."

I concentrate on the sound of his voice and the feel of his strong hand on mine. I stare at the ceiling of the ambulance, but don't really see it. I can't seem to stop my jaw from trembling.

When we get to the hospital, the gurney I'm on bumps and jerks, then glides as they roll me toward one of the rooms. Preston runs beside me, never letting go of my hand. I keep my eyes on his face as the doctors examine me, poking and prodding and taking blood. There's a rush of activity in the room for a while, but I don't listen to anything they're saying. I just watch my brother's face and know that as long as he's still in here, everything is going to be okay. If I was dying, they'd send him away, right?

The Moment We Began

Someone dabs cold liquid on a spot on my jaw and I wince.

I feel like I'm going to throw up. I squeeze Preston's hand harder, every muscle in my body tense with pain and sickness.

I'm glad he's not yelling at me. Or telling me how stupid I am. As time passes and the shock wears off, the consequences of what I've done start to bring up an entirely new kind of fear.

I might be lucky the accident didn't kill me, but I'm going to be even luckier if my parents don't come in here and finish the job.

And oh, god, Mason's car. I close my eyes, the tears coming harder now.

I have no idea what happens to someone who is drinking and totals their car. Am I going to go to jail?

There's nothing about this that's going to end well for me. What the fuck was I thinking? I don't even know. I hardly remember taking Mason's keys, just that one minute he was kissing me and the next I was speeding away. I didn't even make it that far.

Slowly, the piercing pains turn to a dull throbbing.

Preston strokes my hair as I cry, and gradually, mercifully, I finally fall asleep.

Chapter Fourteen

The door to my room sails open and I jerk awake, the sudden motion sending a fresh wave of pain through my sore body.

My father storms through the door, his face filled with rage and worry.

Mom follows him inside. Her eyes are ringed with red and her hair is a wild mess. I've never seen her in public looking like this. She must have gotten out of bed and thrown on whatever was closest without even bothering to brush her hair.

Guilt presses against my chest. They had to have been scared to death to get that call so late at night.

Preston stands, and for the first time in hours, he lets go of my hand and steps away.

I struggle to sit up straighter.

Mom rushes to my side and pulls me into a hug.

"Thank god you're okay," she says, her hand on the back of my head. She presses her cheek to my uninjured side and I feel the wetness of tears on her face.

"What in the hell were you thinking?" My dad's voice booms across the room. He comes to stand on the other side of my bed, his large hands gripping the bed-rail.

I lean back against the pillow and feel the tears starting up all over again.

Mom rubs her hand along my forearm. "You scared us out of our minds," she says. "What happened? The doctor told us you'd been drinking."

They look at me, expecting answers. I don't even know what to say. I'm an emotional wreck, and I have no excuses for what I did. All I can do is find a spot on the wall and stare.

"Your behavior has been out of control lately," Dad says. "But this? This is completely over the line. I won't have a daughter of mine drinking and driving like some lunatic. Do you realize you could have been killed tonight? Or worse, you could have killed someone else? What if you'd hit another car? Or a pedestrian? I can't believe you would be so stupid."

I lean forward and bring my hands up over my face. I don't want them to see me.

I'm sobbing now, thinking about what he's saying.

86

The Moment We Began

He's right. I could have killed someone. I could have died.

Mom puts her arm around my shoulder and kisses the top of my head. She rubs my back as I cry. "Go a little easy on her, Tripp. She's still really shaken up over this," she says. "Come on, Penny, look at me."

She pulls my hands away from my face, but I don't want to look in her eyes. I've disappointed my parents plenty of times before, but after this, I'm afraid they'll never see me the same way again.

Maybe no one will.

"Look at me, sweetheart."

I slowly lift my eyes to hers and she gives me a small smile.

"We'll talk about all this later, okay? Your father and I are just glad you're all right," she says. "The doctor said you're extremely lucky to be alive. Other than a few scrapes and bruises, he says you're going to be just fine. That's what's important right now."

"Am I going to jail?" I ask, my voice trembling.

Her eyes flick toward my father, then back at me. She shakes her head. "We're going to take care of everything," she says. "You just concentrate on getting some rest and getting better."

Relief floods through me, but it's mixed with guilt. I

know they'll have to call in some favors to make this disappear, and it isn't really fair.

"What about Mason's car?"

"Shhhh," she says, patting my hand. "Let us deal with all that."

The door opens and the doctor walks in. Dr. Mallory is about my parents' age, and he's a friend of theirs. He's not usually an ER doctor, and I'm wondering if my parents asked him to come in tonight. He smiles, clutching a clipboard tight against his chest.

"I'm glad to see you awake," he says. "How are you feeling?"

"Sore," I say. "A little bit sick to my stomach."

He pushes his glasses up on his nose. "All very normal reactions," he says. "But I would like to talk to you in private for a few minutes, if your family doesn't mind."

"If this is regarding her injuries, I'd like to hear what you have to say," my mother tells him.

Dr. Mallory clears his throat and lowers the clipboard to his side. "I'd really prefer to talk to Penny privately first," he says. "She could really use some more rest, anyway."

"Of course," Dad says. He releases his tight grip on the rails, then pats my leg as he walks toward the door.

Mom kisses my forehead. "We'll be right outside in the waiting room," she says. "Hopefully we can take you home soon."

"It shouldn't be too much longer," the doctor says.

He waits by the door as Preston, Mom, and Dad all file out. Then, he closes it behind them and even watches through the tiny window to make sure they've gone.

Worry knots in my stomach. What could be so awful that he wouldn't want to say it in front of my parents?

Dr. Mallory pulls up a rolling chair, then sits down by my side. I sit up and he stuffs an extra pillow behind my back.

"Better?" he asks.

I nod. "Am I dying?"

He smiles and shakes his head. "Far from it," he says. "Other than a few scrapes and bruises, your injuries are really very minor compared to the severity of the crash. We can have a plastic surgeon take a look at the cut on your jaw if you'd like, but I don't think it will scar too badly."

I rest my hands on my lap, picking at the white sheets that cover my legs. There's a pulse monitor clamped on my index finger and I tap it against the sheet.

"What's wrong, then?"

"Nothing," he says. "I just wanted to let you know that as a precaution, the first responders took a blood sample and ran a few tests. This is all standard procedure, especially with young women. They often run a pregnancy test just to ensure they don't use any medications or treatments that might adversely affect an unborn baby."

I look up at him, my hands clutching the sheet and my heart stopping in my chest. The room seems to be spinning again, and I blink several times.

"What are you saying?"

"Penny, I'm saying your test came back positive," he says. "You're pregnant."

Chapter Fifteen

I stare at Dr. Mallory, my body rigid. I couldn't have possibly heard him right.

I feel dizzy and press my lips together so tight it hurts.

"Judging by the look on your face, I am assuming you didn't know," he says. "I had a suspicion you didn't, since you were drinking this evening."

My mouth falls open and I raise my hand up to my collarbone.

The world tilts as I try to make sense of all the thoughts spinning through my head. I'm going to have a baby. Mason's baby. And I've been drinking. Tears pour silently down my cheeks. I can't seem to stop them from coming.

"Have I..." my breath hitches and I can't put a voice to my fears. If I've hurt this baby, I'll never be able to forgive myself.

"I'd like to have one of my nurses come in and help me

perform an ultrasound to make sure the baby is okay," he says. "Do you remember the date of your last period?"

I close my eyes and shake my head. I have no clue. "Maybe a month ago?" I say. "Maybe a little over?"

My periods aren't always regular, so I'm not sure and my head is now pounding too hard for me to think straight.

"Do you mind if we roll a cart in here and take a look? I just want to make sure everything looks okay. And maybe we can get a better idea of how far along you are."

I swallow, but my mouth is so dry a lump seems to stick my throat.

"I don't want my parents to know," I say. "I don't want anyone to know."

In such a small town, gossip spreads faster than a wildfire. Get the wrong nurse in here or the wrong person looking at my file and everyone in town will know by noon tomorrow.

How am I going to tell Mason?

What the fuck am I going to do?

"I promise we won't share this information with your parents without your permission," he says. "If we're discreet, you're okay with doing the ultrasound tonight?"

I am dazed, not even sure how to process all this information. This is the last thing I expected to find out tonight.

The Moment We Began

"What about the alcohol?" I ask, panic making my skin feel tingly and cold. "I had way too much to drink. What if hurt the baby?"

My face crumples and I press my fist to my mouth.

"How often do you drink like this?" he asks. "Every night? Once a week? Once a month?"

My hands begin to shake. "I had a lot to drink last weekend," I say. "But before that, it was about a month."

"Your blood alcohol level when you were admitted was less than .10, and if you were only intoxicated twice during your pregnancy so far, I would put your risk of complications such as fetal alcohol syndrome as low," he says. "However, if you continue to drink during your pregnancy, that risk will increase significantly."

I shake my head, relieved but scared. "I won't," I say.

He pats my shoulder. "I'm going to get all the equipment we'll need," he says. "I'll be back in a moment. Is there anyone you want me to call? Someone you'd like to be here with you when I perform the ultrasound?"

I think of Mason. He must be so pissed at me right now. I made a fool of myself, trashed his car, and now this. I want him here, but I don't think he'd want to be here. I have no idea how he would even react to this kind of news. If he didn't even want to be tied down by a relationship with me, he's definitely not going to want to start a family right now.

I bite my lip and run a trembling finger across my forehead.

I don't want any of my friends here, either. They won't understand. There's only one person I can think of that I can totally trust to support me through this.

"Can you get my brother for me?"

Chapter Sixteen

Preston is standing at my side when the image pops up on the monitor.

I have no idea what I'm looking at. The screen just looks like a round black and white blob with a dark black oval in the middle. Nothing in there looks even remotely like a baby.

The doctor moves the wand around, then settles on one location and stares up the screen, his forehead wrinkled and intense.

"What is it? Is everything okay?"

He doesn't answer at first. He moves the mouse around and a couple of measurements pop up on the screen. I squint my eyes, trying to make sense of it. Under the sheet, my toes tap against the bed. Why isn't he saying anything?

"Doctor?" Preston asks. "What exactly are we looking at here? Is the baby all right?"

Dr. Mallory smiles, but doesn't take his eyes from the screen. "See this black part in the middle?" he asks. "That's your uterus."

My heart is pounding and I stare in awe at what he's showing me.

"And here," he says, circling the pointer around a tiny grey blob that is barely sticking out into the black part. "This is your baby."

I can't take my eyes off the tiny little spot. My heart aches and tightens and I think I've never felt so in love with anything in my whole life. I raise the back of my hand to my mouth and exhale, almost laughing.

"So he's okay?"

"He or she," the doctor says, glancing toward me with a smile. "We won't know that answer for a couple of months, yet, but for right now, the baby seems to be doing great. See this little flicker of light on the screen?"

I lean forward and see a pulse of light.

"That's your baby's heartbeat. Nice and strong," he says.

I dissolve into tears for about the tenth time in two hours, but these tears are different. This is a flood of relief and joy and a sudden, paralyzing fear. I am pregnant.

Preston hugs me and we both stare at that tiny flicker, unable to take our eyes off of it.

The Moment We Began

"Holy shit, Penny," he says. "You're going to be a mommy."

I sniff and wipe the tears from my face. I can hardly believe this moment is real.

"From the measurements, I would say you're right at around five and a half weeks pregnant," Dr. Mallory says. He pulls out a little paper chart, moves a few things around and then nods. "That puts your due date in early April."

Five and a half weeks. I try to think backwards to when this happened. I've been on birth control pills for the past couple of years, but I've gotten careless about taking them. I tried setting alarms on my phone as a reminder, but in the past few months, I sometimes missed days at a time. I guess I never thought that much about it, because Mason almost always used condoms, too.

I thought, between the two things, we were being safe enough.

But somewhere along the way, a forgotten pill and a moment of passion came together at just the wrong—or right—time.

Staring at that flickering heartbeat, I know that my life will never be the same again.

Chapter Seventeen

My parents bring me home just after sunrise.

I know they have a lot more they want to say to me, but for now, everyone is just too tired and too drained.

We separate to our own suites, but instead of going back to his apartment, Preston comes with me to my room. I'm so grateful he's here for me. Without his support, I might have already lost my mind.

"Can I get you anything?" he asks. "Or if you want to get some rest, I can sleep on the couch out here for a while."

I reach inside my bag and pull out the bottle of prenatal vitamins the doctor gave me. "Would you mind getting me a glass of water?"

When he disappears to grab some water from the kitchen, I search for my cell phone. I dial Mason's number. I have no idea what I am going to say to him, but we really need to talk. I don't think I'll be able to sleep until I know we're okay. What am I going to do if he hates me?

The phone rings a couple of times. My heart skips a beat when someone picks up, but then I realize it's just voicemail.

"It's me," I say. I hardly recognize my own voice. There's a weariness inside the sound that goes deeper than just being tired. "I don't even know how to begin to apologize for last night. I really need to talk to you. Please, call me."

I hang up and toss the phone on the table beside the couch. I sit down and pull my favorite fuzzy blanket over my legs. I'm not really cold, but having something to wrap myself inside feels good. Like a cocoon. I wonder if I sit here long enough if I'll somehow emerge a better person. Someone who doesn't make such stupid decisions over and over.

I pull my knees up tight against my chest and wrap the blanket tighter.

When Preston comes back with the water, he opens the bottle of prenatals and brings a couple over to me. I take them, finishing off the entire glass of water in one gulp.

"Thanks."

"Anything you need, sis. I mean it."

I feel the tears starting again. It's a feeling that starts deep in my belly. A tightening that spreads upward. I take a deep breath, but I'm too tense and tired. My chest is too tight.

"Do you want to talk about it?" he asks. He sits down against the opposite corner of the couch.

"I think I'm still in shock," I say. I run a shaky hand through my hair. It feels so dirty and heavy. I desperately need a shower, but I don't want to move from this spot. "I don't know whether I'm happy or upset or just really, really scared."

"I think that's probably pretty normal in this kind of situation," he says. He looks away, his lips pressed together and his forehead wrinkled up. "Penny, I don't want to say anything that's going to upset you, but—"

"It's okay," I say. I can tell from the struggle on his face that he wants to ask the tough questions. "I think I already know what you're going to ask."

I think he's going to ask me how I could be pregnant when I haven't really been dating anyone, but he surprises me.

"Are you going to tell Mason?"

My mouth falls open. "How—"

"I'm not blind, Penny. I've seen the way you both look at each other," he says. "I knew something was going on there, but I wasn't sure how serious it had gotten."

"He doesn't want a relationship with me," I say. I fold my arms over the tops of my knees and rest my head against them. "Sex, yes. Relationship? No. He doesn't want to be tied down."

My voice cracks as I say those last words out loud. What am I going to do? Can I really raise a baby on my own?

I hide my face inside my arms, exhausted from crying way too much over the last twelve hours. Eventually, you'd think the tears would stop coming.

"It's going to be okay," he says. He puts his hand on top of my foot.

"How?" I ask. "It's hard to see how this is all going to work out. My mind keeps running through all these possibilities. Mom and Dad are obviously going to be devastated. I mean, I know they'll love their grandchild no matter what the circumstances are, but let's face it. A surprise pregnancy when I'm not engaged or married isn't exactly ideal."

"No, but it's not like you're some teen mom. You're an adult," he says.

I snort. "An adult who still lives at home and who just wrecked her non-boyfriend's expensive car while drunk driving," I say. "This isn't your strongest argument."

Preston smiles and shakes his head. "Well, you do have a point, there."

I smile and straighten my legs across the couch. "And what about Mason? If he doesn't want to be with me, he's not going to suddenly change his mind just because I'm pregnant," I say. "And if he does, that's worse. I'm not exactly hoping for a shotgun wedding here. I want him to be with me because he loves me, and there's nothing I can do to make that happen. Telling him about the baby is only going to complicate that whole situation."

"I know he says he doesn't want to be with you, but I swear, you should see the way he looks at you sometimes when you're not paying attention," Preston says. "There's something there, Penny."

Hope flutters through my stomach, but I try to ignore it. "Yeah, it's called lust," I say. "He's only interested in one thing. I thought that was going to be enough, you know? Just to be close to him."

"I don't think that's all there is for him," he says. "I know him, Penny. I can tell by the way he talks about you and looks at you that he cares about you a lot. And not just as a friend."

"That's not what he says." I'm scared to get my hopes up. I have to remind myself that just last night, he told me we weren't right for each other. He doesn't want me. "He's made it very clear he doesn't want me for anything more than friendship and the occasional sexy times. And weren't you just telling me last weekend that I should forget about him and go out with someone else?"

Preston shrugs. "I just didn't want to see you get hurt," he says. "Mason's... complicated."

To say the least.

"What are you going to do about the baby?" he asks. "You'll have to tell him eventually, I guess."

I lean my head back against the throw pillow. "I have to get him to take my calls first," I say. "I'm sure he's incredibly pissed about his car."

"Insurance will pay for the car. That should be the least of your worries right now."

"There's so much to think about. What am I going to do about school? I'll have to miss the last couple of months of spring semester," I say. "Should I get my own place, or stay here? I am not even remotely prepared for what's about to happen to my body. It's making my head spin just thinking about all of this."

"Maybe you should try to get some rest," he says. "All that stuff will still be here when you wake up. Maybe after some good sleep, you'll be able to think more clearly and make some decisions about who to tell and what you want to do."

"I really wish I could talk to Mason," I say. "He's not answering my calls."

"It might be better to wait until you know what you're going to say to him, anyway."

The Moment We Began

I shrug. "I just want to know he doesn't hate me."

"He doesn't," Preston says. "I promise."

"How do you know?"

"Because we all make mistakes. And because true friends are going to stick by you even when you seriously fuck up," he says. "Mason's been in your life too long and he cares about you too much to turn his back on you over this. You should have seen him out there after your accident. When you drove off, he rushed inside and yelled for help. We heard the tires squeal and all hopped in the back of Knox's truck to come find you. He wasn't mad, Penny. He was terrified."

My eyes widen. So I hadn't dreamed it. "He was there?"

"Yes. He might just be taking some time to work it out in his head. Maybe he thinks you need some space. Get some sleep, okay? I'll stay out here and watch TV just in case you need anything."

I nod slowly and yawn, suddenly so tired I can barely keep my eyes open.

I stand and wrap my arms around him. "Thank you," I say. "I don't know what I would do without you."

"You'll never have to find out," he says. "I love you sis."

"Love you, too."

I disappear into my bedroom, but keep the door cracked. Just knowing Preston's there, watching out for me, helps. When I lie down, all I can do is toss and turn for a while, my mind spinning with questions and fears. Eventually, I fall asleep and dream of what it will be like to hold a tiny baby in my arms.

Chapter Eighteen

That evening, I emerge from my bedroom to find Preston sitting on the couch in my living room watching baseball.

My hair is wild from tossing and turning and my jaw is throbbing. There are bandages covering the worst of the cuts on my face and hands and knees. I walk over to the table to find the extra gauze and bandages we picked up on the way home.

"Hey sleepyhead," Preston says. "Did you get some good rest?"

"A little," I say. "I didn't want to get out of bed, but I desperately need a shower. I stink."

"I thought I smelled something," he says.

I throw a box of gauze at his head, but he catches it instead.

"Lucky catch," I say.

"It's the skills," he says, laughing. He turns around on the couch to look at me. "They didn't want to wake you up, but Mom and Dad want to see you downstairs as soon as you're feeling up to it."

"I don't think I'm ever going to feel up to that conversation," I say, groaning.

"You should just get it over with," he says. "You'll feel better once it's done and they've said whatever it is they need to say."

"I can't tell them about the baby," I say. "Not yet. Please don't tell anyone."

"I won't."

"I'm going to get in the shower and get dressed," I say. "I'll be out in a little while."

He nods and goes back to the Braves game.

I linger in the shower longer than I should, but the hot water feels so good. I let it wash the dried blood from my scratches and the dirt from my legs and hands and hair. When I come out, I feel like a new person. Naked, I stand in front of the large mirror in my closet and place my hand against my tummy. I turn sideways and try to imagine what it will look like when I start to grow bigger.

I've always been a baby freak. I'm always the first person to show up at baby showers. Usually with the biggest, most extravagant gift. Any time one of my cousins

The Moment We Began

or someone else in our family has a baby, I make a beeline straight to them, begging to hold the little one. I love babies so much, and have always wanted to be a mom. I just never thought this would be the way it would happen.

But here, all alone in my own space, with no one watching or judging, I gently rub my hand across my stomach.

And I smile.

Chapter Nineteen

I feel stronger when I walk downstairs to face my parents. Like, no matter what they say to me, I know I have something of my own now. Someone I need to be strong for.

Still, stronger doesn't mean I'm not also a little bit sick to my stomach.

I hate disappointing my parents. I hate it when they're mad at me. They get that look in their eyes that make me feel like I've just ruined their lives or something. Like I am personally responsible for their happiness and instead, all I've done is made them sad.

I've gotten plenty of lectures before, but I've never done anything that has remotely compared to the complete fuck-up of last night.

I'm relieved to see Preston sitting on the piano bench in the great room. Dad is sitting next to Mom on the couch, so I sit down on the chair closest to the piano. I don't know what to say, so I keep my mouth shut and pray this doesn't last long. I'm incredibly tired, which I'm guessing is a side-effect of the pregnancy. I could literally lay my head down on a rock and fall asleep right now.

The tension in the room is thick and sharp and uncomfortable.

I fidget, waiting for someone to say something.

Finally, Dad lifts his head. He waits for me to meet his eyes. When I do, the anger and disappointment I see in them makes me feel like I'm wearing a fifty pound cloak of shame around my shoulders.

"I cannot even begin to tell you how angry I am right now," he says. His voice is calm and even. Controlled and very deliberate. "Your actions have not only put lives in danger, but they've also put our entire family name in the toilet. A drunk driving accident isn't something that can easily be swept under the rug. There are police reports, insurance claims, hospital records. Several documented reports as to what happened last night, which means your mother and I are both having to call in personal favors to try to get this taken care of so you don't have to sit in jail."

My head snaps up at the word. I definitely can't afford to go to jail right now.

"You're lucky you're not losing your driver's license all together," he says. "I managed to get any charges dropped, but believe me when I say that if anything like this ever happens again, you're one hundred percent on your own. Drunk driving is completely unacceptable, Penny. I'm so ashamed of you."

I bite down on my bottom lip.

"I'm not even sure how you got the keys to Mason's car, but you'd better believe I'm going to be questioning him intensely about why he gave you access to his car when you were obviously under the influence," he says.

I sit up. "Wait, it wasn't Mason's—"

He holds up his hand. "Don't speak. Now is when you listen."

I collapse back against the chair, my toes tapping against the hardwoods. He can't possibly blame Mason for this. If he accuses him of being in any way responsible, he's only going to make things worse for me. Dammit. I should have a right to talk, here. I understand them wanting to say their peace, but I'm not going to let him make it worse.

"I'm also having Knox's bar shut down pending an investigation into over-serving," he says.

I shoot up. "No! You can't do that, it wasn't Knox's fault."

My father stands up, too. He towers over me. "I will do what's necessary to make sure something like this doesn't happen again."

113

"If you want to yell at me, go ahead. Rake me over the coals, tell me I'm an idiot, whatever. But don't drag my friends into this and ruin their lives over my mistake," I say. "Knox did nothing wrong. I had been drinking before I even got to his bar. Besides, he had already closed up for the evening. It was a private party. As far as Knox knew, I was there with Braxton. I didn't even have my car there."

I realize I have no idea what happened to Braxton last night. I assume he just headed home after I left the bar, but I hadn't even thought of him until now. I'm sure after the way I acted, he'll never want to talk to me again anyway.

"And as for Mason's car, I stole it," I say. "I got angry, grabbed his keys, and took off. He tried to stop me, but didn't get to me fast enough. You can't blame him for that. It's not like he handed the keys to me. I took them out of his pocket. It was my mistake. My fault. No one else's."

My father clenches his jaw, the muscles in his cheeks tensing. "What were you thinking?"

"Obviously I wasn't thinking," I say, sitting back down in my chair.

"Obviously," my mother says. "Things like this that could ruin your life forever. If you had hit someone else, you could have been charged with a serious crime, Penelope. This is no laughing matter."

"I'm not laughing," I swallow a lump in my throat.

The Moment We Began

"Neither are we," Dad says. "We have given you everything you could have ever wanted in life. Every opportunity to make the most of yourself. When you make stupid decisions, like getting behind the wheel of a car and speeding through downtown, it's like saying you don't care if you throw it all away. How do you think that makes us feel?"

I don't answer. It's not the kind of question that really needs an answer.

"You looked so beautiful and mature last night," Mom says. "When you walked out of this house with that handsome young man, I had this vision of you as a young wife starting out in life. Someone with real dreams and goals and a great future ahead."

She's laying the guilt on thick, and it's working.

"I feel like you just took those dreams and stomped on them." She's crying now. "You've broken us, Penny. The trust between us has been broken, and it's going to take a long time to heal this. You're an adult, so you're free to make your own decisions, but if you want to start building back our trust, there are going to have to be some consequences."

"For the time being, you'll no longer have access to your car," Dad says. "If you want to go somewhere, you'll need to get a ride with your brother or with one of us."

I lean back against the seat. We've made it to the punishment phase of the lecture. I relax because I know this whole thing is almost over. I'll take my punishment and move on. I'm twenty-one years old, so there's not much they can do to me that will make life too hard. I can live without a car for a little while if I have to.

"No more parties. No throwing them or going to them," he says. "You're not to step foot in Knox's bar or any bar for the next six months."

I don't protest. There will be no parties or drinking for me in the coming months, anyway.

Still, I'm caught in a very tricky situation here. I'm old enough to do what I want, but I still live in my parents' house. I drive a car they paid for. I rely on them for a lot of things, including money. I've never had a job and I know I would never be able to do what Leigh Anne did. I couldn't work as a waitress on my feet all day. Especially not pregnant.

"We've also decided to cut your spending down to a small allowance," he says.

I look up. I clutch my hands together so tight, they turn white.

"You're cutting me off?"

"Not exactly," Mom says. "The trust fund from your grandparents has been frozen and we're putting you on a strict budget."

Anger flashes through me. Are they really going to do this to me?

Baby Isaac immediately flashes into my mind. I am supposed to bring five thousand dollars to the hospital tomorrow to pay for his surgery.

My heart tightens in my chest.

"How strict?"

"We've arranged a prepaid card for you that we'll load with one hundred dollars each week," she says.

My eyes widen and my jaw drops. Some days, I spend more than that on lunch. I wasn't expecting them to cut it down so much. This is never going to be enough. "A hundred dollars? Are you fucking kidding me?"

"Watch your language." Dad's voice booms through the great room. "If we wanted to, we could kick you out of the house without a cent to your name. We could have let them put you in jail for a few days until a judge could officially charge you with drunk driving. Trust me; there are a lot worse things that could happen for you here."

"How long?" I ask, crossing my arms in front of me. "How long am I going to be on this budget?"

"Six months," Dad says. "Every expense will need to be accounted for. We'll also pay for your books and tuition once school starts back, of course."

Six months is going to be too late. I drop my head into my hands. This can't be happening. I promised that family I would help them save their son. If he dies, it will be all my fault.

I know that if I ask them for the money, they'll give me the same speech they've given me a thousand times. We can't be personally responsible for every family that falls into tragedy. Our money is better spent going to charities with people who are trained to help families like this. Blah, blah, blah. They'll only be angry with me for promising the money when it was never really mine to give.

Guilt washes over me.

"Seeing your reaction to the idea of a budget just confirms to me that this is the best thing for you right now," Mom says. "We have tried our best to raise children who weren't spoiled by money. We wanted to give you every opportunity without making you greedy or entitled. But it's obvious to me now that somewhere along the way, we made some mistakes with you, Penelope. If money means so much to you that having to go on a budget is the most upsetting part of this ordeal, then maybe you need a lesson on how to go without for a while. Maybe it's time you learned to be grateful for what you have instead of taking all of this for granted."

I bite the inside of my lower lip to keep myself from

talking back. She has no idea what she's saying. Yes, I've gotten used to having nice things, but I'm sure I could handle living on a budget for a while. She has no idea why that money is really important to me.

I've got to find another way to get the money for them.

Not to mention that I'm going to need some way to pay for all the doctor's visits and baby gear. I'm going to need a new car. My two-door sports car isn't going to be very baby-seat friendly. By the time this budget is lifted, I'll only be a few months away from my due date.

I look over at Preston. Maybe I could convince him to take some money to the hospital for me.

"Don't even think about it," Mom says.

"What?"

"I saw that look," she says. "Preston, you're going to have to account for your expenses for the next six months as well. You won't have to live on a budget, but we are going to be checking to make sure you aren't funneling money to your sister."

Preston shakes his head and gives me a sympathetic look.

I close my eyes and pray for this meeting to be over already. All I can think about as they list the rest of their conditions is that tiny little baby in the incubator. What if that was my baby who needed help? No, I can't let this happen.

I'm going to find a way to help, no matter what it takes.

Chapter Twenty

Eventually, I'm going to have to face my friends. Right now, I need them more than ever, but I've never been so scared to make a few calls.

What if everyone thinks I'm a complete loser? What if they don't want to be around me anymore?

One of my worst fears in life is that if I ever lost all my money, I'd find out that none of my friendships were real. I'm not sure I'm brave enough to find out. I want to be very careful who finds out about this. I'd be mortified if the whole town was bragging about how Penny's parents cut her off. Finding out I'm pregnant and alone is going to be bad enough on its own.

Back in my room the following day, I make a mental list of people I feel I can trust enough to help me and not to gossip about this to everyone in town.

Sadly, the list is very small.

Leigh Anne is a no-brainer. She might be angry with me over what happened, but she's not the judgmental type. I just hope Dad never followed through with his threat to have Knox's bar closed down. That will definitely up the anger factor.

Summer and Bailey are on the list, too, but every time I try to write down Krystal's name, I hesitate. Krystal and I have been friends for a very long time, but I have this feeling deep in my gut that she'd turn her back on me in an instant. In fact, I think Krystal might actually be excited if I lost all my money. She'd do her best to try and replace me at the top of the social chain.

I can't think of anyone else who belongs on that list. I would have put Mason on it, but since he's not answering my calls right now, I can't count on him.

Besides Leigh Anne and Summer, I haven't gotten any text messages from friends.

When I have a party coming up, I have people texting and calling me left and right. I'll sometimes get three hundred texts in the space of an evening if word gets out that I'm opening up the pool here at the house the next day, but get in a drunk driving accident and only ten messages come through, six of which are from Leigh Anne.

There's one from Summer. Surprisingly, there's also one from Jenna. I wouldn't have expected to hear from her, but her message was a simple *Let me know if you need anything.*

The other two messages are from random people asking if there's anything going on this weekend. Guess those two are severely out of the loop around here.

So far, I haven't responded to any of them.

I pick my phone up, my palms clammy and my stomach churning. I dial Leigh Anne's number, letting out a long breath while it rings.

"Penny?"

I haven't even had a chance to say hello yet. Leigh Anne sounds scared.

"I'm okay," I say. "I'm sorry I didn't call you sooner, but life has been a little crazy over here."

"I've been so worried about you," she says. "Preston texted me to say you weren't seriously hurt, but I can't even imagine what you've been going through."

"Is Knox okay?" I ask. "I never wanted to get him into any kind of trouble."

Leigh Anne chuckles. "Trust me, Knox has been in worse situations than this. He can handle himself. Don't worry about us, I just want to make sure you're okay. Preston said something about some cuts and scrapes?"

"Just a few minor things," I say. "Listen, I really need to see you. I hate to ask for a favor at a time like this, but I need your help with something important. Can you come over?

I'm currently without car privileges."

"I figured your parents were planning to lock you away for a while," she says. "What is it with our parents still treating us like we're kids?"

"This is what happens when you still rely on them for everything instead of moving out and getting a job," I say. "You seemed to figure that out before I did."

"Barely," she says. "When do you want me?"

"As soon as you can get here." I look around my bedroom, a plan formulating in my brain.

"You sure everything's okay?"

"It's going to be," I say. "I'll see you soon?"

"I'm practically on my way."

I hang up, then go into the bedroom and search my closet for a small bag. The only thing I can find that isn't crazy huge or way too small is my Fairhope High cheerleading bag. I dump my old pompoms and sneakers on the floor and start filling it with anything I think I can sell fast. I search my room for cash, jewelry, expensive clothes, whatever will fit. It's a lot, but I'm scared it isn't going to be enough. Five grand is a lot of money to come up with overnight.

This is my only hope, though. It's either this or go back on my word to the family. And right now, their little baby feels like the most important thing in the world. Like, maybe if I can help him, I can erase the guilt of the danger I put my own baby in. I know that's not how the world works, but my heart is clinging to it.

I'm on my way out the door to wait for Leigh Anne when a plastic bag on my counter catches my eye.

It's my bag of personal effects from the hospital. I pick it up and the diamond bracelet inside sparkles like it's lit up from within. I rub the back of my neck. It's so wrong, I don't even want to think about it. Haven't I made enough bad decisions lately?

The phone rings. It's probably Leigh Anne telling me she's outside, but I can't take my eye off that bracelet.

I bite my lip, then shake my head. I turn toward the door, but as soon as I get my hand on the doorknob, I turn back.

I quickly grab the bracelet and shove it deep inside my bag, then run out to meet Leigh Anne.

Chapter Twenty-One

I'm dying to talk to Leigh Anne about Mason. I want to know if she's heard from him or seen him around town since the accident.

I'm tempted to ask her if she'll drive me by his house so I can hold his front porch hostage until he agrees to talk to me.

But I'm still not a hundred percent certain what I'm going to say to him. I know eventually I'm going to have to tell him I'm pregnant, but I'm too scared right now to even think about that.

A car buzzes at the gate, but when I look out, it's not Leigh Anne. I don't even recognize the car that's out there. I squint at the security cam, but I'm not sure who is inside. The car's an old Toyota that looks like it has seen better days. Definitely not something any of my friends drive.

My cell rings again and I fish it out of my bag, expecting

it to be Leigh Anne.

But it's Jenna.

I'm confused. "Hey, what's up?"

"I'm apparently sitting outside Fort Knox here and your security dude won't let me inside," she says. "Can you see me?"

I look back to the security cam. Jenna leans half her body out the window and sticks her tongue out at the camera.

I laugh. "Hold on a sec."

I hit the intercom button on the security panel. "Jason, can you let Jenna in, please? She's a friend."

"Yes, Ma'am."

"Thank you."

The gate starts to open and I walk toward the front door. My mom's voice stops me.

"Penny? Where are you going, sweetheart?" she asks, her voice tense. She's staring at the bag in my hand like it's a bomb.

"I'm going to go hang out with some friends for a little bit," I say. "Don't worry. No parties or anything."

She walks over and taps on the monitor. "I don't recognize that girl," she says. She crosses her arms in front of her body.

I'm annoyed at the accusatory tone, but at the same

time, I brought this on myself. And I have a stolen bracelet in my bag and am about to break some major rules. So, yeah, I'm not exactly blameless here or beyond suspicion.

"She's a good friend of Leigh Anne's," I explain. "Her name is Jenna and she goes to FCU. She waits tables at Brantley's."

"How come you girls don't just spend some time here? You could use the pool or the game room," she says. "I could have Maggie cook something nice for dinner if you want."

"No thanks," I say. "I'm going to go hang out at Leigh Anne's apartment for a while. It's in the same complex as Preston's. We're just going straight there."

She sighs. "Okay, but please call if you need anything. And no drinking, please."

"I promise." That's an easy one. "No more drinking."

The muscles in her cheeks relax, but she doesn't walk away. She just stands there, staring at me.

"I'll be home later." I give her a weak smile, then bolt out the door.

Jenna's car is idling just beyond the front steps. She gets out and lifts up on her tip-toes, giant purple sunglasses shielding her eyes from the sun. "I hope you don't mind that it's me," she says. "Leigh Anne got a call from her attorney's office that they needed her for a conference call in half an hour. She called me and asked if I'd take over."

I frown and pull the shoulder strap over my body. I clutch the bag. Can I trust Jenna to help me and not blab about it? I barely know her. And I'm not entirely sure she even likes me very much.

She pounds the top of the car. "I know it's not your usually fancy ride, but she's my baby," she says. "She got me here all the way from California."

"I thought Leigh Anne said you were from Macon," I say, walking the rest of the way down the front steps of the house.

She shrugs. "Nah. I went to school in Macon for a year, then transferred here to FCU," she says. "But I grew up in California."

"I don't mind the car," I say, realizing she thought I was frowning about her car not being nice enough. "It's just that I…"

I glance back toward the front door to make sure Mom isn't sneakily standing right behind me listening to every word I'm saying.

"I have something I need to do that's very… secret. No one can find out about this, okay? Can I trust you?"

As I say it, I know it's a dumb question to ask someone directly. People who aren't trustworthy are still probably going to say yes. Who's really going to admit that no, they can't be trusted? Not many people, that's for sure.

And most people really can't be trusted.

"There's only one way to find out," she says. She pounds the top of the car again, then laughs and disappears inside.

I blink and stand there for a second, a little stunned. Was that a yes? Or a maybe?

I get in and she turns the radio up.

"Where to, little lady?"

I bite my lip. "I'm honestly not sure," I say. "Can you just start driving? We'll figure it out on the way."

"Sure," she says.

She rolls the car around the looped driveway, then out the front gate and into the street.

She throws a quick glance toward my bag. "What you got?"

I pull the bag tighter against my body. "This is part of the whole trust thing," I say. "I don't want anyone to find out what I'm doing or why I'm doing it."

"In this town, you realize that's like saying you don't want anyone to know your family has money, right?" She laughs.

"This is important," I say. "I know people talk, but I was hoping we could find a place where people could be persuaded to keep their mouths shut."

Jenna puts on her turn signal and swings her car into the parking lot of McDonalds.

"Listen," she says, turning all the way toward me in her bucket seat, "I know we haven't spent a ton of time hanging out, but I know what you're going through. Whatever you need to do, I'm here for you. Pinky swear. You can tell me, and I promise I'll take it to my grave if you ask me to."

I look down at the bag in my lap. I have no idea if I can really trust her, but right now, she's my best hope of getting this money on time.

I take a deep breath, then tell her about the baby in the hospital and how my parents cut me off.

When I finish my explanation, her eyes are a little shiny and she's staring at me like I'm some kind of alien.

"What?"

She raises her eyebrows and holds her hands up. "I had all these scenarios running around in my head. Like maybe you wanted to run away because your parents beat you when they found out about the wreck or that you had to take this bag full of unmarked bills to some cop as payment for letting you off the hook. I thought this was going to be some shady shit," she says. "I'm not gonna lie. The fact that you're selling stuff to pay for a baby's surgery is probably one of the biggest damn surprises of my life."

I lean my head back against the headrest. "You don't

think much of me, do you?" I ask. "How come you never came to any of my parties?"

"I try to stay away from people who have a lot of money," she says. "In my experience, they end up being egotistical assholes who only care about themselves and will step on whoever they have to in order to get what they want. But since I met Leigh Anne, I've been in constant amazement about how strong and selfless some of the women in this town can be. Even the richest ones. It's truly eye-opening, because I've never met anyone like the two of you in my life."

I study her. She's not afraid to say whatever she's thinking, and I'm not used to that. Most people would have lied and said they like me and that I was being silly for thinking otherwise. Jenna didn't even hesitate to tell me the truth.

"So what would you have done if this really was full of unmarked bills or whatever?"

"I would have driven you where you needed to go, and I would have kept my thoughts to myself," she says. She pulls her sunglasses down over her eyes and turns forward. "Or I would have grabbed the bag, kicked your ass out of the car, and run like hell."

I laugh as she pulls out of the parking lot and heads south on Main Street.

Chapter Twenty-Two

Jenna turns onto the highway and starts heading out of Fairhope.

I turn and look back at the road. "Where are you taking us?"

"I thought you said you wanted to be discreet. That's not happening in Fairhope. Look, if you want to sell your stuff for cash as fast as you can, the best way to do that is at a pawn shop," she says. "You can either pawn it or sell it."

"What does pawning it do?"

She looks over at me, tilting her chin down so I can see her eyes over the top of her sunglasses. "You don't know how pawn shops work?"

I shrug, feeling stupid. "I've watched Pawn Stars before, but usually people just want to sell their stuff. What happens when they pawn it?"

"Pawning is more of a cash advance kind of thing," she

says. "Or a very high-interest loan with your stuff as collateral. Instead of actually selling the item, you'll make a contract with them where they give you cash to borrow for the month and at the end of the month, you either pay them back with interest and get your stuff back or you pay just the interest and have to come back again next month. If you don't pay, you lose the item you pawned and they can now sell it in the store."

"What kind of interest are we talking here?"

"It depends," she says. "Most places, it ends up being something like fifteen to twenty percent after all the interest and fees."

My jaw practically hits the floor. "That can't be right. That's highway robbery," I say, shaking my head. "There's no way they're charging twenty percent interest on a loan for one month."

She raises and eyebrow. "Yeah, it's crazy, but it's true," she says. She eyes my bag. "Do you want to permanently part with the stuff in that bag? Or pawn it?"

"It depends on how much I can get for everything," I say. "I'm willing to sell some of the jewelry and the clothes and stuff, but there are a few items I really can't afford to sell."

"I'm going to take you to a really good place in Savannah," she says. "The guy who owns it is a real character, but he's fair and he'll help you keep this under the table."

I pull the bag closer to my chest. I'm stepping way out of my comfort zone, here. "How do you know all this stuff?"

She smiles. "We don't all have parents who can help us out or pay tuition," she says. "And working at a restaurant means you never really know how much you're going to make every night. Sometimes I come up short on the rent."

I feel like an idiot. It never occurred to me Jenna might be struggling with money. "I guess I just assumed your parents paid for your apartment or something," I say. "Most people I know—"

"Most people you know live on a completely different plane of existence than us mere mortals," she says. "It's no big deal, really. I get by just fine on my own, and I don't have to worry about anyone telling me what to do or yelling at me when I fuck up."

"Must be nice," I mumble.

"It is," she says. "But if I had access to things like tennis courts and private pools and a yacht, I doubt I ever would have moved out either."

"It's a blessing and a curse," I say. "My parents protect me from a lot of things and make sure I have whatever I need or want. But they also shelter me and do their best to control me. I hate to complain about it, because I know how lucky I am to have them. At the same time, though, they've always put so much pressure on Preston and me."

"Your life is your own, though, you know? You can make excuses all you want, but in the end, you're the one who decides the path your life takes," she says. "If you want to be more independent, then do it. What's stopping you? Look at Leigh Anne. Her mom's probably one of the meanest people I've ever known in my life. She did everything she could to control Leigh Anne, and it worked for years. But as soon as she decided to get a job, get her own apartment, start thinking about what she really wanted out of life, she kind of broke free from all that. Her mom still says mean things sometimes, but now Leigh Anne just doesn't put up with it."

"I wish I could be more like that," I say. "My mother isn't mean. My parents are great, really. They just want the best for us and have these set ideas about what that means."

I think about the baby growing inside me. This is seriously going to rock my parents' plans for my future.

"Just because they want it, though, doesn't mean you have to do it," she says. "It's your life, not theirs."

I stare forward as we cross into downtown Savannah. Jenna makes it sound so easy. Like all I have to do is move out, get a job, start living the life I want, and I'll be happy. But I know it's a lot more complicated than that. I'm afraid I would need a level of strength I just don't have inside me.

We sit in silence as she navigates the streets. She hasn't taken us to the pretty River Street area of Savannah. The streets here are full of brightly-colored houses with damaged roofs. Gas stations. Liquor stores. Fast food restaurants. I've never been to this part of the city.

She pulls into the parking lot of a dirty strip mall and parks in front of a tiny little shop called Gold-Silver Pawn. It's the kind of place you might overlook a thousand times. I'm starting to doubt trusting her with this. I don't have much time and I can't see how a small, seedy little place like this is going to get me five grand.

Jenna laughs and I turn to look at her.

"What's so funny?" I ask.

"The look on your face," she says. "It's going to be okay. I promise."

She snatches the bag from my lap and gets out of the car. I follow her inside where it's dark and cluttered. Tall silver racks hold junk from floor to ceiling. DVD players, Xbox's, CD's, clothes, lamps. Nothing's really put in any kind of logical order. It's more just scattered and thrown across the shelves in basic groupings. The path through the racks is narrow and we have to carefully scoot through so we don't knock anything off.

There are only two other people in the store that I can

see. There's a black guy with a shaved head sitting on a stool near the front counter. He's got one foot up and one foot flat against the floor and he's wearing a black jacket that's hanging open just enough for me to see he's got a small gun tucked into the waistband of his jeans.

He catches me staring and he adjusts his jacket to hide the gun.

I look away as fast as I can. I have no idea what I'm doing in a place like this.

Behind the counter is a really short, fat guy who looks like he could be a mobster or something. He's wearing four or five ridiculously big gold chains and he's got a Yankee's baseball cap on that's turned to the side.

He smiles at us. "Jenna, baby, how you doin'?"

"Heya, Rocco," she says. She jumps up on the counter and reaches across to give him a huge hug. "This is my friend Penny."

Rocco lifts his head up once in greeting. "What brings you two in here?"

Jenna puts my bag up on the counter. She turns and looks around the store. "Just us in here right now, right?"

"Looks like it," the guy on the stool says.

"Okay, good," she says. "Here's the deal. My friend here needs cash fast. Off the record."

"Whoa, now," Rocco says, holding both hands up

defensively. "Off the record isn't something I do for just anybody. You know that."

"You owe me, Rocco," she says. "I'm calling in a personal favor. Please, you gotta help her."

"I don't gotta do nothin'," he says. He shrugs and eyes the bag. "But for you, I'll take a look."

I step closer. The diamond bracelet is still in the bag, and I don't really want to just offer that up first thing, but I have no idea how to do this and I don't want to say something wrong or piss these guys off.

I tap Jenna's arm and she ignores me.

I tap it again.

She jerks her head toward me. "What?"

I lean toward her and whisper in her ear. "There's a bracelet in there that I'm not sure I can sell. Can I just get that out first? Then he can look at the rest of it."

"Yeah, sure." She scoots the bag toward me and I unzip it. I have to dig through to find the bracelet. I close my fist around it, and stuff it in my pocket.

"Done," I say with a smile. I've never felt more awkward in my life.

Jenna pushes the bag toward Rocco.

He opens it and starts laying items out one at a time. He makes notes on a pad of paper. It takes him about twenty minutes, but he finally circles something, then turns the paper around and scoots it across the counter toward us.

Jenna looks to me, an eyebrow raised in question.

The notepad has a bunch of figures written on it. The one that's circled is $1600.

I close my eyes and let out a frustrated rush of air. "That's for everything?" I ask.

"That's for even exchange," Rocco says. "Cash in hand."

Fuck. I need a hell of a lot more than that.

"There's got to be at least ten thousand dollars' worth of stuff in there."

"Look, this ain't a department store," he says with a laugh. "You want cash, this is the best I can do. Unless you wanna show me what's in your pocket?"

I swallow. I know I should just take whatever he's offering and walk out the door, but I can't. It's not enough.

I slowly pull the bracelet out of my pocket and lay it across the counter.

Rocco whistles and reaches under the counter for a small black box that has what looks like a metal pen top on one end. He switches it on and presses the metal probe onto the top of each diamond. He waits for a beeping sound, then moves to the next until he's tested every single diamond on the bracelet.

"This is really something special," he says. He looks up and lets his eyes drift from mine all the way down to my knees. "Where did you get this?"

"It's mine," I lie.

"Bullshit," he says. "Where'd you really get it? I can't buy stolen merchandise."

My shoulders slump and I press my palms against the edge of the counter. "It's my mother's."

"You stole it from her?"

"Not exactly," I say. "She let me wear it a few nights ago. I got into an accident and it ended up in a plastic bag inside my purse. For all she knows, it was lost in the accident."

"So she doesn't know you still have it?"

I shake my head. Guilt churns my stomach, but what choice do I have? My mother has hundreds of these kinds of things. Bracelets, rings, earrings, watches. Does she really need another diamond bracelet more than this baby needs his surgery? No way.

It's easy to rationalize in my head, but I know what I'm doing is still wrong.

"Two thousand dollars," he says, running the bracelet through his hand.

"I need five thousand dollars," I say bluntly. "For all of it."

"Don't dick around with her, Rocco," Jenna says. "Give her the five grand. This stuff is worth a hell of a lot more than that and you know it."

He lets a burst of air out through his lips, then raises his hands and backs away. "That's a lot of money for something under-the-table like this. I'm the one taking all the risk."

"Please," I say, meeting his eyes straight on.

Rocco sighs and looks at the guy sitting on the chair. They exchange heavy looks until finally, the other guy shrugs.

Rocco holds his hand over the counter to me.

I put my hand in his, and we shake on it.

Chapter Twenty-Three

Nurse Valerie takes the envelope from my hand, tears shining in her eyes.

"Are you sure you don't want to talk with the family yourself?" she asks. "I'm sure they'd love to know who donated this money. They're going to want to say thank you."

I shake my head. "I don't want to bring any extra attention to it," I say.

She smiles. "You've done so much for so many families here. How come you don't ever want anyone to say thank you?"

I look down at my feet. I think about all the money I've spent on myself in the past couple of years. New clothes. A new car. Anything and everything I wanted. "Because I do so much less than I should," I say, looking up to meet her gaze. "Keep me updated on how the baby does, okay?"

"I will," she says.

I keep my head down as I make my way back to the parking lot. I know Jenna's waiting for me, but I step to the side and lean against the brick wall. I pull my phone out of my pocket and dial Mason's number again.

Please answer.

I tap my toes inside my shoes as the phone rings. The line picks up, and I expect it to be voice-mail again. But it isn't.

"Hey," he says. He sounds tired.

"Hey," I say. My heart beats fast in my chest.

Silence passes between us. Two days of not talking felt like an eternity, but now that I have him on the phone, I have no idea what to say.

"How are you feeling?" he asks.

I lean my head back against the rough bricks. "I'm okay," I say. "I'm sorry about your car. Are you pissed?"

He hesitates and my chest tightens. "Yes," he says. "But not about the car. Fuck the car. I'm pissed at myself."

"No, this was my fault, Mason. I'm so sorry. I can't believe I did that. I don't know what I was thinking."

"You were angry," he says. "Frustrated. That's on me. I'm not good for you Penny, can't you see that?"

My insides tighten and knot. "That's not true."

The Moment We Began

I want to tell him we belong together, but the harder I cling to him, the faster he pulls away.

"It is," he says. "The last few times we've been together, you've gotten out of control. I don't want to be responsible for that. You deserve better than me, Pen. Better than what I'm able to give you. Look, there are things you don't know about me. If you knew what kind of guy I really was, you'd be running."

I slide down the wall, my legs not wanting to hold me up any longer. I can't lose him now, but I have no idea how to turn this around. I don't want better. All I want is him.

"I'm not perfect, either," I say.

"I gotta go," he says. "Take care of yourself, Pen. I mean it."

It sounds like a goodbye. I bury my free hand in my hair and pull. What do I do? What can I do?

"Wait," I say, my voice shaky. "I need to see you."

"I can't," he says. He draws in a long breath. "I'm sorry. I don't want to do anything that's going to hurt you more than I already have."

"This was my fault," I say. "Dammit, don't push me away just because you think that's what's best for me. That's not for you to decide. If you don't want to see me, that's one thing, but don't say it's because you don't want to hurt me. That's bullshit. Not being able to talk to you the past few days has hurt me more than anything. How can you not know that?"

He groans. "Tomorrow night some of us were talking about getting together at Knox's lake house," he said. "I wasn't planning on going because I figured you'd be there, but if you really want to talk, I'll go."

I breathe out and the tension I've been holding in my body releases. "Thank you."

"I really do need to go," he says. "I'll see you tomorrow."

"Okay."

"And Penny?"

"Yes."

He pauses. "I'm really glad you're safe."

Chapter Twenty-Four

It's nice to be able to skip out on dinner with my parents the following night. They aren't speaking to me. Their anger and disappointment hangs like a Georgia heat in the air, suffocating me.

I am nervous about seeing some of my friends again, but Leigh Anne promises tonight will be close friends only. No big parties. No drinking.

No judgment.

She picks me up at six-thirty and my stomach is in nervous knots the entire ride to the lake house. For some reason, I feel like tonight could make all the difference. Like, when I see Mason's eyes, I'll know if there's hope or if I'm going to have to do this on my own.

When we get there, though, I'm disappointed to see he's not there yet.

Knox, Leigh Anne, and Jenna are here already. Preston

joins us half an hour later. By the time Summer's car comes bouncing down the path, I'm starting to feel anxious.

What if he's not coming?

Knox and Preston cook chicken on the grill with fresh vegetables and bread. I'm relieved when no one brings up the accident. Conversation is easy and relaxed. Mostly, we talk about the upcoming school year.

I take my time eating, one eye on the road leading up to the house.

As the sun disappears behind the trees, so does my hope.

"Thanks for not being completely pissed at me," I say as I stand to help Knox bring the plates inside to the kitchen. "I never wanted to get you or the bar in any trouble."

Knox shrugs. "I was honestly more worried about you than anything," he says. "I had no idea you'd even left. I thought you were just going outside to talk. I never would have let you drive home. Not in a million years."

"I know." My cheeks warm and the food in my stomach turns. I've barely had an appetite the past few days. Every time I eat, my stomach hurts like this. I'm not sure if it's the start of morning sickness or if it's just the constant nervous anxiety. "I didn't mean to drive off, either. I was just so mad, I wasn't thinking straight. I'm really glad you didn't get into any trouble over it."

The Moment We Began

He takes the plates from my hand and runs them under the water, then sets them into the open dishwasher. "Me too," he says. "To be honest, it's been a really crazy summer. Ever since all the publicity from Leigh Anne's case, people have been packing into the bar every night. It's been great for us, don't get me wrong, but man, dealing with all the fake ID's and attention has been a real nightmare."

"Have you had a lot of fake ID's coming through there?"

"More than you want to know," he says. "I know it sounds awful, but I never really cared so much before. I knew all the regulars and didn't care if one of my twenty-year-old friends wanted to grab a drink or two. But now? We aren't exactly flying under the radar anymore. The money's good, but the attention sucks. Rob's used to have this very laid back atmosphere, but now it's gotten fast-paced and hectic, everyone pushing to get a table or angry they didn't get their drinks fast enough. It's exhausting. It makes me feel like I'm back in Chicago. Back in the rat race."

I sit down at the small table in the kitchen and watch as he finishes rinsing off the dishes. I hadn't realized how unhappy Knox was about the bar getting busy. I would have thought it would be exciting for their family to start bringing in some good revenue. It never occurred to me they liked it the way it was.

"What if you hired someone for the door," I say. "A bouncer who's in charge of checking all the ID's. Twenty-one and up only or maybe armbands for underage people. That way you wouldn't have to constantly check them at the bar. Then you can limit how many people can be inside at once, too. Keep the crowd as big or small as you want."

Knox throws the wet dish towel into the sink and turns around. His eyebrows are cinched in the middle, like he's thinking it through for a minute. "You know, that might actually help," he says, giving me a little smile. "Dang, I never thought about that, Penny. It's been the three of us working the bar for so long, I didn't really think about hiring help. You're a genius."

I smile back. God, it feels good to be praised for something after the week I've had. "I don't know about genius," I say. "It's basic business, really."

"What is?" Leigh Anne asks, stepping into the kitchen.

"Penny had a great idea about hiring a bouncer for the bar," Knox says. He starts to tell her more when headlights flash through the windows. The road leading up to the cabin is bumpy and rough and the lights bounce up and down like search lights.

I stand, my heart in my throat.

Leigh Anne comes to stand beside me. "Is it Mason?"

I can't answer. I can only wait and watch. And hope.

The Moment We Began

I am trying to judge the shape and color of the car, but then realize I have no idea what he'll be driving. I completely totaled his car.

Preston and the others walk into the room, their laughter carrying through the hallway.

I don't even turn to look at them. My eyes are glued to the car outside as it stops and the lights cut off.

From the lights mounted on the sides of the lake house, I can see enough to make out that it isn't a car at all. It's a truck.

When the driver gets out and stands up, I instantly know it's him.

I know the movement of his body as if it were my own. I've spent so many hours watching him and loving him that I'd know him by a single turn of his cheek.

"Let's head outside," Preston says, patting Knox's shoulder. "I've got a cooler full of sodas. We can get a fire going and sit out there for a while."

As Leigh Anne passes by me, she grips my shoulders and gives me a hug.

Most of the group heads through the house toward the front porch, but I hang back to talk to Mason.

My hand trembles as I turn the knob on the back door and pull it open.

He freezes when he sees me. His face is half in shadow,

but his eyes are on me. And mine are on him.

"You're late," I say, breathless.

"I almost didn't come," he says. There's a sadness in his voice that can't be denied, and I wonder if everything is broken between us.

And if there's any way to fix it.

"I understand if you're mad at me," I say, nervous. "If you didn't want to see me."

He shakes his head, then looks down at his feet as if he'll find the right words down there. "I'm not mad at you. Believe me, I wanted to see you more than ever," he says. When he looks up at me, there's something in his eyes that scares me. "I'm going to be taking off for a while, Pen."

The words make my knees almost give out. My entire stomach lurches and I struggle to breathe in. "What do you mean?"

I'm hoping he's going to say something like he's going on a three-day trip to Vegas, like he's done a few times before, but before he answers I already know it's going to be more than that. This is why he wanted to see me tonight. To say goodbye.

He steps onto the porch and his face comes into the light. There are circles under his eyes. "I've got to get out of this town for a while," he says. "I've been thinking about it for months, honestly. It's just time. Things have gotten stale for me here."

"How long is a while?" I ask, my hands shaking a little. I shove them in the pockets of my jeans so he won't see. "A week or two?"

He shakes his head. His eyes are full of apologies and regrets. "I was thinking maybe a few months or so."

Months? As if my world hasn't shattered enough in the past week, Mason's just taken a hammer to it.

I want to sit down right here on the floor and lay my head against the smooth, cool wood of the door frame. I hear laughter out on the front side of the house, but I feel like I will never laugh again. All I want to do is sit down and disappear.

I want to go to sleep and wake up a week ago so I can fix all this and go back to the way things were.

I want to tell him don't go, but I know I have no power over him. I never have. Instead, I ask, "Are you leaving because of me? Because of what I did?"

"It's complicated," he says.

My heart sinks low in my chest and I feel hope draining from me. He fiddles with the keys in his hand.

"I'm so sorry about your car," I say. "You loved that car."

His head pops up and he looks me in the eyes. "Love is a strong word for a car," he says.

I've never heard him say anything like that in his life. He's babied that damn car for the past two years.

"What did you get instead? Is that a truck?"

He gives me a half smile and glances back. "Come here," he says. He holds his hand out to me. "I'll show you."

My heart skips a beat as I reach for him.

When our hands touch, he rubs his thumb softly against the top of my fingers. That's when I know, for the first time, that my brother was right.

There's more here than lust. There's a tenderness to Mason's touch that sends shivers down my spine.

For him, it might not be love. Not yet. But it gives me hope.

Chapter Twenty-Five

Mason leads me back outside to where the cars are parked. I don't know exactly what I'm expecting, but a rusted beat-up Ford pickup is probably the last thing. It doesn't seem like Mason at all.

Mason's the guy who likes flashy cars with perfect red paint and sleek shiny lines.

He's the guy who once nearly punched a random stranger for touching his car in the parking lot of a concert.

He's not an old Ford pickup kind of guy.

Mason walks up to it proudly and pounds the hood a couple of times. A huge smile spreads across his face.

"What do you think? Pretty cool, huh?"

I'm literally speechless. I walk around the back of the truck and study its dirty bed that still has gravel and woodchips between the treads. Dried mud is splattered across the back and the tires are covered in red clay.

I open the door and pull myself up into the driver's seat. The windows are both already rolled down.

Inside, the upholstery is actually patched in places with duct tape. On the dashboard, there's an old, yellowed Polaroid picture of two kids with bright blond hair. They look almost the same age except the girl is maybe a year older than the boy.

I pick it up. "Who's this?"

Mason's face darkens for a brief moment. He hops into the passenger seat and takes the picture from me. "Just someone I used to know."

He seems so sad and serious. Not like Mason at all. I don't know how to make sense of it. There's something more going on here than just my accident.

No, this is something else.

I've been so wrapped up in myself and my own problems, it never occurred to me that he might be going through something of his own right now. And I have no idea how to push past his walls to find out how to help him. After what happened between us this past week, I'm probably the last person on earth he wants to talk to about it.

He puts the picture back up on the dashboard, then shrugs it off.

"What do you think of the truck?"

I put my hands on the steering wheel and try really hard to see what it is he's so excited about. "I think you got screwed by your insurance company."

He rolls his eyes and shakes his head. "Well, I didn't

want to spend all that money on another brand new car," he says. "I took some of it and bought all kinds of gear for my trip. Camping stuff, like a tent and some backpacks. A hatchet. A camping stove. Stuff like that."

I have to look twice to make sure he's not kidding. "A hatchet?"

He lifts one eyebrow and slowly nods up and down. "Oh yeah, baby. And it's a real beauty. It's used, but it's freshly sharpened and really great quality."

"Mason." I turn all the way toward him on the seat. "What the hell are you going to do with a hatchet?"

He stares at me for a long minute. "You don't get it, do you?"

I study his face, not sure what he expects me to say. "I get the urge to leave town, believe me. But why this truck? Why camping instead of hotels? If it was me I would fly somewhere exotic like St. Lucia and stay at a resort with room service."

He presses his lips together tight and turns his body away from me. "I guess I should have known someone like you couldn't understand what I'm trying to do," he says.

"What's that supposed to mean?"

He slaps his hand against his thighs. "I don't know, maybe that you act like a princess sometimes," he says. "Penelope Wright couldn't possibly understand why someone would willingly camp out in nature or want to just hop in a truck and head west."

I grip the steering wheel. "Explain it to me, then."

Mason turns to me. "Don't you see what's been happening to us?" he asks. "We party and spend money and drink like it's nothing. We take everything in life for granted, which means we're always on the verge of losing it and we don't even realize it."

"I thought you said this had nothing to do with the accident," I say.

He runs a hand through his dark blond hair. "It's not just the other night," he says. "It's everything. Every night. I feel like it's gotten completely out of control. I don't want to be this person, Penny. The more time goes on, the more I become someone else. Someone I really don't think I like anymore."

My shoulders slump and I take my hands off the wheel.

"So this is really some kind of pilgrimage?" I ask. "Some kind of journey to salvation? What do you think is really going to change?"

He looks up and our eyes meet. "Everything," he says. He shifts on the seat, moving closer to me. "Have you ever wondered what it would be like to pull into a town where no one knows you and just set up camp? To walk around without all the expectations that comes with being a rich kid? Look at Knox. When he moved to Fairhope, no one gave a shit about him. He didn't have a fancy car. He didn't flaunt his dad's money. He just came in as himself."

"And everyone treated him like crap," I say, not understanding what he's getting at.

He shakes his head. "Not everyone," he says. "The

people who mattered saw past it all. It was people like us who judged him for what he didn't have or what he might have done. But the people who were going to make a difference in his life just saw him for who he was. Money didn't factor into it, because he didn't let it. Don't you ever think about how that would feel?"

I have no idea how something like that would feel. I've always been recognized as Tripp Wright's daughter. Every friend I've ever made has known how much money my family has and there's no way to know if their friendship is real or if they only want to be part of the rich crowd.

Then it hits me.

He's really leaving.

This isn't just some spur-of-the-moment thing for him. He's been thinking about this for a long time. My accident simply became the catalyst that made him finally do it.

Silence stretches between us. I can almost feel the miles passing, putting distance between us that we'll never get back. By the time he comes home, the world will look completely different. He'll see it with a whole new set of eyes. He'll see me with new eyes.

And maybe he won't like what he sees.

"Please, tell me you're not doing this just to get away from me," I say.

He reaches across the duct tape and takes my hand. The warmth of his skin on mine is like medicine to my soul.

"Leaving you is one of the hardest parts," he says softly.

I look over and see that he's staring at me with an

expression that's full of affection and almost… regret?

"I don't want you to go." I can only whisper. My heart is breaking inside. If I tell him about the baby, he might agree to stay, but what good would that do me? I don't want him to feel trapped here by some feeling of responsibility. He'll come to resent me for that, I know it.

But if he leaves, I might lose him forever.

He runs his index finger along each of my fingers, one at a time. Back and forth, the lightest whisper of a touch.

"If I don't get out of this town, I'm going to suffocate here," he says. "In some ways, you're the only thing that's been holding me to this place."

I sniff and my throat constricts. "Are you saying you're ready to let me go?"

He's all I ever wanted, and with each moment that passes between us, I feel him slipping away.

"I'm saying I finally realize that if I stay, I'll destroy you," he says. His eyes shine in the dim light. "You want so much more than I can give you, Pen, but when I'm here—when I see you every day—I can't stay away from you. I try, but I always keep coming back. The only way I can think to save us both is to put some distance between us. To let you move on with your life. Find someone else."

"I don't want someone else."

"You've never given anyone else a chance," he says.

I look away, tears welling up in my eyes. He's right, but that's not the problem. The problem is that he's never given me—us—a real chance. He's been too busy pushing me away to really explore what could be between us. But when I'm in his arms and it's just the two of us, I know it could work between us.

Maybe there's another way to save us both. To find out, once and for all, if we are meant to be.

I'm going to go with him.

Chapter Twenty-Six

My heart races and my head spins. Could I really do something so crazy?

I'd have almost no money to my name. I'd be camping in a tent, sleeping on the ground, eating out of cans or something. But I'd be sleeping next to Mason. If I could have him all to myself for a couple of months, maybe I could break down his walls long enough to make him see that we belong together.

Just thinking about it makes me feel twenty pounds lighter.

Of course, walking away means leaving my entire support system behind. It means walking on a tightrope without a net. It means missing my mother's annual end-of-season charity ball. And if we're really gone for months, it means missing the start of the new semester at FCU. It would mess up my entire schedule and plan.

Of course, isn't that going to happen when the baby comes anyway?

And when am I ever going to have another opportunity like this? I only have a few months until my belly starts growing, and by then it will be too late to find out if he's with me because he loves me or because he wants to do the right thing.

This is my chance. My one chance.

I look up at him, shadows dancing across the dark stubble on his jawline.

Would he let me come with him?

Mason looks down at me and his deep green eyes hit me straight to my core. I want him more than ever.

I need him more than ever.

His eyes narrow and he turns his head, questioning. I smile and he studies me. "What?"

"When are you planning to leave?"

"Tomorrow," he says. "First light."

"Can you wait for me? I want to come see you off."

His lips part and he studies me again. "What for?" he asks.

I know I should tell him what I'm thinking, but I'm scared he'll say no. "Just promise me you won't leave until you see me."

166

The Moment We Began

He hesitates. He wants more specific answers, but I'm not giving them.

"Please," I say, and it's the one word that breaks him.

"Yes," he says. "I'll wait for you."

Chapter Twenty-Seven

After everyone else has left for the evening, Leigh Anne offers to take me home.

We spent a few hours around the fire talking. Everyone had a ton of questions for Mason once he told them about his plans to take off for a while. Preston kept looking at me like he was scared I might lose it. He wanted to drive me home, but I didn't want to risk blurting out the truth to him. He'd only try to talk me out of it.

"You aren't spending the night with Knox out here?" I ask Leigh Anne as we climb into her car.

"Not tonight," she says. "I've got to work a double shift tomorrow, so I want to actually get some rest for a change."

"Well, considering it's already after midnight, I think you're already screwed," I say.

She giggles. "Not as screwed as I would be if I stayed."

"Haha," I say, slapping her arm as she gets in and starts

down the bumpy dirt road leading to the highway.

We ride for a moment in silence, but as soon as she pulls out onto the main road, I turn toward her in my seat.

"Thanks for tonight," I say. "I really needed a night to just chill without anyone looking at me like I'm some horrible person."

She crinkles her face and pats my leg. "We've all messed up, Penny. We've all got regrets."

"Thanks," I say.

She frowns. "How are you taking Mason's news?" she asks. "Are you okay?"

"Yes," I say. "No. I don't know, really."

"Did you get to talk to him much about what happened last week?"

"A little."

She clears her throat. "Penny, what exactly did happen last week?" she asks. "One minute you were kissing Braxton and having a good time, then the next Mason was dragging you out into the parking lot. What happened between the two of you out there?"

As far as Leigh Anne knows, Mason is nothing more than a dream to me. I've never told her the truth about us sleeping together for the past year.

Maybe it's time.

I lean back against the seat and play with a strand of my

hair, twirling it around and around my finger. "My hair used to be so long," I say. "Remember how Mason used to tease me about it?"

She smiles. "He used to call you Rapunzel. He said if your parents ever locked you up in a tower, he would come save you."

"My knight in shining armor," I say. "Last summer Preston and I had some friends over on the boat. Mason and a few others. We stayed up really late drinking and playing cards. Watching movies. After everyone left and Preston went to bed, it was just me and Mason."

I take a deep breath in, remembering that night like it was yesterday.

"We must have stayed up talking until five in the morning," I say. "I had my hair in one long braid down my back and out of the blue, he asked me to take it down. I remember feeling something shift between us. Like a wall coming down. I pulled the braid apart and he ran his hands through it over and over. That was the first time he ever told me I was beautiful."

Leigh Anne looks over at me, a small smile tugging at the corners of her lips.

"He kissed me," I say, running my hand through my hair. "And then he did a whole lot more than that."

I watch for her reaction, hoping she's not going to be

angry at me for not telling her sooner. Her mouth falls open slightly, but she doesn't say a word. She just listens.

"He told me right from the start that he wasn't looking for a serious relationship," I say. "I didn't want to freak him out, so I said I wasn't either. He told me up front that he didn't intend to be exclusive, but I thought I could handle it. I thought it would be worth it just to be with him."

"Oh, Penny," Leigh Anne says. She reaches for my hand and I take it. "I had no idea."

"Two days later he showed up at a bonfire on the beach with another girl," I say, laughing. The sound is hollow and joyless. "The next day I walked into the salon and told them to chop my hair off."

She pulls up to the gate at my house and the night guard waves us through. When she stops in front of the house, she turns and pulls me into a hug.

"I can't even imagine how hard that must have been," she says.

"I've been caught in that same cycle ever since," I say. "When it's just the two of us, it's like magic. But every time I see him with another girl, it breaks my heart."

"This has been going on for over a year?" she asks.

I shrug.

Her eyes widen. "Penny, how come you haven't told him how you feel about him? You can't live like that," she says. "You deserve better than that."

I suck in a breath. "I know," I say. "I tried to call it off with him at the boat party just before you came home. That's why I went out with Braxton. I was trying to move on and have fun. But Mason walked in and saw me kissing Braxton and he freaked out."

Leigh Anne leans her head against the back of the seat. "Oh, my god," she says. "That's why he took you outside to talk?"

"Yes," I say, my nose starting to run from holding back tears. Saying all this out loud makes me sound like a fool, but there's no way anyone else can see what Mason and I share when it's just the two of us. If they could see that, they'd understand why I can never let him go. "We kissed, but he gave me the same speech he always gives me about not being able to offer me what I want. I guess I couldn't take it anymore. I grabbed his keys and drove off, not really thinking about what I was doing. All I knew was that I was angry and I wanted to get away. It was stupid."

"I can't believe you've been going through this alone," she says.

I shrug. "It's nothing compared to what you were going through. I chose this, you know?"

"You love him," she says. "Love makes us do crazy things."

173

I smile and wipe my eyes. "Yes, it does," I say. "So if you find out I've done something crazy in the name of love, don't judge me, okay? Promise?"

She cocks her head to the side and narrows her eyes. "Crazy like what?"

I laugh. I shake my head. "I really need to get inside," I say. I wrap my arms around her. "I love you."

"I love you, too," she says, hugging me back. "I'm here for you if you want to talk about it, okay? You don't have to go through the hard times alone. I learned that the hard way."

"I know," I say. "Goodnight, Leigh Anne."

"Goodnight," she says. "And for what it's worth, I really like your hair like this. It suits you."

I smile. "Mason said the same thing," I say. "And here I thought cutting it would piss him off, but he actually liked it."

"Sometimes men don't really know what they want until they see it for themselves," she says.

A nervousness flutters through me as I realize that's exactly what I'm counting on.

Chapter Twenty-Eight

I can't sleep. There's too much to do and it's already late.

I take a shower, dress as simply as I can, then stare at the set of Louis Vuitton luggage I usually take with me on trips. It's a ten-piece set that cost a fortune. My parents gave it to me as a graduation present after high school, along with a month-long trip to Europe.

I can't pack in this.

I pull my closet apart looking for something else I can use, but I can't find anything suitable.

It sort of defeats the purpose, though, to go on a back-to-basics trip with luggage that costs more than the truck we're riding in. Besides, the idea of lugging a huge suitcase into a camp site is just ridiculous. If I'm going to do this, I want to do it right.

My cheerleading bag is still on the floor of my closet. I

pick it up and groan. This thing is tiny, but I can't find anything else.

Never in my life have I packed in something so small. Not even for an overnight trip.

I'm not sure I can do this.

Part of me says to lift my chin and just do it. I can live in the woods, right? I don't need all this fancy stuff.

But part of me says I'm insane for even considering it. What if I start throwing up with morning sickness? Am I really going to want to be without basic comforts?

I shake my head and take a deep breath. I'm not going to talk myself out of it before I've even given myself a chance. Maybe I'll be a natural outdoors-woman.

It'll be an adventure.

And most importantly, it will be my only real chance to find out if there's potential for a future with Mason.

I square my shoulders and set the bag down on my bed, then get to work choosing what I'm going to take.

First, the very basics. I'll need underwear. I can probably make do with seven pairs. Enough for one week and then I can either wash them in the sink or find a place to do laundry. Maybe we'll stay in a hotel that has laundry service. I stuff them into the bag.

What else? I'll need shampoo and deodorant and stuff like that. But when I walk into my bathroom, I feel like I'm going to cry. I use more products on a daily basis than I could fit in two of those bags. I don't want to look gross the whole time.

I have a few travel bottles of shampoo, so I put those into a small makeup bag. I take my brush, deodorant, moisturizer, toothpaste, mouthwash... crap. It's already too much stuff.

My muscles tense. This shouldn't be so hard! It's stupid! If I can't pack light enough to go on an outdoor adventure, then I really am a snotty rich girl.

Come on, Penelope, get it together.

I compromise and decide to pack my clothes in the cheer bag and my makeup and stuff in my Louis Vuitton train case. It's not ideal, but at least I'm trying, right?

I am able to put most of my makeup and essentials in the train case, but the clothes bag is a nightmare.

I finally narrow it down to one pair of jeans—the ones that really hug my butt because Mason always comments when I wear them—a pair of cutoff jean shorts, khaki shorts, a short black dress that rolls into a teeny little ball, ten basic colored tanktops, a couple of pairs of flip-flops, two bikinis, and a black mini-skirt. I have to really squish the bag together to get it to zip, but when it does, a triumphant smile breaks out across my face.

See? I'm not so terrible at this after all.

I look around my room, trying to figure out what else I can't live without for the next couple of months.

I grab the bottle of prenatal vitamins the doctor gave me. I dump them into a plain plastic bag and toss the bottle into the trash. This is only a one month supply, so I'll have to pick some up when we're out on the road if we're gone longer than that.

I know I won't be able to stay gone too long. I'm going to need to come home and get a proper appointment with an OBGYN and make sure I'm taking care of the baby. Dr. Mallory told me most people schedule their first visit for between eight and ten weeks along. According to the measurements of the baby, I'm a little over five weeks now.

Which means I've only got about five weeks before I absolutely need to get back home for an appointment.

I take a deep breath and touch my belly. It's hard to believe there's a tiny little baby growing inside of me. I feel completely normal, but there's this fluttering heartbeat deep inside. It's such a strange thing to create a life. Strange and beautiful and terrifying all at once.

I know I'm taking a huge risk leaving my comfort zone and the shelter of my parents' house right now, but I'll do anything to give this baby a chance to grow up with two parents who love each other.

I have to know if there's a chance for more between us.

The Moment We Began

I glance at the clock and see that it won't be long before the sun starts coming up.

I grab a pen and notepad from my desk and walk out onto the balcony. I sit down in the chair and look out over the garden. It's dark outside, but in the distance, there is a tiny haze of light beginning to show. I don't have much time.

There's nothing I can say to my parents in a note that will keep them from freaking out over me being gone, but I know I can't just leave without saying anything. They'd come after me.

I need them to give me space and respect my decision to leave.

But I've never done anything like this before, and I don't even know where to start.

Finally, I just scribble the following note:

Dear Mom and Dad,

I know I've disappointed you lately, and I'm sorry about everything I've put you through.

I need some time away to think through some things. I need to be on my own for a while, and I need you to respect my privacy.

I'll be out of touch for a while, but I'm with a friend who will take good care of me. I'll try not to stay gone too long. I can't tell you where I'm going, because I'm not exactly sure yet. It will be a true adventure!

I need some time to step away from my life here and really think about what I want for my future.

I hope you'll understand that I'm not doing this to hurt or scare you. I'm doing this for me.

I'm not sure when I'm coming home, but if I'm going to be gone longer than a month or two, I'll make sure to call and let you know that I'm safe. Please don't look for me.

All my love,
Penny

I leave the note on my pillow, grab my two bags, and tiptoe down the stairs. I go out the back door, avoiding the night guard out front. I climb over the fence near the pool, feeling equal parts devious child and determined woman.

Chapter Twenty-Nine

I walk to Mason's in the semi-darkness of the morning.

I'm glad it's way too early for anyone to be up and about, or I'm sure I would look like a crazy person walking out here in a pair of Docs and cut-offs with a cheerleading bag slung across my shoulder. Especially in this neighborhood of million-dollar houses. I hear a few dogs barking, but other than that, it's crickets out here.

For the first time since I decided I wanted to go with him, I'm nervous. Now that I've got a second alone with my own thoughts, I realize just how insane this is. How it's totally possible he was just being nice, and that I really am the reason he's skipping town in the first place.

What am I going to do if he won't let me go? It's going to be depressing if I end up sneaking right back into the house.

And I don't even want to think about how I'll handle

not seeing him for months.

It takes exactly six minutes to get to his house and by the time I can see his truck in the driveway, my hands are sweaty. I rub them against my shirt and take a deep breath. I straighten my shoulders and throw my head back, flipping my hair over my shoulders. I'm here now, so I simply won't take no for an answer. I'll make him take me, whether he wants to or not. Once we get on the road, we'll be having so much fun and feeling so free, he'll be glad I came.

At first, I don't see him and I think I'm going to have to go knock on the window of his room, but just as my feet hit his driveway, he comes out the side door near the garage with two large duffel bags in hand.

He doesn't see me at first, and I watch him. He's got headphones on and is mouthing the words to some song I can't hear. His head is bobbing up and down. He steps forward, then back, then turns around, dancing his way to the truck. I stand there, giggling. This is the carefree Mason I've loved most of my life. Not a care in the world. Light as air and not giving a shit what anyone thinks of him.

He tosses the two bags into the back of the truck, then finally looks up.

I'm smiling and he returns the smile at first. He reaches to pull off his headphones, then his eyes go to the bags in my hand and his smile fades.

The Moment We Began

My stomach turns. I push the nausea down and act confident, like I couldn't imagine he wouldn't want me here. I learned a long time ago that sometimes the best way to get what you want is to act like it's already yours. People have a hard time saying no to that.

I walk up, putting a bounce in my step, and sling my cheerleading bag into the back next to his. Mine looks so tiny compared to his. I could have fit a lot more clothes in one of those.

He pulls the headphones from his ears so that they hang around his neck. "What are you doing?"

"I'm coming with you," I say, as if it's already been discussed a thousand times. "And really, Mason, I'm surprised at you. Look at all this stuff you're bringing. I thought you wanted to get back to basics? I packed better than you did."

"Wait, uh-uh," he says, shaking his head. He leans over the side and grabs my little bag. "This is not happening, so get that in your head right now."

I swallow, fighting to not let any disappointment show on my face. "Oh, it's happening," I say, taking the bag from his hands and throwing it back into the truck. "When are we getting out of here? I need to make one stop by an ATM before we leave town. What time do you think fast food places open? I'm starving."

His mouth gapes open. I've completely thrown him for a loop, but at least he hasn't grabbed my bag again.

Yet.

"Pen, listen. This is not a good idea," he says, leaning against the side of the truck. "I need some time alone to get my head straight."

"You said you wanted to get away from the partying and the money and the expectations, right? You wanted to stop taking life for granted and learn to appreciate what you have. Well, I want those things, too."

He runs a hand through his hair. "Penny—"

"You also said leaving me was one of the hardest parts." I move closer to him. "So don't leave me. Take me with you."

He inhales slowly, his eyes on my lips. My heart races.

"I don't know that this is a good idea," he says, slightly breathless now. "Plus, I don't think you've fully grasped what kind of road trip this is. I'm not going to be staying in luxury hotels and flying to exotic locations. We're talking tents and bugs and public restrooms."

I cringe a little at the word bugs, but I'm willing to brave the wild in the name of love and adventure.

I think.

"I know that," I say. "I've done luxury hotels a thousand times, but not once in my entire life have I ever

184

camped out under the stars. It sounds romantic."

He laughs, but turns his body toward me, which is a good sign.

"It can be," he says. "It can also be smelly and dirty and rainy. You can't handle it, Pen. No way are you cut out for this."

I lift my chin. "Just because I've never done it before doesn't mean I can't handle it. Besides, it's not like you grew up camping out either." I nod toward his house, which is almost as big as mine. "We'll figure it out together. It'll be fun."

"I used to go camping all the time with my family growing up," he says, surprising me.

I press my lips together and narrow my eyes at him. "When? I remember your family taking vacations to the same resorts in Hawaii and the Caribbean my family went to. I never remember you guys going camping."

A faraway look takes over and he pauses, remembering something. "No, not after we moved here," he says. "Everything was different after my dad got that job working for your family. The last time we all went camping was the summer before…"

His voice trails off and he looks down at his feet and scuffs them back and forth against the asphalt.

"Before what?"

He looks up and shrugs again. "Before we moved here, I guess. It's been a long time, but I remember being really happy. It was a lot of fun back then."

I smile and lift one shoulder, trying to be cute. "I can do fun," I say. "Besides, you never went on any of those camping trips alone, right? Maybe it's not as fun all by yourself."

He scratches the side of his neck and avoids my eyes, but he's laughing. I'm definitely getting through to him and the knots in my stomach are loosening. He's going to take me with him. He just needs one more little push.

"I can handle this, Mason. I won't complain once, I swear." I make a criss-cross over my heart and he looks down, staring a moment too long at my cleavage.

I take another step closer to him and we're practically touching now.

"I'm no good for you, Penny. Can't you see that?"

"That's not true," I say in a soft voice. "Maybe it's this town that's no good for either one of us."

He's so tall I have to lift my chin to look up at him. My breath is shallow as I wait for him to speak. I wish I knew what to say to convince him this is the right thing.

"It's not a good idea," he says, turning away. "Trust me. Every time you get close to me, I end up hurting you. Or you end up hurting yourself."

The Moment We Began

I swallow and step back. I can't let him leave without me. "I need to go on this trip with you, Mason," I say.

There's more desperation in my voice than I intended and he picks up on it.

He turns, worry in his eyes. "What's wrong? Did something happen?"

I close my eyes. I can't tell him the whole truth, but I can at least tell him part of it.

"After what happened the other night, my parents cut me off," I say. "They said they'd let me live at the house and would make sure I had a car to drive, but that there would be no more credit cards, no more unlimited cash and nothing but a tiny monthly allowance to help me pay for school stuff."

Mason leans his head back. "Jesus, Penny, from the devastated look on your face, I thought you were going to tell me something horrible," he says. "You do realize this trip is all about getting away from the money, right?"

"I know, but it's also about getting away from Fairhope," I say. "Didn't you say this was about learning to appreciate life? I want to learn to do that, too. I can't live the rest of my life being so dependent on my parents and their money that they feel they can control and manipulate me by holding it over my head. Most people's parents don't still control them at my age."

"Most people's parents aren't multi-millionaires," he says.

"Yours are," I counter. "You still get to make your own decisions. I don't see them out here telling you not to leave."

Mason clenches his jaw and looks up toward his house. "Things are complicated at my house right now," he says. There's a darkness in his eyes. Pure anger.

I know he's never really been a huge fan of his dad, but he never wants to talk about it so I don't push the subject. I wonder if they got in some kind of fight.

"What you said to me last night meant something to me," I tell him. "When you said you wanted to have some adventures of your own so you could figure out who you are without all these expectations and obligations on your shoulders? That really got to me. I want that, too, more than I ever realized. I don't want my parents holding their money over my head for the rest of my life."

I lean against the side of his truck, the words flowing out of me.

"The only way to prove to them that they don't own me is to leave," I say.

"I hope you're not saying you intend to use me to get your money back," he says, crossing his arms in front of him. "This trip is about something real, not about you manipulating your parents or trying to teach them a lesson so that you can come right back here and pick up right where you left off."

I stop and put my hands on my hips, anger flushing my cheeks. "Are you seriously accusing me of that when I just poured my heart out to you? I'm trying to be honest with you here."

One corner of his mouth lifts up in a half-sneer, half-smile. "I know you better than you know yourself, sometimes, Pen. You're very good at manipulating people to get what you want. And it works every damn time. But I'm not going to let you ruin this trip for me when three days in you want me to turn back around because your parents are begging you to come home and offering the world on a silver platter to get you back."

I walk right up to him and point my index finger right at his chest. "Don't you dare accuse me of being the only one here who is good at manipulating people." I press my finger hard against his chest. "As if you haven't charmed every girl in this town and the next. The simple fact that you can date a different girl almost every weekend and never have any of them come after you with a shotgun is a miracle in and of itself. I think that's more than enough proof that you're the one who's the master of manipulation, and don't try to pretend it's not true."

I'm hyper-aware of my hand on his chest and how close

my face is to his.

"Besides." I soften my hand and lay it flat against his chest, feeling the defined muscles underneath. His heart is racing just as fast as mine. "It doesn't work every damn time. It's never worked with you."

He's standing almost perfectly still, except that his breath is coming fast and his shoulders are moving up and down with each inhale and exhale.

"That's because I know you," he says. "If I gave myself to you, I mean truly gave my heart to you, I'd never be able to let you go. And I can't afford that in my life."

His words are both heaven and hell to my ears. He wants me, but won't have me. He pulls me to him, but pushes me away in the same breath.

"This isn't really about your parents, is it? Why do you really want to come with me?" he asks in a whisper. He lifts his hand to my face and pushes a strand of hair back behind my ear. His fingers run lightly across the healing cut on my jaw.

I raise my hand to his and press it against my cheek. I lean into him and close my eyes, my heart racing.

"Because I can't imagine my life without you," I say. "And I know that scares you. I know you think we're not right for each other, but you can't deny that there's something more between us. I can't let you walk away just because you're scared."

He doesn't speak, but he also doesn't pull away.

"I know I've made some stupid decisions lately, but you have to understand how frustrating this has been for me," I say. I've never been this honest with him before. I've always been too scared of pushing him away. Right now, there's nothing to lose. He's leaving either way. All I have is honesty at this point. "When we're together and it's just me and you, there's something special. I know you have to feel it too. And I know we agreed that it would just be physical, but I think we could have something more than that if you would only give it a chance."

He takes a deep breath in and pulls his hand away from my face. "We've been over this," he says.

"I know you say you don't want to settle down, but you also say you don't want to leave me," I say. "You can't have both anymore. We've been through too much and I care about you too much for that."

"So what do you want from me?" he says.

"I want you to give this one real chance," I say, my heart aching with need. My eyes search his. "I want you to take me with you. Be with me and only me. Let's leave all our money, all our distractions behind. Let's explore each other and see if there's something real here. Something that could last. And if there's not, I'll let you walk away. I swear.

I'll never ask anything from you ever again. I won't get mad and drive off in your car. I won't try to kiss you or call you or manipulate you. If at the end of this, you don't want to be with me, I'll let you go."

I swallow, my mouth suddenly dry from the thought of exactly what I'm offering him. I already know something like this could break my heart forever. But I'm willing to sacrifice forever if it means one real moment with him.

He presses his hands against my hips and pulls me all the way against him.

"You're saying I can have you all to myself on this trip and if I'm still not ready for a relationship at the end of it, we can just part ways? No questions asked?"

Our eyes meet and passion for this man consumes me. I've never been this close to having him. Or losing him forever.

"Yes."

"And what if I don't want to walk away? What then?" he asks. His hands grip my waist tighter and my knees tremble.

"Then we live happily ever after," I say, a smile playing at my lips.

"Is that a promise, too? No matter what else happens?"

I move my hand up the length of his chest, then up across his neck, pulling him closer to me, my fingers gripping the side of his neck and my thumb resting on his cheek. "If you take me with you, it's one hundred percent your choice what happens between us," I say.

I made my choice a long time ago.

He leans his forehead against mine and groans. "How am I supposed to resist you?" he says.

"You're not," I say. I grip his shirt into my fist, wanting him closer. Wanting him to stop denying that we belong together.

He lifts me slightly off the ground as he lowers his lips to mine. He takes them passionately, dipping his tongue into my mouth, devouring me in a rush of need. I wrap my arms around him, giving myself to his kiss. He spins me around and presses my body against the side of the truck. My legs go up, wrapping around his waist as he grinds into me.

He breaks away and I gasp for air, my hands digging into him. Needing him. His lips move across my jawline and down to my neck. I lift my chin, giving him access and moaning when his teeth graze my skin.

I rock against him, feeling him grow hard against me. Our bodies have taken over the conversation, the deal closed between us. I've sold my soul for this, and I don't regret it for a second.

All I want is him.

He places both hands on my face and turns my head so

that we're looking directly into each other's eyes. We're both breathing hard, our bodies sweating in the already humid early morning air.

"Are you sure you know what you're getting yourself into, here?" he asks. "I don't want to break your heart."

I swallow back tears and breathe out in a half-laugh. I shake my head slowly back and forth. "You've already broken my heart a thousand times."

His eyes move back and forth across my face and his eyes wrinkle with a mix of sadness and worry.

"At least I know this will be the last time," I say in a whisper, not fully trusting my voice. "Will you take me with you, Mason?"

He holds me to him for a long moment, then finally says the one word I am longing to hear.

"Yes."

Chapter Thirty

Mason lets me down slowly. He holds me in his arms a few more seconds, then kisses the top of my head and lets me go.

"You realize how crazy this is, right?" he asks. "If we're really going to do this, we'll need some rules."

I crinkle my nose. "I thought we were trying to get away from all the rules."

He smiles. "We're making our own rules," he says. "First, no whining about where we're staying, what we're eating, or what you're wearing."

I roll my eyes and lean back against the truck. "I already told you I wouldn't complain."

"Okay, well just expect me to remind you of that after a few nights of sleeping in a tent."

I laugh. "What else?"

"No cell phones or calling back home," he says. "What

did you tell your parents about where you were going?"

"I left a note on my bed," I say. "I just told them I was going out of town for a little while and that I was fine, but I needed some time on my own. I told them not to come looking for me and that I'd try to check in if I wasn't back in a month or so."

He nods. "That's good. At least they won't think I've kidnapped you," he says with a laugh. "That could get pretty ugly."

I giggle, picturing a SWAT team outside our tent.

"This isn't going to be a luxury trip, so you've got to learn to be frugal. I'm sure that's a word you've never had to deal with, but we're going to be on a very tight budget if we're going to make this last," he says. "I've got about two grand, which sounds like a lot, but it's got to really last. Gas is going to be really expensive if we're driving a lot. Plus food. And camping isn't free. How much do you have? And I'm asking about cash. No using credit cards or anything that can be tracked. Part of the whole adventure of this is no one knowing where we are at any given time."

I smile big. I've never had that. Even when I was in Europe, I was on a strict itinerary and my parents were constantly checking in on me to make sure I'd arrived at each location safely with my friends.

"I don't have nearly as much as you do. I have three

hundred bucks in cash on me right now, but if we get to the bank before my parents read that note, I think I can take out another hundred or so."

He nods. "That'll work," he says. "We'll make it work."

"I have a rule too," I say, hoping this isn't too much to ask of him. And if it is, I'm not sure I can go.

"Okay, what?"

"No other girls," I say. "I know you were originally planning to be alone, so I'm sure you had some grand dreams about leaving a string of broken hearts from here to Los Angeles and back, but if I'm going to offer myself to you like this, I want you to really give it a chance. There can be no one else as long as we're together."

"Done," he says. "Of course, I say that fully expecting that you'll be on the first flight home after a few nights in a tent."

He winks and I punch him in the arm.

"You're going to eat those words, mister, just you wait."

"I'm looking forward to it," he says. "To all of it."

Chapter Thirty-One

After a brief stop at the bank, Mason pulls into a gas station on the edge of town.

"You want anything from inside?" he asks. "I don't plan on stopping anywhere for a while after this."

I crinkle my nose. "Not even for breakfast?"

He jerks his thumb in the direction of the convenience store. "You can have anything you want from inside," he says.

I start to pout, then remember my promise not to whine. I can't very well break that promise before we've even left the Fairhope city limits. "Just get me a bottle of water and a granola bar or something that doesn't look too gross."

I'm already getting the feeling this trip is going to kill my diet, which is already a daily struggle.

Oh well, maybe I'll learn to actually enjoy food again. Isn't that supposed to be one of the perks of being pregnant?

Eating whatever you want and not worrying about your weight?

Too many comments from my mother about my weight while growing up killed my joy for eating. I couldn't put a cracker in my mouth without her yelling at me about how many carbs it had and how it would just end up on my ass a few minutes later.

Mason fills the tank, then disappears into the store.

I take out my cell phone and compose one quick email to my brother.

You're going to think I'm nuts, but Mason and I have run away together. No, not to get married or anything, ha! Just to have some fun and get away for a while. I haven't told him about the baby, so please keep it just between us. I need to find out for myself whether there really is something more between us. I promise I'll be safe. Don't miss me too much. Love, Penny.

I hit send just as Mason opens the door of the truck. He's got a bag of chips hanging from his teeth and his hands are full of junk food.

I laugh and grab the chips. "What did you do?" I tease. "I thought we were supposed to be on a budget."

"We can't start a road trip without munchies," he says with a laugh. His eyes are shiny and happy and I can't remember the last time he seemed so light.

He dumps everything onto the seat between us. Energy drinks. Nuts. Water. Candy. "Take anything you want," he says. "But leave me the Junior Mints, I love those things. Oh, and one more thing."

Before I can stop him, he snatches my phone from my hand.

"Radio silence from here on out," he says. He pulls the back case off and fishes out the sim card inside. He holds it up, then ceremoniously tosses it out the window.

I lean over, watching it fall to the pavement. "Hey, what if I need to make an emergency call?"

"You may have told your parents not to come after you, but that thing is like easy tracking 101," he says. "It takes some of the adventure out of this thing. Besides, if there's an emergency, the phone will still work to call 911."

I sit back, feeling more nervous by the second. There's that last flash of panic, knowing this is really it. I've never done anything like this in my life.

"What about your phone, then?"

He lifts an eyebrow at me, then lifts up and pulls his cell out of his back pocket. He hands it to me with a half-smile. "You want to do the honors?"

I press my lips tight, trying not to smile back, but I'm kind of glad he's letting me do this. It takes me a second, but

I finally get the back cover off and find the sim card. I bite my lip and meet his eyes, then throw it past him through the window.

As we drive off, two lonely little sim cards litter the pavement at the Solo on Highway 64 on the way out of Fairhope. To me, they serve as proof of a commitment the two of us just made to each other.

I turn to him as we approach the county line. "It's just you and me now," I say, which isn't exactly true.

"You ready for this?" he asks.

"Are you kidding? I've been waiting for this my whole life."

With that, I roll down the window on my side of the truck and stick my head and both arms out into the rushing wind, watching the Fairhope sign as we blow right past.

Chapter Thirty-Two

"Where are we heading?"

Mason has a small map on the seat between us. He hands it to me. "Pick a place," he says.

"Seriously?"

He shrugs, then pops a few Junior Mints into his mouth. "Sure," he says. "Why not?"

I smile. This is so crazy. I'm used to over-planned trips without much room for freedom. After all the drama and worry of the past week, I feel free and daring and happy.

I spread the map open and start looking.

"What's the general plan?" I ask. "Are we camping out tonight? Because we'd need to stop somewhere early enough that it's still light outside, right?"

"Well, we can't drive all the way to Mexico today, if that's what you're asking," he says, laughing.

I roll my eyes. "I know that," I say. "I'm just trying to

get an idea of how far we should go. And when we get there, then what? Do we just plant ourselves somewhere for a week? Or are we going to drive every day?"

"Whatever we want to do," he says. "That's the beauty of this."

"I'm not used to having so much choice," I say.

"You realize how crazy that sounds, right?"

"What do you mean?"

He turns the radio down and keeps one hand casually on the steering wheel. "Think about it. You come from one of the wealthiest families in the South. You could have just about anything in the world you want. You could afford to go anywhere in the world you've ever wanted to go. And you just told me you're not used to having so much choice?"

I lay the map down across my legs. "Well, you know what I mean."

"Yes, but I want you to really think about it," he says. "This is the kind of thing that's been on my mind a lot lately. Why would a girl who could literally have anything she wants be limited on choices?"

I shrug. I've never really thought about this before. "I guess because I don't always feel like my choices are my own."

"Exactly." He adjusts his weight and sits up straighter. "See, money doesn't always open the world up to you.

The Moment We Began

Money can be a strait-jacket sometimes, too. This is
something people don't always realize. They think that
because we have money, we're lucky and free. But
sometimes the money is what ties us down. Let's say I
wanted to work on a construction site. Say I like working
with my hands and working outdoors, so I want a job where
I can be outside in the sun and build things. If my dad
wasn't Nathan Trent, do you think anyone would give a
shit? No, it would be normal. It would be an honest way to
make a living and that would be that. But, because my dad is
rich, I have to consider how it looks for me to have a job like
that. People suddenly judge me, like I'm only working that
job to make a point or stick it to my dad. Or they assume my
parents are going broke. It can't just be something I wanted
to do."

I lean back. I think about school and how my mom
wanted me to be pre-law because she was. I never really felt
like I had a choice.

"If Penny Wright didn't want to finish college, it would
be a scandal, right? That's such bullshit," he says. "Our lives
are dictated by how things look, and I'm so tired of it."

"What brought this on?" I ask. "Why has this been on
your mind so much? I mean, it's not like you actually want
to work construction, right?"

"No," he says. "But if I did, I want to be free to make

that choice without being judged for it."

"So, what then?"

He licks his lips. "Honestly?"

"Yeah," I say. "I want to know what made you start thinking about this."

"My parents have been having some financial problems," he says. He glances over at me, watching for a reaction. "It's been going on for a while, and all they ever do is fight about it. Mom keeps trying to convince Dad to put the house on the market and look for a smaller place. It's not like they'd have to move into a studio apartment. She's talking about downgrading to a five-bedroom house or something, but Dad acts like it would be the end of his reputation in the community. He thinks it will draw all this attention to our family. So instead of making a change that would take away some of the financial stress, they put themselves deeper in the hole just to keep up appearances."

I frown and stare at the map, not knowing what to say.

"There's more to it than that," he says. "But that's really what got it started for me. Then, the more I started looking around at all our friends and the things people do to one-up each other or show off, the more I started thinking about just getting away from it all for a while."

"I didn't know your parents were having a hard time," I say.

The Moment We Began

"No one does," he says. "And I didn't want to bring it up to you, because your dad's the one who pays mine. It's awkward."

I shrug. "Still, I'd rather you felt like you could talk to me instead of keeping it to yourself and dealing with the stress of it yourself."

"It's hard to complain to you or Preston about money," he says. "I was afraid if I said something, you'd want to do something to fix it."

I bite my lower lip. "It's my first instinct," I say. "I can't help it. When someone needs money, I feel like it's one of the few things I can do that will really make a difference."

"I know you don't mean it as an insult, but you can't throw money at every problem and expect that to be enough," he says. "Anyway, my point was that it's not the money that's the problem. It's the fact that my parents are willing to sacrifice everything we have to try to keep up the appearance of having money."

I nod. "And in response, you decided to strike out and do the opposite," I say. "Drive to a place where no one knows you in a truck that pretty much guarantees no one will think you have money. Then what? What's the goal?"

He leans back against the seat. "To just live," he says. "To experience a simpler kind of life where the only thing that matters to people is what kind of person you are. Not how much money you have or what kind of house you live in."

It seems like such a foreign concept to me, I can hardly wrap my mind around it. "I've lived my entire life opposite of that. I've made friends by inviting people to parties on the yacht. Trips to Europe. I've always worn expensive clothes and driven fast cars. People flock to me because of those things, I think. I've always been scared that if I took all that away, maybe there wouldn't be much left to like about me."

He shakes his head and reaches across the seat to grab my hand. "You're so much more than all those things, Pen."

"I guess we'll find out," I say with a laugh.

"Let's pick a place and settle in for a while, then," he says. "We'll be Penny and Mason, drifters with no money, looking for a good time. Maybe without all those other things to hide behind, we'll learn all kinds of new things about ourselves."

I raise my eyebrows. "You have no idea how scary that sounds."

"Yes, I do," he says. "But it'll be fun, too. I promise."

I let go of his hand and lift the map up, studying all the possibilities.

My eyes land on the beach. I've always loved the ocean more than anything, so why not, right? "Can we camp on the beach?"

The Moment We Began

He smiles. "Maybe not directly on the beach, depending on where we go, but I bet we could find a few campgrounds that are close to beaches," he says. "Look around the gulf. Alabama, maybe? If you look, camp sites should be marked on the map."

I run my index finger along the gulf coast, then see a little tree icon. "What about Gulf State Park?" I ask.

"Sounds like a great place for a new start," he says. He takes my hand again and I get butterflies in my stomach at his touch.

"I couldn't agree more," I say, then scoot across the seat and turn the radio back up.

Chapter Thirty-Three

Mason's hand is warm against my arm.

I shiver and lift my head. My neck is stiff from leaning against the door frame for who-knows-how-long. My arm is freezing from where the air conditioning has been blowing on it.

"I fell asleep," I say, stretching.

"I noticed," he says with a smile. "You're cute when you drool."

My hand flies to my mouth to wipe away any drool. I'm mortified, but when Mason clutches his stomach in laughter, I give him an eat-shit look and punch his leg. "Jerk. I don't drool."

"Yes, you do," he says, moving away fast so I don't hit him again. "Next time I'll get pictures."

"You'd better not," I say. I chase him out of the truck, crawling across to the driver's side and climbing out the other side.

The sun hits me full in the face and I lift my hand to shield my eyes. It feels so good after the cold air inside the truck. I'm surprised the air conditioning on that thing works, but I'm glad it does.

The sound of waves crashing on the shore brings goosebumps to my arms.

I look around, my heart lifting. "Are we here?"

"Close," he says. "I thought we'd grab a late lunch and then go see if there's a spot at the campgrounds."

I bounce up and down in my boots and clap my hands together. The breeze lifts my hair off my neck and I lift my face to the sun.

Mason puts his arms around me and I lean into him.

"How long was I sleeping?" I stayed awake as long as I could, but eventually the adrenaline wore off and I crashed.

"About four hours straight," he says. "Didn't you get any sleep last night?"

I rub my face with both hands and shake my head. "Not a wink," I say. "I spent half the night trying to figure out how to get all my belongings into that tiny little bag."

"I was wondering how you did that," he says. "I'm half-expecting you to start unpacking it Mary Poppins style later." He stands up straight and I laugh at his Mary Poppins impersonation. He pretends to be holding a large bag, then opens it wide and peers down inside.

His eyes get wide and he puts one hand over his mouth. Then, he pantomimes reaching in and pulling something out.

"What'd you find?" I ask, playing along.

"A king-size bed," he says, then looks inside again. "And about sixty pairs of shoes."

I laugh and realize I'm using muscles I didn't even know I had. I've never laughed so free and so pure in my life. I feel like a new person. A completely different version of myself.

"I swear, there's no king-size bed in my bag," I say. "But if I had known you had those huge duffel bags, I would have stolen one."

"I bet," he says.

He throws an arm around my shoulder and I love the weight of it against my neck. I reach up and grab his hand in mine and we walk together toward a small strip of beach-front restaurants and bars.

This place is nothing like Fairhope. Most of the shore-line in Fairhope is crowded with boutique shops and bars that cater to the wealthier college kids with lots of disposable income. There are shops where you can buy things like expensive sea shells and original beach-themed art by local artisans.

Here, everything is run down and battered. There's a short boardwalk that has seen better days, the wood washed out and worn. I don't see any tourist traps or art galleries. Instead, there's a bar that just has a simple red sign that reads "Open" and a bait and tackle shop leading up to a decrepit old pier that looks like it could fall back into the ocean at any moment.

There are a couple of places that look like they've been closed down for a while, judging by the spider webs and grime on the windows.

I start to wonder if there's going to be any place to eat around here when finally, down on the end, there's a restaurant called Dottie's Diner. Mason opens the door for me and I walk in. I've never been in a place like this. If I thought Knox's bar was a dive, then this place is whatever comes three steps below dive.

A few rickety tables are arranged haphazardly around the room. The chairs are all mismatched and dingy.

The floor of the place is some kind of institutional-looking tile, like something from public school, only worse. I think it might have been white at some point, but it's scratched and stained and dirty now.

Along the right side is a counter where three scruffy-looking men sit drinking coffee.

The bell dings as we walk in and a couple of the guys

turn to look, then do a double-take. I don't know whether to smile or run.

And we're supposed to eat in this place? I seriously would not be surprised to see a roach crawling across the floor at any second. But I promised Mason I'd be a good sport. And we are at the beach, at least. I'll just eat something light and relatively safe and we can get the hell out of here.

"Hey there," Mason says, nodding toward the woman behind the counter. "Sit anywhere?"

"Yes, sir," she says. The woman is wearing a pair of baggy jeans and a t-shirt that's covered in flour and grease splatters.

Mason leads us to a table in the middle of the room. He pulls a chair out for me and I thank him and sit down. There's no silverware on the table, just one of those silver napkin dispensers with tiny little napkins and a couple of plastic salt and pepper shakers.

I can feel his eyes on me, studying my reaction. I am trying very hard not to have one.

I clasp my hands together and set them on the table, then think better of it and move them to my lap. "This looks nice," I say.

"Liar," he says, leaning forward. He grabs a laminated menu from the table next to ours. "You said you were

215

hungry, right? You'd be surprised what kind of food you can find in a place like this."

I desperately want to make a joke about roach salad or rat soup, but I restrain myself and opt for a lame nod instead.

"I'm serious. Southern cooking at its best. And I bet the seafood is really fresh. Here, take a look."

Mason hands me the menu. There's something sticky on the side of it. I'm going to hope it's syrup.

The menu lists everything from breakfast to steak. I search for the most harmless item. My stomach growls. All I've had to eat today is half an oatmeal breakfast bar. I'm starving.

The waitress from earlier comes around the corner with a notepad and pencil. She's middle-aged with graying hair. She's not unattractive, but she's also not trying very hard. "Hi folks, what can I get ya started with today?"

"I'll take a Coke," Mason says, then looks to me.

"I'd like a bottled water," I say.

"We got tap water," she says, her voice flat.

I shake my head. No way I'm drinking tap water in a place like this. "I guess I'll just take a Sprite, then."

The waitress gives me a look. I know that look. She's annoyed by me. She thinks I'm acting like I'm too good for this place.

The Moment We Began

Am I? I have been trying my best not to show any kind of dislike for it.

I smile at her to try to get her to warm up to me, but she's already looking at Mason. Her eyes have stayed on him most of the time we've been here.

And I honestly can't blame her. He looks so good in those tight jeans, and his green t-shirt shows off the deep emerald of his eyes. His hair is a touch longer than normal and he's got two days' worth of stubble on his chin. He looks like the kind of guy who belongs in a beach town in California. A bronzed surfer god.

And I'm just the snotty bitch he walked in with.

I decide to try harder.

I study the menu, doing my best to be optimistic. I could get pancakes and eggs or something, but the pancakes might be too heavy for my stomach if we're going to spend the rest of the day on the beach. My mom has been a carb-nazi for years, though, so the thought of a really good pancake sounds amazing.

They offer a couple of different sandwiches, but neither of them sounds very good. I know Mason says the seafood is fresh, but the thought of a fish sandwich turns my stomach. You'd have to be really brave—or stupid—to order fish in a place called Dottie's Diner.

"Do you kids know what you want? Or do you need a

few more minutes?"

"I think I'm ready," Mason says, but looks to me questioningly.

I smile politely. "I could use another minute if you don't mind."

She does everything but actually roll her eyes, but from her slumped shoulders and the long sigh, I know she hates me. And I've only been in here for two minutes.

She walks away and Mason grabs the menu from me. "What are you thinking of?" he asks. "Or do you just want me to order for you?"

I snatch it back from him. "I was thinking about the pancakes, but—"

"No buts," he says. "Do it. Gotta go with your first instinct in a place like this. Whatever sounds good probably is."

"What are you getting?"

"The fish sandwich," he says.

And I start laughing.

Chapter Thirty-Four

Half an hour later, almost every pancake on my plate has been devoured. I lean back against the chair. "Oh, my god, I'm so full."

Mason nods. "I told you," he says. "Sometimes the places you find off the beaten path are the best in the world. You find some real duds here and there, but there's just something about finding a place like this that's part of the adventure. See, the secret is that these mom and pop diners use a lot of homemade recipes and tricks. Stuff passed down for generations or developed by the cook after years of working the same menu. You don't get that at chain restaurants where half the food is frozen and exactly the same as everywhere else."

I look down at my plate and am honestly tempted to lick the rest of the syrup off of it.

"Did you folks enjoy your meal?" the waitress asks. She

comes up and grabs all the plates at once. No tray. She just keeps stacking them on one arm like a pyramid of dishes.

"It was so good," I say. 'Those were the best pancakes I've ever had in my life."

She actually smiles at me.

"Those are my secret recipe," she says. "I'm really glad you liked 'em."

I look at Mason and he gives me an 'I-told-you-so' look.

"Are you Dottie?" I ask.

She smiles. "Oh, hell no," she says. "Dottie's been dead goin' on five years now. Mean old bat. But I bought the place from her greedy son when he inherited it. I've worked here since I turned sixteen and this kid from St. Louis we've never seen comes in here in his suit and tie, telling us he's going to close the place down if he can't find a buyer."

She shakes her head.

"I didn't think we'd be able to come up with the money at first, but I really think he was just glad to get the place off his hands. Sold it to me and Buddy there real cheap," she says. She points toward the counter and one of the men sitting there with his back to us raises his hand in greeting, not even bothering to turn around. "My name's Delores."

"Well, it was really great, Delores, thank you," I say.

"You two just passing through?" she asks, still balancing all those plates and silverware like it was nothing.

The Moment We Began

Mason leans forward. "We were actually hoping to find a place along the beach where we could camp out," he says. "Is the Gulf State Campgrounds around here?"

"Oh yeah, that's just a few miles on down the road," she says. "Might not be lots of room there this time of year, though. Lots of folks make reservations and come stay for a while. You might have better luck at the smaller one right here in town. It's privately owned and usually has more of a community atmosphere to it. You guys in tents? Or you got an RV?"

"A tent," Mason says.

She looks at me, and I get the distinct feeling she's doubting my ability to sleep in a tent. "I wouldn't have guessed that," she says. "But I think you might want to try Little Lake campsite. The state one is real commercial outfit. Lots of RV's and noise and such. Our little one here is real close to the beach and is a lot quieter. More off the beaten path, so to speak."

"Do they have showers?" I ask.

She laughs. "Oh yeah," she says. "They got all the modern conveniences a girl like you could need."

She's messing with me, and to be honest, it kind of scares the crap out of me. I'm tempted to tell Mason we should try our luck at the bigger site, but I can tell from the smile on his face that he's already sold on this other one.

221

"Sounds perfect," Mason tells her. "And if we stay, I'm sure we'll be back for more of your amazing food."

The woman smiles from ear to ear and I swear to God I see an actual blush creep across her cheeks.

I sneak a look over at Mason. I always knew he was a charmer, but this is a side of him I've never seen. He's more humble and a lot less flashy. The Mason I have known has always been more aggressively flirtatious. He's usually the center of attention. Loud and pushy.

But this Mason is a real gentleman.

And I like it.

Before the waitress walks away, she pulls the check out of her apron and lays it face-down on the table. Mason turns it over, then throws a ten dollar bill down on the table.

"Ten dollars?" I grab the check and turn it over. Dang, no wonder this place is practically run into the ground. "All that food was only seven bucks? You've got to be kidding me. She didn't even charge us for our drinks."

"This place is a real find, huh? What did I tell you?" he says. "Let's go check out the beach, then we'll head down to the campground to see if there are any spots left for the night."

"How long will we stay?" I ask as we get up and head out the door.

Mason turns to wave at Delores and Buddy before he

The Moment We Began

leads us back out into the sunshine.

"As long as we want."

Chapter Thirty-Five

Mason and I walk out toward the beach. It's a sunny morning, but there aren't very many people on this side of the beach. Pretty far down one side, we can see a colorful cluster of umbrellas and towels and bodies. On the other side, there's the small, weathered pier.

"Which way?" I ask.

Mason studies them both. "Let's check out the pier," he says. "These old ones can be really cool sometimes."

We step into the sand and I realize it's going to be a tough walk with these boots on. "Hold on a sec," I say.

I hesitate, looking around for a place to sit down. There's no curb or anything. Just sidewalk and sand. I plop down on the beach, then nearly jump up as the hot sand practically burns the back of my legs.

"Whoa," I shout, crouching down. "It's super-hot."

Mason pulls his t-shirt off and lays it down on the sand

for me. "That should help."

I stare up at him, wide-eyed. My pulse quickens at the sight of his defined abs and perfectly tanned skin. "When did you become such a gentleman?" I ask. "First you're so sweet to the lady inside and now you're being really nice to me."

I sit down on his shirt and begin untying my laces and pulling off my boots and socks.

"Don't act so surprised," he says. "I've always been a gentleman at heart."

I snort, but then see by the look on his face that I've hurt his feelings.

"Oh, Mason, I'm sorry. You know I didn't mean it." I pull my other boot off, then stand up, the hot sand burning the bottom of my feet as I approach him. "It's just that back home, you're usually all about the hit-it-and-quit-it mentality with women. I mean, I've seen glimpses here and there of how sweet you can be when we're alone together, but you can be a real asshole sometimes and you know it."

He shrugs. "This is different," he says.

"How?"

He leaves his shirt on the ground by my boots and we take off toward the pier. "Besides it being just you and me, I guess this is just more of my comfort zone," he says. "This is more of how I grew up. The party guy got to be more of an act. It just felt like that was who everyone expected me to be, you know? That's part of why I needed to get away. I was tired of being me, if that makes sense."

My shoulder brushes against his as we walk. I want to lean in to him. To be in his arms. But he takes one step apart from me and our skin loses contact.

"It makes a lot of sense," I say. "I feel that way all the time."

"How is that possible?" he asks, shaking his head. "You're perfect, Penny."

"Ha! I'm far from perfect," I say, leaning down to grab a pretty shell that caught my eye. As soon as I pull it from the sand, though, I see it has a huge hole in it. I throw it back down and keep searching. "You're talking to the girl who got drunk and wrecked an eighty thousand dollar car. I've made so many mistakes it's not even funny."

I step into the waves, then jump back when the cold water splashes against my feet and ankles.

"Brrr. That's colder than I thought it would be. I thought the Gulf of Mexico was supposed to be warmer water."

"It is warmer," he says. "It just feels cold because the sand was so hot."

Another wave breaks and rushes toward us. I squeal and run around him, heading back to the warm sand. Now that I'm wet, the sand sticks to me.

"Wimp," he says. He moves toward me and before I realize what he's doing, he lifts me over his shoulder and runs toward the water.

"No!" I scream, kicking and giggling.

I expect him to stop when he reaches the water, but he doesn't. He keeps going, running in slow motion through the waves until they cover his knees. Then, he dives forward, taking me with him as he plunges into the water.

I scream just before I go under. A wave crashes on top of us and my head is pushed beneath the surface. At first, the water is freezing cold, but it's more like a jolt that hits and then disappears. I flail my arms to swim away from him, then find the sandy bottom with my feet and push up out of the ocean.

I wipe the water from my eyes and push my hair back from my face. Mason comes up laughing, then looks at me with a terrible grin. I open my eyes wide and start backing up.

"Don't you dare," I shout.

But he does. He jumps across the space between us, hooking his arms around my waist, and dragging me under again. This time he holds on to me. I spin around to face him as we both come up out of the water. We stand, our bodies half-in, half-out of the gulf waters. My tank top clings to my body, but rises up every time the water laps at the edge of it.

Mason sets both hands on my waist, his fingers brushing against the bare skin as my tank top lifts up, leaving my skin bare to him.

I wrap my arms around him and lay my palms flat against his muscled back. We're breathing hard from playing in the water, but my heart is racing because of how close he's standing. Every time his fingers move against my flesh, my insides flash with fire.

A bigger wave breaks just before it gets to us, knocking us slightly off balance. Mason pulls me closer, tighter in his arms. He dips his head and I rise to meet him, our lips eager.

My mouth opens slightly and I lick his bottom lip with my tongue as he kisses me. He tastes of salt. I open wider and let his tongue explore mine. I rake my nails across his back and he moans, pulling me tighter against him. His kiss becomes hungrier, more passionate. I lift up with the next wave, wrapping my legs around him in the water and grinding my body against him.

He reaches around to cup my ass, holding me to him as the waves break over and over again, never interrupting our kiss for even a second.

Eventually, I pull away, out of breath and wanting more.

"Is this real?" I whisper.

229

Sarra Cannon

He kisses the side of my mouth, my cheek, my temple. "It's real for now," he says.

I cling tightly to him, but his words echo in my heart. For now. He's already leaving room for a time when it won't be real, won't be us, anymore. But that's what I offered him, didn't I? A chance to walk away when this is over?

It's only day one and already I'm falling deeper. I have no idea how I'm going to survive this.

I know I can't spend the next few weeks dwelling on what's going to happen at the end of all this. I'll drive myself crazy and I'll end up pushing him away. What I need to do is just take it one step at a time. One moment at a time.

I kiss him again, the sound of the waves roaring in my ears and my heart thundering in my chest.

And I let myself fall.

Chapter Thirty-Six

After an uneventful trip down to the pier to watch old men fish, Mason and I dry off and drive south toward Little Lake Campground.

We miss the small sign for the place and have to turn around. The road leading to it is narrow and sandy, but well-traveled.

I hold on to the window-frame as the truck bumps up and down along the road. Mason slows when we come to a small gated outpost. Behind it, there's a wooden fence marking off the campgrounds. There are two square wooden buildings off to the left marked with male and female, and I really hope those aren't the only showers and bathrooms they have here. The buildings are tiny and weather-beaten. The roof of the Ladies room is covered in leaves and the overhangs are covered in giant cobwebs. I don't even want to think about the spiders that could be lurking under the toilet seats.

I shudder.

"You okay?" Mason asks. He follows my gaze to the bathrooms and chuckles. "Not exactly the Ritz Carlton, I realize, but at least there are showers and toilets. That's better than some campsites I've stayed in."

My eyes grow wide. "Please tell me you're not planning on taking us to a place with no bathrooms," I say. "I'm not complaining, just politely begging you with all that I am."

He laughs. "Nah, not anytime soon, anyway. Let's get your feet wet first."

He parks just outside the gate and goes out to talk to a guy sitting in a lawn chair outside a small wooden building. They nod and carry on a conversation I can't hear, then finally Mason shakes the guy's hand and hands over some cash from his wallet.

I relax a little. At least we seem to have a place to stay. I think I'd definitely prefer camping out in a tent to some of the shady motels we saw near the beach.

When Mason comes back, I ask him how much it costs to camp here.

"It's twenty-five bucks a night to pitch a tent and use the facilities," he says. "If we decide to stay, we can get a discount if we pay for a week up front. Not bad, huh?"

"Only twenty-five dollars? You're kidding me?"

The Moment We Began

"Nope."

I clap my hands together. "With our money, we could stay here for months."

He lifts one eyebrow. "Are you saying you're so incredibly excited about camping out now that you're willing to stay for a month?"

I slide across the seat toward him and run my hand up his leg slowly. "Do I get to stay in a tent snuggled up next to you?"

He bites his lower lip and sucks a loud breath in through his nose. "Do you have any idea what you're doing to me right now?"

"I could make a guess," I say.

"Come on, let's find a parking spot and find our camp site," he says. "There will be plenty of time to talk about tent snuggling after dark."

I laugh again and realize my cheeks hurt from spending the entire afternoon smiling like a lunatic.

Guilt stabs me as I think about what must be going on back home, though. I'm sure my parents are mad as hell and chances are most of my friends are really worried about me. At least they know I'm with Mason. Those closest to me will know just how exciting that is for me and they'll be happy.

My parents? Not so much.

Mason gets in and pulls the truck through the wooden

233

gate. He drives around the area for a minute, then finally stops. He looks down at the piece of paper the guard gave him and shakes it in his hand. "This is it," he says, putting the truck in park and turning it off. "We can't park the truck here long term, so we need to grab our stuff and get started putting it together. It's only a couple of hours until it gets dark and we want to have everything set up by then."

"Okay." I get out and reach into the back, pulling out everything I can get my hands on. I try to lift one of the bigger duffel bags, but it's way too heavy. "Do we need all this stuff?"

"Yeah, if you want to be comfortable," he says. He makes a face and spins in a circle. "Shit. I totally forgot that you didn't bring your own sleeping bag or pillow or anything like that."

I shrug. "Can't I just share with you?"

He takes both big duffel bags out and throws them to the ground near our numbered site. "That should be okay for tonight, but believe me, you're going to want your own bag if it starts getting cool at night. Plus, have you ever slept in one of these?"

I grab a couple of the smaller bags and carry them over. "A tent? Or a sleeping bag?"

"A sleeping bag."

I search my memory. "I think I used to have a pink

The Moment We Began

Barbie sleeping bag that I took when we had birthday party sleepovers and stuff," I say. "But I'm guessing that's not really the same thing."

"Not exactly," he says, shaking his head. "Grab that last box and I'll drive the car over to the parking lot."

I set the box on the ground and look around at all this stuff. "I don't have the first clue what to do with this."

"I figured," he says. "Just wait for me. I'll be right back."

Mason kisses my forehead, then gets into the truck and drives away.

I sit down on one of the bigger bags, then take a minute to really look around at the other campers. There are a couple of empty sites around us, but most of the places are taken up by tents in a variety of shapes and sizes and colors. Down at one end, I see a tent that looks like the freaking Taj Mahal of tents. It's huge and looks like it has several partitions inside. An older woman in overalls and a tank top is standing at a card table that's been set up in front. She pours vodka into a red cup, then adds a tiny splash of something that looks like lemonade. She finishes it off with a couple of ice cubes from her cooler, then takes a long drink.

When she's done, she looks up and our eyes meet.

I look away, realizing I've been staring. I'm already completely out of my element here, the last thing I want to do is make enemies or come to be known as the rude girl in camp.

Mason said we would stay as long as we want, but I have no idea what that really means. I'm usually more of a planner, so not knowing if we're here for one night or ten makes me feel anxious.

I glance back toward the big tent and the woman waves. I lift my hand and smile. I feel completely awkward here. I probably look like a complete mess after our swim, too. My shorts are still wet.

But, oh god, it was amazing to be in his arms after all this time. Yes, we'd had a few moments in the past where we gave in to each other, but nothing like today. Mason's different here. The second we left Fairhope, some of his walls came down. Maybe some of mine too. I don't know if it's the freedom of being gone or the fact that I came with him or what, but he's being so sweet and attentive.

And those kisses.

I lift my hand to my mouth, remembering.

He's pushed me away for so long, this feels like a dream. I just pray it doesn't turn into a nightmare. With Mason, I feel like I can never completely know what to expect.

And right now, there's so much on the line.

I expected him back by now, though. I stand up and

look in the direction he drove off. The campground has a lot of large trees, so I can't see too far, but I think I can make out some cars in a parking lot a ways down. It shouldn't have taken him this long to park and walk right back. I don't want to risk getting lost or missing him somewhere along the way, so I decide to start unpacking some of these bags. I may not know how to put the tent together, but I can at least pull out the pieces so that when he gets back, it's ready to go.

The bag the tent comes in is cinched together by a black cord. I pull on it and the mouth of the bag opens wide. I turn it over, dumping the contents out onto the ground. Metal pieces clang against each other and fall hard into the sand and dirt at my feet. A few people at the site across from ours look up. One of the guys stands up from his folding chair.

"You need some help?" He's got a long beard and is wearing a flannel shirt with the sleeves ripped off.

I make a face. "Um, no thanks," I say. I look down the path again, but still no sign of Mason. "It just slipped right out of my hand."

The man smiles and raises his can of beer in a salute. I wave back to say thanks and take the rest of the pieces out of the bag. More carefully this time.

Once it's laid out, the whole thing looks very complicated. I had considered taking a stab at it, thinking

Mason would be so surprised if he came back and the tent was set up. But knowing there are people watching me, I don't dare. I'd probably end up making a big mess, and it would suck if I ruined the tent.

What else can I do?

I have no idea what's in the rest of the bags, so I take a look around. One of the boxes has a full set of kitchen-type stuff. Pots and pans, some kind of stove, maybe? One of the grocery bags has hotdog buns, peanut butter, plastic cups, that sort of thing. He probably doesn't want me taking that stuff out, so I just set it back down.

I look over at the campsite across from us to see what they have set up. Their party seems to take up two spots and there are three different tents set up between them. Their tents are much smaller than the one at the end, so I think it must be more like ours. Three men who look to be in their late thirties or so are sitting around a small fire, and I wonder how they can stand it when it's so hot and humid out here.

I study our site. Do we need a fire? Maybe, if he plans on cooking hotdogs or something for dinner. Plus, he said it might get cooler in the evenings. There's a ring of big rocks filled with the ashy remnants of past fires in the center of our site. I don't know where everyone's getting their firewood, but that would at least be something useful I could do.

The same man who offered to help before is looking at me again. "You sure you don't want some help? You look a little lost."

I cross the path toward him. "Do you know where I can get some firewood?"

The man looks at me, then looks at his friends. They all laugh. My cheeks flush and I tug on my hair. What did I say?

"I'm sorry, I didn't mean to bother you." I turn around, mortified.

"Now, wait a minute," the man says. "I'm sorry, I honestly didn't realize you were serious."

I can't just ignore him, so I turn back. "I really don't know where to get it," I say. "It's my first time camping. Is there a little store or something?"

The man's belly jiggles even though he's trying to keep a straight face.

I clench my jaw tight. If he's not planning on helping me, why does he keep offering? Asshole.

"No, there's no store," he says. "But you do realize you're standing in the middle of the woods, right? There's firewood all over the ground."

I close my eyes, feeling like a complete idiot. I was thinking they were using firewood like you'd use in your house. The kind you find in a grocery store or someone selling on the side of the road during the winter months. I wasn't thinking I'd have to actually walk around and collect it myself. And what in the world are the rules on something like that? Can I only take wood that's on the ground near my site? Or can I just walk around everyone's sites and pick up random sticks?

I'm too scared to ask. I don't want to be the source of entertainment out here tonight.

"Thanks," I say. I turn away and walk straight back to go sit down on the bag. I'm completely useless out here.

I look down the path again and this time, I see him and my stomach lurches.

He's not alone.

A girl who looks about our age is walking next to him. She's tan and has a rockin' body that she's obviously not afraid to show off. She's smiling and flipping her hair back. Major flirt-mode. And worse, Mason's smiling back. The girl stops and points to a green tent that's already set up. Mason stands and talks to her for what feels like an eternity.

I know I can't stand there staring at them forever. The guys behind me are surely watching me. I'm like a reality TV show to them at this point, probably. Survivor Idiot or some shit.

I walk over and sit down on the duffel bag, but I can't

help watching Mason with her. What the hell could they possibly be talking about?

This is just like him, too. Even though he promised no other girls, here he is on the first day obviously hanging out with another girl who is way too hot for my comfort level. Of course, how could I have expected him to really keep to that promise? He's a player. I know this. It's in his nature to flirt with hot girls. Hell, it's in every guy's nature.

But part of me had been hoping that our kiss in the ocean today meant something to him.

I watch as he hugs the hot girl, then walks back down the path toward me. I pick at the edges of my fingernails, not even wanting to watch him walk over here. I'm totally pissed and he's smiling like he just won the damn lottery.

"Hey, guess what?"

You've found someone hotter to sleep with tonight?

I force a smile. "What?"

"I just met these girls who said there was a big music festival going on this week just up the road a few miles. Apparently there was some big bonfire and lots of local musicians and stuff," he says. "We just barely missed it, but she said there's another one in a couple of weeks in Gulf Shores that they're coming back for."

"And you want to go with them?"

"Well, yeah, don't you?"

I swallow, thinking about the way that girl was looking at him. "I guess," I say. "I thought we were just going to play it by ear for a while."

"We are," he says. "But if we stick around, I think it could be cool to hear some people jamming out on the beach."

I shrug. "Okay, whatever you want."

I am trying so hard to act normal. I don't want to fight with him and ruin our first night. But at the same time, I kind of want to punch him in the nuts.

"Hey, what's wrong with you?" he asks. He puts his hands on my shoulders and turns me to face him. "Why are you upset? I thought this would be part of the adventure. Let's see where it takes us."

"Nothing," I lie. "I'm fine. I'm just ready to get things set up so we can relax."

"I see you started working on the tent," he says smugly, staring down at the scattered pieces.

"I took it out so you could put it together easier," I say. "I was going to get us some firewood, but I don't know the rules about that kind of stuff."

"Rules?"

"Yeah, like whether I can pick it up from just anywhere, or if I have to find some at our own site, or what?"

Mason picks up a large leather case and flips it open.

The Moment We Began

Inside is a small axe with a worn wooden handle. The blade, though, shines like it's just been sharpened. "Firewood is really more of a man's job," he says. "But you can come with me, if you want. Help me carry it."

"No, thanks," I say. "I'll stay here. I just need a little direction on what you want done."

"Are you sure you're okay? Because when I left you were smiling and when I walked back…" His voice trails off as points toward the path. He presses the palm of his hand against his forehead. "You're mad because I was talking to that girl?"

"Is that what you call it?"

He makes a frustrated noise in his throat. "Yes, that's exactly what I call it," he says. "She was telling me about the festival. I thought you'd be interested in it too."

"And you didn't notice how hot she is? Or how much she was flirting with you?"

He sighs and picks up the hatchet. With one hard swing, he buries the tip of the blade into a stump. "Is this how it's going to be, then? The whole trip you're going to be watching me like a hawk, freaking out every time I talk to another girl?"

"I'm not freaking out." I struggle to keep my voice down. From the corner of my eye, I can already see our neighbors turning around in their chairs to listen. "I just thought we agreed you weren't going to flirt with other women while we were together."

"Then I guess we damn well better define what you mean by flirt, because in my mind, that's not at all what I was doing with her," he says. He steps closer to me, not trying at all to keep his voice down. "Now, if I'd told her she was a fine piece of ass, that would be crossing the line, but as I see it, talking to a nice girl about an upcoming music festival, that I would like you and I to attend together, is completely harmless. And if you're going to hover over me the whole time, then maybe you should get on the next bus back to Fairhope."

I stomp one foot in the sand. "You're the one turning this into a big deal," I say. "I was doing my best to ignore it and keep a good attitude. You're the one who disappeared for more than half an hour, leaving me here to fend for myself."

He opens his mouth and lifts his hand like he's going to say something, then makes a fist and shuts his jaw with a snap. He takes a deep breath, then leans down and pulls the hatchet from the stump. "I'm going to get some firewood," he says. "I'll be back later."

Regret seeps into my bones. I didn't want this to turn into a big argument, but I've seen him parade girls like that right under my nose a thousand times. I don't want to see it happen again. Not now. Not when I have so much to lose.

"Wait," I call out to him. He turns. "What am I supposed to do while you're gone?"

"You're a big girl," he says. "Figure it out."

He walks away, heading into the wooded area past the camping sites. I stand there staring after him until he's too far in for me to see him through the trees.

I turn and the woman with the big tent is just standing there, staring at us with a big grin on her face. When I narrow my eyes at her, she just shakes her head and lifts her red cup toward me in a salute.

I'm pretty sure I've never felt more lost in my life.

Chapter Thirty-Seven

I stand there, staring at the scattered tent pieces and the bags all around me. There's a tug deep inside my gut that says I should just give up and go home. That Mason was right. I'm not cut out for this. I have never really lived without my parents standing right behind me, ready to pick up the pieces when I fall apart.

That's what they did when I was eight years old and fell out of a tree. I had been climbing high, trying to prove to Preston and his friends that a girl could climb just as well as any boy. I got almost as high as Preston when I lost my footing and fell to the ground. I broke my leg and hit my head on a rock. My mom was more worried about the future scar that would be left on my forehead than anything else. The leg would heal, but she was horrified by the thought of that scar.

She was on the phone with a plastic surgeon in the

ambulance on the way to the hospital and by morning, I'd already had surgery on my face.

I lift my hand now and feel the place where the scar would have been. Instead, the skin is smooth and perfect, almost no sign of the mistake I'd made when I was a little girl.

And they'd done the same thing a few days ago when I crashed that car. Driving drunk is one of the dumbest things I've ever done in my life. I could have died. I could have killed someone else. I probably deserved to go to jail or to have my license suspended.

But Tripp Wright's daughter can't have a spot on her record like that. So they fixed it.

Money can fix almost anything.

But it can't fix your heart. And it can't make you a better person.

I want what Mason wants. I want to be a better person. The kind of person who appreciates what she has and who sees the best in others instead of someone who automatically assumes everyone has ulterior motives.

I stare down at the tent and know that if I give up now and go home, I'll spend the rest of my life under the wings of my parents and their money. I'll never really learn to do anything for myself. I'll never have the chance to really know what I'm capable of.

The Moment We Began

And what is that going to teach my child someday?

I'm being pulled in two different directions. I don't want life to be hard. I like having money. But at the same time, I don't want to be the kind of person who never really experiences life. I don't want to live on a pedestal anymore.

I bend over and take the first piece of metal in my hand. I can do this, right? How hard can it really be to put a tent together? I study the various pieces, putting myself into it. I figure out which side is the bottom of the tent and spread it out on the smoothest part of the ground. Then, I start putting the stakes in the ground, tying them off. The ground is soft, so getting them into the ground turns out to be a lot easier than I thought it would be.

The whole thing falls over on me twice before I really figure out how it works, but I'm getting there.

I see the men by the fire have all turned their chairs around to watch me and the woman with her red cup is still standing there with that grin on her face. They might be getting a kick out of this, but at least I'm not giving up.

By the time Mason comes back, the tent is more than halfway put together. I'm sitting on the ground unraveling the last part of the rope when he comes up. My hands are super dirty, so I stand up and rub them against my shorts.

He's got firewood piled up high in a stack against his chest. I rush over to take some and after a brief look of surprise, he unloads a few pieces onto my arms.

"Thanks," he says. Then he notices the tent. "Holy shit, you did this?"

I stand straight and proud. "Yep, all by myself. I had a couple of false starts, but it started making more sense the farther I got into it."

"It looks great. I'm impressed."

"Thanks," I say. "Looks like you got a lot of good firewood."

"Should be enough for a couple of nights, anyway."

He dumps all the wood onto the ground near the fire pit, then starts stacking them up in a neat pile. I go back to finishing up my work on the tent while he gets a fire going. The sun is starting to set in the distance and the woods take on a pink and orange glow. I hear the crackling of several fires around us and as I look out across the park, I can see at least ten different fires and campsites with families, friends and couples all enjoying one last vacation before the end of summer.

"I'm in shock that you pulled this off," Mason says.

He walks around checking the stakes and pushing them down just a little further into the ground. He takes one completely out and backs it up about an inch. "You want to make sure the tension is nice and tight," he says. "That way the top of the tent is completely raised up. See?"

The Moment We Began

The side of the tent comes out and the fabric is more taut. I nod, then stand back and take in the whole scene. "I can't believe I really did that on my own," I say. I run a weary hand across my forehead and smile. "I'm camping."

He laughs and steps closer to me. He runs his hand over my forehead and little pieces of dirt fall away. I make a face and reach up to rub it clean, but my hands are so dirty, I think I'm only making it worse.

Mason puts his arm around me. It's the first time he's touched me since our argument. "No matter how long I've known you, Penny Wright, you keep finding ways to surprise me."

Chapter Thirty-Eight

"Dog me," I say with a giggle, holding my stick out toward Mason.

We're sitting together on a large log Mason brought over from the empty campsite next to ours. He takes a hotdog from the cooler and spears it with the end of the stick. I hold it over the fire.

"I haven't had a hotdog since I was little," I say. "My mom never lets us eat stuff like this."

Mason puts a hotdog on his own stick and puts it practically into the fire.

"You're gonna burn it," I say.

"No, I won't," he says, bumping me with his arm. "Mine will just be ready faster. Yours is the one that's not going to be ready until midnight with as far as you're holding it up."

I scoot a little closer to him, wanting to feel the warmth

of his body against mine. I regret not packing a sweatshirt.

"Hey, I'm really sorry about earlier," I say after we've been quiet for a minute. "I am just so used to seeing you with other girls that I just assumed you were flirting with her. I hope you can at least try to see it from my point of view."

"I know," he says. "I'm sorry I got so angry. I made a promise to you, though. No other women. I'm going to stick to that, Pen. You have to trust me."

I suck in a breath. Trust. That's a very tricky word, especially when it comes to Mason. I know he cares about me and would do anything in the world to keep me safe. But when it comes to my heart, he's broken it too many times to count.

"I want to trust you," I say. "But at the same time, we're doing something crazy here. At the end of this, no matter how I feel, you can just walk away."

"If that's all you're going to think about this whole trip, then it's over before it really begins, isn't it?"

I look over at him. Shadows dance across his features. Is he saying he wants to give this a real chance? I have no idea how I'm going to survive this when it's over. I think about raising a baby on my own and it's almost too much to take.

But how can I expect him to change in just a few short weeks?

The Moment We Began

Maybe I've gotten us into an impossible situation here.

He pulls his hotdog from the fire and studies it. "Dammit."

I look over and see that one entire side is burnt to a crisp and I laugh. "Ha! Told you you'd burn it."

I pull mine from the fire and look at it. It's a perfect brown all the way around. He looks over and before I can stop him, grabs the hotdog off my stick and stuffs it into his bun and takes a bite.

"Hey," I shout. I drop my stick and tackle him.

He falls to the ground, the half-eaten hotdog still in one hand. I straddle him and put my hands against his chest.

"Give me my perfect hotdog," I say.

"Or what?" He lifts one eyebrow and even in the dim light of the fire, I can see his eyes are filled with mischief.

"Or I'll keep the sleeping bag all to myself tonight," I say.

"Well, that's not an option," he says.

Under my hands, I can feel his heart racing as his eyes search my face.

He drops the hotdog into the dirt and grabs my hips. He lifts up and crushes my mouth with his, pressing hard against me, exploring me with a hunger he's never shown.

I respond with my whole body. I can't get close enough to him. He pulls me into his arms and I wrap my legs

255

around him. My hands run over his arms, his face, through his hair.

He parts his lips, drawing me in with his tongue. Passion explodes in my core, and I want more. I want all of him.

I tug on his hair and grind my body into his, feeling him growing excited through his jeans as he presses against me. He groans and moves his kisses to my chin and neck. His hands play with the hem of my tank top, then slip underneath, caressing the skin on my back and at my waist.

I lean my head back, giving him access, but it's not enough. I pull his head back and take his mouth again.

Behind us, the fire roars. Sweat trickles down the back of my neck and down the center of my spine.

"I want you," he says, pulling away. He's out of breath.

"Then take me." I meet his eyes. "I'm yours, Mason."

He stands, lifting me in one smooth, strong motion, then carries me into the tent. He doesn't even bother zipping it back up behind us.

He lays me down on the sleeping bag, then lifts his shirt over his head and throws it to the side. The light of the fire flickers against the tent, illuminating the shadows around his muscles.

His body is perfection and even though I've seen it a thousand times, I want nothing more than to touch him again. Consume him. Explore every inch of him.

I lean up, reaching for the button on his jeans.

He moans and I look up, meeting his eyes in the semi-darkness as I unbutton, then unzip his pants. His eyes are dark and full of need. It's the most beautiful thing I've ever seen. I'm addicted to that look. I'd let him break me a hundred times as long as I never had to live without that look.

I know it's wrong, but I can't help it. I love him. Tonight, I feel it more than ever.

Impatient, he finishes for me, pulling his pants off, and tossing them in a pile with his shirt. I touch the band of elastic on his boxers and help him pull them down over his erection. I'm instantly wet at the sight of him, needing to touch him and feel him against me. But when I reach for him, he gently pushes me back, delaying my touch.

I'm breathless, gasping for air, but only needing him to survive.

My body burns for him. Exists for him. And when his hands find me, my body trembles at his touch.

He undresses me with furious urgency, and in seconds I'm lying under him, naked and begging. I writhe against the ground, my hands reaching up to slip around his waist. My nails scratch against his back, pulling him down until his skin meets mine.

I open for him. Ache for him. And finally, he lowers himself fully onto me, slipping inside. The first seconds are full of a beautiful ache as my body stretches to receive him, then welcomes him as he pushes all the way.

We move together with passion and need. A push and pull that somehow feels different this time. I'm not sure if it's because of the way we opened up to each other or if it's from the excitement of being alone on this adventure, but we're more connected. More in sync with each other, our bodies moving to meet each other's needs at every turn.

And when he comes, he's looking deep into my eyes. The passion there sets off fireworks of emotions inside of me. Our bodies tremble together and I cling to him with the hope of the last few years, wondering if maybe, for the first time since I've loved him, he's feeling something like love for me, too.

Chapter Thirty-Nine

The next morning, I wake up in his arms.

All the times we've been together, we've never actually slept together like this, and I want to enjoy these first few moments before he wakes. I snuggle into the crook of his arm and look up at his face. He looks so peaceful and perfect.

His dark blond hair is a mess, and I smile as I think of how many times I must have run my hands through his hair last night.

At some point in the night, he must have zipped up the tent and pulled the sleeping bag over us. We're still naked and one of my legs is looped with his. I realize the best feeling in the world is the warmth of his naked skin against mine.

Even if this can't last, I think, it was all worth it for this moment right here. For this one night we shared when I felt love from him. Even if he never admits it or says it out loud, I felt the stirrings of it, and I will never forget it as long as I live.

His eyes flutter open and he smiles when he sees me watching him.

"Morning," he says. He kisses my forehead and I snuggle my face against his chest.

"Good morning," I say.

"Last night was amazing," he says. His voice is husky this early in the morning and it sends an electricity through me.

"Yes," I say. "If I had known how much fun camping out in tents could be, I would have suggested this a long time ago."

He sits up a little. "Hey, that's right. You survived your first night in a tent," he says. "Penelope Wright slept naked in the great outdoors. No one back home would believe me."

I laugh and sit up, the sleeping bag slipping down to my waist as I lift my arms and stretch. My body is a little achy from sleeping on the hard ground, but mostly I just feel happy.

"You've got to stop that," he says.

When I look over, I see that he's staring at my breasts.

"Stop what?" I ask, playing innocent.

He groans and pulls me into his arms. "You know

what."

He kisses me, but it's not the same hungry kind of kiss from last night. This is a soft kiss that says he's exactly where he wants to be.

"If we don't get up now, we're going to lose the whole day," he says. "Because I'm never going to want to leave this tent."

"Who says we have to leave?" I ask.

"Don't tempt me," he says. He gets up and pulls his discarded clothes back on his body.

He searches the sleeping bag for my clothes, then tosses them to me.

"Come on, get dressed," he says, a smile playing at his lips. "I don't know about you, but I'm suddenly very hungry for pancakes."

My stomach growls at the thought, but I frown at the clothes in my hand. "We can't go back to the same diner wearing the same clothes we wore yesterday," I say. "Plus, I desperately need a shower."

Mason shakes his head and laughs. "If this trip is about pushing boundaries, then I dare you to forget, just once, what other people might think of you," he says. "We can grab breakfast, then come back and shower, I promise. But just this once, screw what anyone else thinks about what you're wearing or what you look like and just go with the

261

moment."

"I'm all for pushing boundaries," I say, "but this is not just about what other people think. This is about feeling clean and not totally disgusting when I'm eating breakfast."

He rolls his eyes. "Fine," he says. "I'll get your bag so you can change clothes, but the shower has to wait."

"Deal."

He unzips the tent and steps outside. I lie back against the ground and pull the sleeping bag up to my chin. It smells like him and I breathe in, a satisfied grin playing at the corners of my mouth.

Chapter Forty

Mason and I decide to stay for a while.

We fall into a rhythm in this little beach community. A lot of the campers are there for just a night or two, but a few of them, like us, are there for a week or two. The lady in the Taj Mahal tent with her red cups and vodka is named Linda. She and her husband, Dodger, are from Indiana, but they like to spend a few months every summer here on the gulf. We've spent several nights over by their tent playing cards. Linda keeps trying to get me to drink some of her vodka, but I keep playing it off, saying I don't drink anymore. Mason doesn't question it.

The girl Mason was talking to that first day, left at the end of the weekend, and I was honestly glad to see her go. There was something about the way she looked at Mason that made me want to drop-kick her.

Most of the people we've met have been super nice,

though, and I realize Mason was right. People do treat us differently than they would if they knew we came from money. It's a strange thing, really. I'm the same person either way, but the way they see me is different. To them, I'm just a normal girl hanging out with her boyfriend on a camping trip. There's nothing to prove. I can just be myself.

Back home, I was always special. People were afraid to insult me or get on my bad side, but these people just say what they want to say and they aren't worried about what I'll think of them. They just act like themselves.

It's hard to pinpoint the exact difference, but I feel like I'm one of them rather than always apart. I also feel like I don't have to constantly work so hard to impress everyone. I can just sit back and not be the center of attention and it's okay. It feels good, really.

We spend a lot of time on the beach and every time I put on my bikini, I stare at my belly, expecting to see some kind of change. It's still flat, but for how much longer? My breasts have definitely gotten more tender over the past few days.

I've noticed a few other changes, too. Like little cramps and tugs in my belly. And I get tired a lot easier. Some days after spending an hour at the beach, all I want to do is curl up in the tent and sleep for the rest of the day.

Nighttime is my favorite. Mason and I snuggle up next

to the fire talking for hours. Some nights we have sex and some nights we just hold each other, but I feel closer to him with each passing day.

Every morning we get up and head to Dottie's for breakfast. Mason gets coffee every day, but I lie and say I'm trying to cut back. I don't think it's good for the baby and I don't want to take any extra risks.

We've gotten to know the regulars there pretty well, but mostly, I've fallen in love with Delores.

Or rather, Delores' cooking.

She's an artist. I've eaten food cooked by some of the world's premiere chefs and have never had anything taste so amazing as what she cooks right here in her greasy little kitchen.

Her husband, Buddy, is often the one cooking, but I've learned that almost all of the recipes belong to Delores. She's been cooking since she was ten years old, because her mother had a degenerative bone disease and was in a wheelchair through most of Delores' childhood. That left Delores, as the oldest of five children, to take on chores like cooking and cleaning and when she was old enough, driving.

She's unlike anyone I've ever known. She has a lot of attitude and pretends to be tough, but on the inside, she's a jelly donut. So stinking sweet.

More than once, I've seen her handing out food to children out back. This, above all things, makes me love her. When I ask her about it, she always tells me to mind my own business, but I know what she's doing. None of those children ever pay for the food and sometimes she loads them up with bags and bags from the kitchen. The grateful look in the eyes of those kids tells the real story there.

This morning, while Mason and I are finishing up our food, I overhear a piece of a conversation between Buddy and Delores about the diner's finances. They aren't arguing, exactly, but I can tell they're stressed about something.

Delores is sitting at the counter with a stack of receipts. Buddy is on the kitchen side, leaning over the counter. Sometimes Delores says something that makes Buddy lower his face into his hands.

"What's up with you this morning?" Mason asks. "You're so quiet."

I lean closer to him. "I've been trying to listen in on their conversation."

I nod my head toward the counter, trying not to be too obvious. Mason turns and looks, and I cringe.

I grab his hand. "Don't look," I say. "I don't want her to know I'm listening."

"I can hear you, girlie," Delores says, not even bothering to turn around. "Don't think I haven't noticed you eying me

The Moment We Began

all morning like a nosy-pants."

I twist my body to the side. "You've been turned around the whole time," I say. "There's no way you've seen me looking."

She taps the shiny napkin dispenser with her pencil.

"Oh," I say.

"Oh," she repeats, mocking me.

I grab my juice and stand up. I walk over and sit a couple of seats down from her. "Since I've obviously been eavesdropping anyway, you want to tell me what's got you guys whispering so much over here?"

She frowns at me. "How many times do I have to tell you that you need to stay out of my damn business?"

"Maybe I can help," I say.

She rolls her eyes and throws her hands up. "Well, Buddy, we didn't realize we've had a financial consultant eating breakfast in our diner every day for the past week and a half."

Buddy eyes me. "I don't know, Delores. She looks like she might be the college type. She might be camping out at our beach, but she's wearing three hundred dollar boots. Maybe she could help. God knows we need somebody's help."

Worry gnaws at my stomach. "What's wrong? Is the diner in some kind of trouble?"

267

Delores clenches her jaw and the muscles in her face tense.

Mason comes to stand beside me. He puts his hand on my arm. "Don't be rude, Pen. If they wanted to share their private business with you, they'd have asked for your opinion. Come on, let's get out to the beach. It's supposed to rain this afternoon and I want to enjoy the sun while it's out."

I'm not giving up that easily. Maybe it's really none of my business, but I probably could help them. My dad taught me a lot about money management growing up. Besides, she's doing something good for those kids and now I have a soft spot for this run-down place.

"I know a thing or two about running a business," I say. It's just about the most personal thing I've told them about who I am. "I'd be happy to take a look if you want."

Delores looks at me, then at Buddy. He nods at her and she throws her hands up in the air.

"You might as well," she says. "But the numbers are going to add up the same whether it's me doing them or some fancy college girl."

She stands and pushes the stack of receipts toward me.

I look to Mason, eyebrows raised.

"Go ahead," he says. "I don't know that you should get involved, but if you want to try, go for it. I'm going to go swimming for a while. Maybe stop by the dock and see if anyone's catching anything today."

"Okay," I say. I grab his hand and give it a squeeze. "Say hi to Malcom for me, will ya?"

Malcom is one of the old guys we've made friends with while we've been here. He's out there fishing every day, rain or shine.

"Will do," he says. I can tell from the tone of his voice that he's not happy with this, but he's just going to have to deal with it.

This place has become a home away from home for us. I would hate to see it close down.

When Mason leaves, it's just me, Buddy and Delores left in the place.

"So tell me, how long do you think you've got?" I ask.

She eyes me. "What are you talking about?"

I narrow my eyes at her. "I heard you tell Buddy that you thought you didn't have much time left before the bank came calling. I want to know how long you've got."

She looks to Buddy and again, he nods.

"If we're going to let her take a look, we might as well tell her the whole deal."

"Fine," Delores says. She pulls a pack of cigarettes out of her apron and lights up.

There's no smoking allowed in restaurants in this state,

but I'm not about to say anything. Besides, it's her place. I just don't know how bad second-hand smoke would be for the baby. I stare at the cigarette and she raises an eyebrow, then puts it out without saying a word.

"According to this letter we got this morning, we've got sixty days until they start proceedings to shut us down," she says. Her hand trembles slightly as she pours herself a fresh cup of coffee.

I don't show it on my face, but only having sixty days means it's gotten pretty bad. A lot of times, the bank will work with a small business like this for a long time as long as they can pay a little bit. Especially when it's one of the only businesses of its kind in such a small community.

"Well, let me take a look and see what I can find."

I get to work for the rest of the morning and Delores brings me any paperwork I ask for along the way. By noon, I've determined that Dottie's has been losing money consistently for about three years now. Just a slow trickle, but over time, they've managed to dig themselves into a pretty deep hole.

I think about all those kids who bring home food to their families because of Delores' kindness.

"How long have you been giving food to the kids?" I ask when Dottie comes to sit back down beside me.

She hesitates. This is obviously something she's been

doing under the table, and I can see she doesn't want to talk about it.

"How long?" I ask again.

She closes her eyes and takes in a breath. "Three years," she says. "Give or take. I used to sneak some food to some of the poorer families in town when Dottie was still alive, but if she'd ever found out, she would have fired me in a heartbeat. But when Buddy and I took over, it started small and just grew."

I nod. Her voice is wobbly, and it's the first time I've seen her close to tears.

"I know I shouldn't give away our profits like that, but if you saw the way some of these kids live," she says. "It would just break your heart, I'm telling you."

"Okay, but you've at least got to start charging for everything people order. Like drinks and sides and stuff." I look at my notes again. "I've looked at all the numbers, and I'm telling it to you straight. Unless you have some miracle surge of tourist to this area, you're going to fold."

Buddy rubs his forehead and Delores grips the counter.

"This place is all we've got," she says. "We took out a second mortgage on our house just for the down payment on this place. I'm scared if we lose Dottie's, we're gonna lose our house, too. I don't know what we're going to do. We've been struggling for so long, just to stay afloat, but this summer just wasn't what it needed to be. Too much rain this season and too many businesses along the strip closing down. Everyone's been moving on to the bigger coastal towns. Now that we're getting toward the end of the season, I'm scared as hell. We don't get any visitors around here during the winter months and there's really only a couple of weeks left of the summer rush, and that's if we're lucky."

"If you stopped giving food away for a few months—"

"No," she says. She puts her hand on my arm, and I think it's the first time she's ever actually touched me.

I look up and meet her eyes. She wants me to see how serious she is about this issue.

"Without this diner, those kids would near starve in the summers," Buddy says. "When school's in, the kids get breakfast and lunch, but during the summer, they're lucky if they eat once a day. What Delores does for those kids is…"

His voice trails off.

"Yes, but if you lose the diner completely, you'll never be able to help them," I say.

My heart is breaking for them. This is the kind of thing I have been telling my mom about forever. She's so set on sending money to help starving children overseas when there are kids in our own communities who go without eating for days.

The fact that Delores helps so much when she has so

little makes me feel guilty for not doing more with my own money.

I really want to help them, but their finances are a serious mess. Since their income varies wildly depending on the season, they really should have been doing more to cut expenses during the colder months. I look over my notes several more times, looking for anything that might be able to help them.

Finally, I see something tucked under one of the bank notices that catches my eye.

"Wait," I say, pulling the paper out to examine it more closely. "What is this license here? It's some kind of beach permit? Does that cover the entire beach area?"

Delores takes it from my hand. "Oh, that's just a license to operate a food cart. We had to get it for this year's Spring Break festival down in Gulf Shores. We thought it would be a good business idea to go over there, because they had all these vendors participating and my friend Sara Jane said she could get us a booth at the fair."

"Did you make good money?"

Buddy shakes his head. "Not too bad, but it wasn't what we'd hoped for. We ended up spending a lot carting everything down there and then there ended up being this big storm that week and a lot of the spring break crowd didn't show up. It was a real mess."

"But you guys have a cart?"

Delores nods. "Yeah, we got it stored in the garage at our place," she says. "It belonged to Dottie. She used to sell food to tourists out on the boardwalk during the busy seasons. Why? What you got cookin' in the brain of yours?"

"I might have an idea, but I don't want to get your hopes up before we've had a chance to really make sure it'll work. I'll come back this afternoon if I can."

I try to keep the excitement in my voice down, but I can't help it. Delores looks at me with such hope in her eyes.

I throw my arms around her. I can't believe I've gotten so attached to her in such a short period of time. I don't usually let my walls down around people this fast, but she's a genuinely beautiful person. Her entire body stiffens, but then she relaxes and laughs. When I pull away, there are tears in her eyes.

"Get on out of here and enjoy what's left of the sunshine," she says. "Don't you go worrying about us anymore, okay?"

I roll my eyes and give her a look. "I'll be back as soon as I can," I say. "All we have to do is raise enough money to pay the bank for a couple of months to get you back in their good graces. Then maybe they'll hold out until the next tourist season before they act on any of this."

She nods at me, but then turns away and lights another

cigarette.

I smile at Buddy and he winks as I turn and head out to the beach to find Mason.

Chapter Forty-One

I step onto the beach and feel the first drops of rain on my face. I stop for a moment and lift my face to the sky. I love the rain.

I've always been such a water baby and this past week of living outside and being able to hear the water every day has been great. In Fairhope, the beach is always so crowded. Here, it's a completely different experience. Some days, it's like we have the whole ocean to ourselves.

I wonder how the rain will affect our tent. I'm guessing the thing is waterproof. Surely it is, right? People camp out in the rain, don't they? I hope. I need to go find Mason and make sure we don't need to get back to our camp, but for now, it's heaven to be standing on the beach with the wind blowing over my skin and the sound of the waves in my ears.

It's only been ten days since Mason and I left Fairhope,

but I feel like it's been months already. I had expected us to be traveling more, but we lucked out when we found this place. We're the best we've ever been in this little nowhere town.

I know it can't last forever, and we've already been talking about wanting to move on and see more of the country, but I want to do this one last thing before we leave. I want to help Delores and Buddy keep their diner if I can.

I know that all it would take is one call home and I could have all the money I wanted at my fingertips. I'm sure by now my parents are freaked out enough about not hearing from me that they'd do anything I asked. But I like being anonymous here. I like being my own person and not depending on them for anything. Camping hasn't been easy and I did eventually make Mason drive to a camping store to buy an inflatable bed, but overall, I've been enjoying it.

I'd enjoy anything as long as I could wake up every morning in Mason's arms.

The rain begins to fall harder, and I decide to look for him before it gets too bad out here. I look both ways down the beach and don't see him anywhere. He mentioned the pier, so I start walking in that direction. Just up ahead, I catch sight of a red shirt in the sand. That's the same color Mason was wearing this morning, so he must have been swimming and then made a run for it when the rain hit.

The Moment We Began

But as I get closer to the shirt, I see that there are two shirts sitting there in a pile. Mason's red one. And a blue one I don't recognize. I pick it up from the sand and a knot forms deep in my stomach. It's a size small and has a picture of a Care Bear on the front.

I drop it to the sand, the rain pouring down my face. I don't want to rush into any kind of judgment. It could be anyone's shirt. Well, any girl's shirt. But Mason and I have become way too close for him to do something like that to me. He wouldn't. He promised me. Maybe this is just some kind of coincidence.

I rationalize it out, but inside, my heart is racing.

I need to find him. And if he's with someone else, I need to know.

I take off at a run, heading for the pier. There's a tiny bait and tackle shop just at the entrance to the pier and I collect myself before walking inside. I expect to see him standing there, maybe chatting with a group of tourists or maybe some of the fishermen. It doesn't take me long to walk through the whole place.

He's not here.

Panic fights its way up through my throat, but I push it back down and force a smile as I walk to the front counter.

"Hey Walt," I say.

"Heya, Pretty Penny," he says. Walt owns this shop. He

stays open until midnight every night, so Mason and I have made more than one late-night run here for water or a snack here and there. He always calls me Pretty Penny, and it always makes me smile, but right now all I want to do is cry.

"Looks like the ceiling fell out."

"Yeah, it's really pouring," I say. Then, casually, I ask, "Have you seen Mason?"

He looks up toward the ceiling. "Not today," he says. "Did you lose him? I don't think I've ever seen the two of you apart."

I try to smile, but I think it comes out more of a lopsided grimace. "Just misplaced him for a few minutes," I say. "If you see him, let him know I'm looking for him, please?"

"Not a problem," he says. "You're welcome to wait here until the rain lets up a bit. Or I could let you borrow my umbrella."

"Oh, no thanks," I say. I'm already half-way out the door. I raise my hand in a wave, then head back out into the rain.

I look both ways down the beach, but don't see any sign of Mason. Maybe he went back to the diner looking for me? That's the only thing I can think of unless he already walked back to the campsite.

Still, I can't imagine he would have just left his shirt behind. It's not like we have an infinite supply of clothing

The Moment We Began

with us.

I start to head back to the diner, and I'm not sure why, but something leads me to look back toward the pier one last time.

That's when I see him. Standing underneath the wooden slats of the pier.

Holding a girl in his arms.

Chapter Forty-Two

I stop dead in the sand. The sky grows darker as the storm clouds roll across the gulf, but there's enough light for me to see the two of them huddled close under the pier, a towel wrapped around their shoulders.

I choke back a cry.

Thunder rumbles in the distance, but I can't move. I'm paralyzed with fear.

Despite all my talk about letting him walk away at the end of this, I know it isn't possible for me to ever let him go without a fight.

I thought I loved him before we left Fairhope, but I realize now that what I felt was nothing compared to what has grown between us in the past ten days. Spending every moment of every day laughing and getting to know him, breaking down the walls he's guarded so tightly around his heart, has sent me to a place I can never come back from.

I'm way past the point of no return.

And if he's not in love with me, I don't know how I'll survive it.

I force myself to move forward, and every step feels like a death march.

When I'm close enough for him to notice me, his face turns ghost-white. He takes his arm from around the girl's shoulders and when she turns her face toward me, my world shatters.

It's the same girl he'd been talking to that first day at our campsite.

I don't even know her name. She was only camping there for a few nights before she and her friends moved on. I hoped to never see her again in my life. But here she is, squeezed so tight to Mason in her tiny little bikini.

She smiles at me, and I just want to run forward and rip her hair out. To tell her she's killed me.

But I force a smile as I step under the pier.

Mason scoots to the side, leaving his towel over the girl's shoulders. I want to laugh. Or scream. He's already been caught, what is he trying to do? Pretend I didn't see him?

I stare into his eyes, searching for an answer about what he's doing, but all I see there is fear.

"I've been looking for you." My voice stumbles over the

words, but I hope he can't tell over the sound of the rain against the wood above.

"I was out on the beach swimming when the storm came on," he says. "Harley and I ran under here, thinking maybe it would pass quickly."

"Harley?"

She holds her hand out toward me, but all I can do is stare at it dumbly. "You must be Penny," she says, awkwardly pulling her hand back under the towel. Her voice is extremely bubbly for a girl whose been snuggling with someone else's man. "Mason was just telling me you guys have been here the whole time."

A nod is all I can manage. I want him to say something. Anything. To apologize or at least try to convince me there's nothing going on here.

But he doesn't. He just sits there, speechless.

I'm surprised I can manage to keep standing. With every second that goes by, I'm losing more and more hope about what was really going on between them. Have they been out here all day together while I was inside working on the diner's papers?

"When did you get back to town?" I ask. "I thought you guys left."

She wraps the towel tighter around her shoulders. "Oh, yeah, my friends all ended up going home to start back at school, but I already graduated earlier this summer, so I thought I'd just set out on my own for a while."

"Oh," I say. "What made you come back here?"

Mason clears his throat. "Did you just get finished up inside with Delores?"

I wonder why he's changing the subject.

My heartbreak is mercifully turning into rage. Rage I can handle much better than pain and devastation. I harness it.

"Yes, I did," I say. "I wish you had just come in there when the rain started. I'm sure it would have been a lot more comfortable in there. We could have warmed you up with some coffee. Of course, you two looked like you were getting warm just fine on your own."

He brings his knees up and rests his arms against them. He's fidgeting with his hands, and I know there's more going on here than just an innocent chance meeting. I want to ask him and just have it out right here, but it's just too much. I don't want this stranger to see me crying.

I just want to get the hell out of here.

"Well, you two have fun," I say. I'm on the verge of a major shit-fest, and if I don't leave now, I'm going to say something I'll regret.

I turn fast and start walking as fast as I can back down the beach. The rain is coming hard now and it stings my skin, but I keep walking.

I feel like a fool. How could I have believed he felt the same way about me? Has this just all been about sex to him? Did I just convince myself things were changing between us?

The floodgates open and tears stream down my face. A sob shakes my body and I lift my hand to my mouth to muffle the sound. I don't want him to know. I don't want him to hear me.

I think I hear my name on the wind, but I don't turn around. I can't. I just keep walking. I'm almost running now, my boots caked in wet sand and my clothes and hair completely drenched to the core.

Then I feel a hand on my shoulder. He spins me around and takes both of my arms in his strong hands.

"Penny, please, don't go," he says. "Let me explain."

I hope the rain hides my tears. When I open my mouth to respond, my breath does this double-hitch that gives me away. I close my eyes and try again, summoning whatever strength I have left to get through this moment.

"Don't bother," I say. "Just let me go."

"No," he says. "It isn't what it looks like."

I pull away and wrap my arms around my body. I'm shivering in the rain and wind.

"Isn't that the line every guy gives when it's exactly

what it looks like?" I say. "Do you think I'm stupid?"

He closes his eyes and rubs his forehead. "Shit," he says. He looks up at me and I'm surprised to see his eyes are filled with tears too. "Penny, I swear to God, I would never do something like that to you. Not after I made a promise to you. Not after—"

"Please don't lie to me, Mason," I say. "I am on the edge here, and I just need to know the truth. If something happened between the two of you or if you're attracted to her, then you'd better tell me right fucking now. If you want to sleep with her, you need to tell me the truth."

"Sleep with her? Are you crazy?" He's shouting over the sound of the storm and the waves crashing against the shore. "I was just sitting on the beach watching the waves come in and thinking about some shit when she just came up and threw her arms around me. I thought it was you at first, so I hugged her back. But when I turned around, I see this girl I barely know and she's smiling like crazy. She kissed me on the cheek like we were old friends."

I'm listening but my body is shivering both from cold and fear, not sure where this conversation is going. Not sure where we'll be at the end of it. Or if my entire world is about to come crashing down.

"I talked to her for a few minutes, just to be nice and before I know it, she's stripping down to her bikini and saying she wants to get in the water," he says. "I told her I was heading back up to see you in the diner and that she was welcome to tag along if she wanted, but that's when the rain came. The clouds had already been gathering, but it was like it all just came out of nowhere. Before I know it, she grabs me and starts shivering like crazy, saying she's deathly terrified of storms. I didn't know what to do. I felt like an idiot.

"She pointed to the pier and begged me to walk her over there and make sure she was safe," he says. "I didn't know what to say. She railroaded me. I felt like a puppet, just doing whatever she told me to do."

"I saw you," I shout. "I saw you under the pier with your arm wrapped around her. Her face was inches from yours."

"Dammit, I know," he says. He runs a frantic hand through his hair. "She gave me some line about being so cold. It just sort of happened. I didn't do anything other than exactly what you saw."

"Why did she come back here, Mason? Why this place? And why did she seek you out?" I'm crying again. I can't help it. I want to believe him, but I don't know if I should. If he's lying to me, I'll be the biggest fool to ever for live if I don't walk away from him right now. After all the times he left my bed only to show up at a party the next night with some dumb whore, I'm stupid if I give in to this story.

But his hands are trembling. He's never done this before. He's never denied what he's done. He's always just put it out there, right in my face. He's always made sure I understood that he didn't care about me the way I cared about him.

For once, he seems to give a shit, but I'm too scared to think straight.

"The second I saw you standing there in the rain, I knew what you would think," he says. "Penny, I was wrong. I should have come straight to the diner to find you. She had my mind all twisted up. She told me she hasn't been able to stop thinking about me since the day we met and that she came back to find me. I was trying to explain to her that I'm with you, but she kept pushing me. I didn't know what to do."

I turn toward the ocean, watching the violent waves of the tide as it rolls in on the storm. I feel sick.

Mason comes to stand behind me. He wraps his arms around me and pulls my body close to his. His skin is cold at first, but our body heat quickly warms us. I'm tense in his embrace.

I'm in too deep to let this go. I need more from him, but I have no idea how much he's willing to give.

He dips his head and I can feel his breath close to my

ear.

"I don't ever want to hurt you again, Penny," he says. "But I'm not good at this. I've never gotten close enough to a girl to want to make any kind of commitment. I don't know how this works or how to be what you need me to be. Please don't let this ruin what we have."

"What do we have?" I ask. I don't turn around, because I'm scared to look into his eyes. I'm scared I'll break open and melt into the sea if he tells me we're just friends.

He turns me around, his arms still tight around me. "Do you really have to ask me that?"

"Yes," I say. I struggle against him, but he's not letting me go. "I have loved you for most of my life, and I think you know that. I think you've always known. But you never wanted me. Not the same way I wanted you. Maybe I was a fool for thinking this trip could change that. And I know you told me to trust you, but you're the one who has taught me not to trust you, Mason. All this time, do you know how much it has hurt me to have you in my bed one night and in another woman's bed the next? It's been torture. I can't go back to that. Not anymore."

He pulls away and places his hands on my cheeks, lifting my eyes to his. "Penny, I'm not attracted to her. You're the one I want. You're the only one. What can I do to prove that to you?"

I close my eyes and let my head fall back against his arm. I want him to tell me he loves me, but it can't happen like this. Not if I have to force it. I don't want him to say it because he felt he had to just to keep me here.

But more than ever, I wish he would say it on his own. From his heart.

I'm beginning to wonder if those are the three words I'll never hear him say.

"Let's leave, then," he says. "Would that show you I don't want to be with her? We've been in this town for almost two weeks. There's so much more we could see and do. Let's just pack up and go. Start again somewhere else. We can make this work."

I pull away and look up at him. The rain is dying down, but the wind is blowing his hair all around. There's hope and fear in his eyes, and I want to trust him. I want to believe him.

"Where would we go?" I ask.

His lips curl into a small smile and he wraps his arms around me. "Anywhere you want," he says. "I just want to be with you. Please say I didn't fuck this up."

I can't help but smile. Out of all the times he's hurt me, he's never offered to make it up to me or given me any hope that there was something between us worth not fucking up. I slide my arms around his waist and press my head against his chest.

"Is that a yes?" he asks. "And can we go inside to get a cup of coffee and talk the rest of this out? I'm freezing."

My teeth are chattering, so the thought of a hot cup of coffee sounds amazing right now. Maybe I could convince Delores to make a pot of decaf for me.

"Okay," I say. "Let's go by the store and grab a new map first, though. Maybe while we're there, we can figure out where we're heading next."

His face breaks out in a huge smile and he lifts me up off my feet.

I laugh and the sound carries in the wind.

I can't help but hope it carries all the way to the space under the wooden pier.

Chapter Forty-Three

Mason and I sit in the diner drinking coffee and trying to dry out.

Delores comes over to fill our cups and eyes the map spread out on the table. "Don't tell me you guys are getting the itch and are thinking of leaving us already?"

Guilt tugs at my insides. I promised to help her keep the diner, and I don't want to leave her hanging. But I don't want to have to stay here when Harley the Harlot is in town, either.

"We're considering it," I say. "But don't worry, I'm not abandoning you."

A few tourists walk in and Delores steps away from our table to grab a few menus for them.

"Did you figure something out that might help?" Mason asks. "I forgot to ask."

"The diner is really in trouble," I tell him. "They've only

got sixty days to make a balloon payment and they just don't have the income. With the end of the season coming up, they're terrified."

"That sucks," he says. "This place is a real treasure."

"Exactly," I say. "I'm so used to being able to just write a check and help someone out. I've never helped a business like this, but I've written more checks than I could count."

"For who?" he asks, an eyebrow raised.

I shrug and take a sip of the coffee. I forgot she just refilled it and it burns my tongue. "The homeless shelter. A couple of families around town. The elementary school a couple of times. I give a lot of money to families of sick babies at the hospital when they don't have insurance to pay for treatments."

He draws in a loud breath and his mouth drops open.

I look up and see that his eyes are wide and filled with tears. I put my hand on his. "What's wrong?"

"Are you serious?" he asks, his eyes wide. "You do all those things?"

"I don't really advertise it," I say. "I don't want my parents to find out. Dad says our family business isn't a charity and if we started giving away money to everyone who needed it, we'd be broke by morning. I know he has a point, but at the same time, why do we need so much? My parents are so set on giving to these big national charities.

The Moment We Began

They completely ignore the fact that there's a real need for help in our own community."

I look up and see that Mason is really affected by this. He's in shock or something.

"What?" I ask, my cheeks flushing. "I'm not the world's most shallow person after all, huh?"

He shakes his head. "You know I've never thought that about you," he says. He takes my hand. "I just think that's really great what you've done."

"I know a lot of people in town think my family is greedy," I say. "They don't see the whole picture, though. Even though I might not agree with all their choices, my parents donate more than a million dollars a year to various charities and organizations. But because he drives an expensive car and lives in a big house, people call him greedy."

"My dad is the greedy one," he says.

Mason doesn't talk about his father much, so I'm surprised when he says this. I've tried several times over the past week to get him to open up about what's really going on at home, but he always closes up and refuses to talk about it. I glance over at him and see there's some kind of battle going on inside his eyes. There's a mix of anger and hate and something like fear.

I'm scared to ask him more. This is when Mason always

shuts down. He opens the door, then when I take a step inside, he slams it right in my face.

So I wait. When and if he's ready to say more, he will.

"You know how you said you were so tired of people judging you the second they found out whose daughter you were?" he asks.

"Yes, it's like I'm Penny, the normal girl until someone says my last name and suddenly it's like, Oh, you're Tripp Wright's daughter? The bazillionaire? That's when they start asking about my trust fund and assuming that I'm just another spoiled rich girl with a credit card. They automatically act like I'm shallow and superficial."

"It's been easier here, though, right?"

"It's been amazing," I say. "To be judged solely on who I am and not what I have."

"That's what I want more than anything," he says. Sadness seeps into his voice and it scares me. "I don't want to be judged for who my family is. Or what my family has done."

"What are you so afraid of?" I ask him softly. "What's really going on at home?"

Mason lowers his head into his hands. When he comes up, his eyes are vacant. The moment has passed, just like that.

My heart sinks. I don't want to let this go. I need to

know what's bothering him so bad. Why he really wanted to get out of town.

"Mason," I say. I put my hand on his and he looks up at me. "I know there's something going on that you are scared to talk about for whatever reason. But you know you can trust me, too, right? I'm not going to judge you or be upset with you. I just want to know so I can help. So I can be here for you. You don't have to deal with everything alone."

He shakes his head. "There's nothing to talk about," he says, and I know the discussion is over. He's closed up again and there's no point pushing him. "Let's just map out a route. I'm thinking it's too late to really get on the road tonight, but we could head out at first light."

"There's something I want to do at the bank first," I say.

He eyes me. "I know you want to help them, Pen, but if you call your parents or try to wire money here, your parents are going to come here to find you. You know that, right?"

I shake my head. "I'm not going to call them. I'm not even going to use my family name. I just want to see if I can talk to the loan officer and get another thirty day extension on their loan. I have some ideas for how they can help their business, but I'm going to need some time tonight and tomorrow to get it set up before we can leave."

He sets the map down flat on the table and nods. "Do

what you gotta do," he says. "I can get things packed up while you head to the bank in the morning."

"Have you two decided which direction you're headed?" Delores asks, dropping off our check.

"West," I say. "Always west."

She looks down at the map and points to a town in Texas called Beaumont. "If you guys end up around this area, you'll want to stop into a little country bar called Knockin' Boots," she says. "My brother Lester and his wife Caroline manage it. They have live music and they'll set you up with some free drinks if you tell them you know me. Might even let you get up on stage and sing if you want."

I laugh. "No," I say. "Trust me, no one wants to hear me sing."

"I can sing a little," Mason says.

I laugh at first, then realize he's not joking. "You're serious?" I smack his arm. "You never told me that. How come you've never sung for me?"

He shrugs. "You've never asked me to."

"I don't believe you," I say.

He smiles. "Someday, I'll prove it to you," he says.

"Is that a promise?"

"Yes, it is," he says. "Just you wait."

I smile and look down at the map. Beaumont, Texas it is, then.

Chapter Forty-Four

I spend the rest of the afternoon going through my ideas with Delores and Buddy.

They have an old computer in the back room, so we get on and map out all the different big events and festivals coming up in this area over the next couple of months.

"See, there are a lot of end-of-summer events coming up on the bigger beaches," I say. "With your license, you should be able to contact them and see if you can get on as a vendor. If nothing else, you could take your food cart up there and set up somewhere in town unofficially."

"You don't think it's going to be a big risk to spend all that money getting the menu together and gas for the trip and everything?"

"The key is to be smart about what you serve. Only stick to your simplest, best items," I say. "A few things you can make ahead of time and then just heat up on demand.

Things that don't take too many expensive ingredients. The kinds of foods that will appeal to people outside enjoying a day on the beach."

"Crab cake burgers," Buddy says. "It's one of Delores' most popular summer dishes. We could freeze the patties ahead of time and just heat them up on the grill when we get there."

I nod. "Exactly. If you can come up with three or four good items like that where you won't be wasting any food if you don't sell out, you won't be in danger of losing any money," I say. "And at these festivals, you can charge a premium. One of the problems I see from the menu you used at that spring break event is that you were really undercharging for everything. No one charges less than a dollar for a can of soda at these things. You could probably sell cold bottles of water for a dollar each and if you get bottles of Coke instead of cans, you could probably sell those for two dollars each."

"Two dollars?" Delores asks. She presses her lips together and settles her hands on her hips. "We can get those wholesale for less than forty cents a bottle."

"Right, so each one you sell at two dollars is major profit," I say. "Which you desperately need right now."

"Well, I don't want to be screwing people just to get ahead," she says.

The Moment We Began

I want to laugh at how innocent and perfect she is, but this is a serious matter. "Delores, you aren't screwing people. Two dollars is a fair price at an outdoor event like this. Besides, you're not trying to just get ahead. You're trying to save your diner."

Her face becomes serious and she nods. "Okay, what else?"

I go through the rest of the menu with them while Mason creates a calendar of all the upcoming events along the Alabama coast for the next two months.

"The more of these you can get to, the better," I say. "And when you get a little bit of money, I want you to spend some of it on flyers you can hand out, telling people where to find this diner. Trust me, when they taste your food, they're going to want to stop by and visit this place. And if you get ahead, maybe you can invest a little bit of money into having the floors cleaned up or putting in new tables and such."

She nods, but I see fear in her eyes.

"Try to keep an eye out for any catering jobs. Parties, birthdays, that sort of thing." I put my hand on hers and squeeze. "It's going to be okay, Delores. I won't let you lose this place."

"Heaven must have brought you through those doors to me," she says, squeezing my hand. "And here I thought you were just some snooty little tourist when I first met you, thinking you were turning your nose up at my tap water."

I laugh. I don't tell her that's exactly what I was doing.

But who knew how much ten days could really change a person?

I'm kind of starting to like the person I'm becoming.

Chapter Forty-Five

By the time I get back from the bank the next morning, Mason has the whole camp packed up and ready to go.

There's no sign of Harley at the campgrounds today, and she's lucky she didn't show her face.

"How did it go?" he asks.

"Good," I say. "I laid out my ideas and asked him to extend the loan an extra month and see how it all pans out."

"And he agreed? Just like that?"

I lift my hands up. "Just like that," I say. "He thought the plan had real potential. Of course, they're still going to have to pay what they owe, but the bank wants to see them succeed so they can get their money back. He said he's willing to give them the time to turn things around."

Mason smiles. "I always knew you were beautiful and smart, but who knew you had such a great mind for business?"

I roll my eyes. "Not my parents, that's for sure," I say. "I've tried bringing up some of my ideas to my dad, but he always waves me away. He's always asking Preston for ideas and Preston could care less. But you know how it is. The son has to be the one to carry on the family name and tend the family business. It's a Southern tradition."

"It's bullshit," he says. "If your dad can't see how good you'd be for his company, he's blind."

I climb into the truck and Mason gets behind the wheel. "It's okay," I say. "I've been thinking of taking some time off from school anyway."

"Why?" he asks. "Because of this trip?"

"That and some other things," I say. "No big deal."

But it is a big deal. It's a very big freaking deal. I've been avoiding thinking too far into the future, but eventually I'm going to need a plan.

I fold the map so that the route from Alabama to Texas is open on my lap as he pulls onto the road leading out of town. "I feel like we've gone back in time," I say. "This is probably the longest either one of us has ever gone without checking email or using a GPS to get where we're going."

"I know, but that's part of what makes it so fun."

I nod and stare out the window. Thinking about the future also has me thinking about what's going on back home. Are they out looking for us? Is everyone worried about us?

Will my parents ever forgive me for leaving without talking to them about it first?

For now, Mason and I are living in this little cocoon. It's just us and the rest of the world fades away, but in a few weeks, I'm going to need to go home and face reality again. When I get home, there are going to be a lot of decisions to make. For now, though, I'm going to concentrate on making the most of our time together. If it works out the way I'm hoping, Mason will be by my side and we'll be making those decisions together.

Chapter Forty-Six

Mason and I take our time on the road. We decide to play it by ear, stopping at a few different campsites along the coast on our way toward Texas.

"I've never been to New Orleans," I say, studying the map at breakfast a few days later. "It's only a couple of hours from here and I've always wanted to see it. I doubt there are many places to pitch a tent in the middle of the city, though."

He laughs. "No, I imagine they generally frown on that sort of thing," he says. "Not that people probably haven't tried during Mardis Gras."

"I bet," I say. "Can we go? Even just for the day?"

"Anything you want, baby," he says.

He's never called me baby before and for some reason, it makes me giddy. Other than being the only person in the world who calls me Pen, Mason has never had a real pet name for me. I could get used to swapping terms of endearment with this guy.

"Next stop, The Big Easy," I say. And just for fun, I throw in, "Sweet cheeks."

He cocks his head to the side and his eyes narrow to threatening slits. "Don't press your luck, missy."

I stand and toss my dirty napkin at him. "What would you prefer, then? Sugar-lips? Pumpkin? Love muffin?"

He groans and pulls a few bills out of his wallet. "Can't you at least try to think of something a little more masculine?"

"Hot stuff? Lover boy?"

He's trying to act annoyed, but his lips curl up on the corners. "I like Mason," he says. "Let's stick to that."

I put my hand in his and we walk out to the truck together. "For now," I say. "But you can still call me baby."

He leans down and kisses me before opening the door on the passenger side. "You like that, huh?"

"I love it," I say, wrapping my arms around him and going in for another kiss. What I really want to say is I love you, but I hold back. Things are going so well since we left Little Lake that I don't want to push my luck.

It only takes us an hour and a half to get into the city. We park in a public parking lot downtown that only costs ten dollars for the full day, then walk around, exploring the city hand-in-hand. We walk around the French Quarter, have lunch and beignets at Café du Monde, and spend the rest of the day walking around the St. Louis Cemetery.

"I know it's strange to say a cemetery is pretty, but it is," I say.

The stone crypts are all above ground. Some are plain, but others are ornate, decorated with beautiful artwork and sculptures.

"They're like little houses for dead people," Mason says.

I step around one of the tombs and my foot catches on a stone. I push my hands out in front of me to catch my fall, but my hip slams hard against a stone vase. I cry out and clutch my side, fear rushing through me as I fall hard against the ground.

Mason rushes to my side. "Are you hurt?" he says.

"I don't know," I say, tears filling my eyes. My hands are trembling and I can't catch my breath.

I sit there for a long time, not saying a word. Terrified I may have hurt the baby, but not able to tell him what's wrong.

"Penny, you're scaring me. What's wrong?"

I shake my head and lean against him. "I'm okay, I think," I say. "Just a little shaken up."

He helps me stand and I slide the edge of my shorts down. There's a long scrape across my hip and stomach that's bleeding a little. It stings, but it's nothing serious. At least not from the outside.

I try my best to shake it off and go on with our day, but it stays in the back of my mind. I can't stop worrying about the baby.

After that, the carefree atmosphere of the day is gone and Mason suggests we get back on the road to find a place to stop for the night.

When we stop for gas a few miles outside the city, I get out of the truck and tell Mason I'm going to use the bathroom.

I go inside the small restroom and shut the door, then lean back against it, trying to calm myself down. If this baby could survive a major car accident, surely he can survive a little fall. I'm sure it's no big deal, but I can't shake the feeling that something's wrong.

I splash cold water on my face and take several deep breaths. I'm probably just overreacting.

But when I go to use the bathroom, there's a little blood on the tissue.

My heart nearly stops. I'm not going to be able to go on pretending I'm okay, and there's no way I'll be able to hide my worry from him.

But if I tell him now, I'm afraid it will ruin everything. I'm not ready yet. I know he cares about me a lot, but until he tells me he loves me and wants to be with me even after we decide to go home, I don't want him to know about the baby.

I step outside of the bathroom and glance through the window at Mason. He's still standing by the truck filling the tank. I walk to the clerk at the counter.

"Do you have a payphone here?"

He shakes his head. "No, sorry."

I bite my lip and run a hand through my hair. "I really need to use the phone," I say, pleading with my eyes. "It's an emergency. Can I use yours?"

He sighs. "Is it long distance?"

"Yes, but it's really important," I say. I search my pockets for cash, but I must have left it in my bag. The only other thing I can think to do is use my calling card. I have the number memorized. "I can use a calling card. It won't cost you anything."

He thinks it over, then finally hands me the cordless phone from under the counter. "Be quick, though, just in case someone calls the store," he says. "The owner will be pissed if he calls in and it's busy."

I thank him and glance out at Mason again. I know I don't have much time. Using the card goes against our rules, but we're just passing through here anyway. By the time anyone tracked us down, we'd be gone.

My fingers are shaky and I mis-dial a couple of times before I finally get it right and the line starts ringing.

When the operator answers, I ask her to connect me with Dr. Mallory's office. It's after five in the afternoon, but miraculously, he picks up on the second ring.

"Dr. Mallory? This is Penny Wright," I say.

"Penny? Oh, my goodness, are you okay? Your mother told me you'd left town and that no one's heard from you," he says. "I've been very worried about you."

"I'm sorry, I don't have a lot of time to explain, but I need to talk to you." The words are rushing out of my mouth so fast, I'm stumbling over them. I tell him about the fall at the cemetery and the spotting.

"I really don't think you have anything to worry about," he says. "Spotting can be totally normal at this stage in your pregnancy, but it would be best if you could come in and get things checked out just to be safe."

"I can't come in," I say. "I'm not even close to home right now."

"What about a local clinic where you are? Or even an emergency room? Any place that could do a quick exam or ultrasound to make sure everything's okay. That would at least put your mind at ease."

I close my eyes. I have no idea how I would pull that off without Mason finding out. "I don't know if I can get in to

314

see anyone right away."

"Everyone here is very worried about you, Penny," he says. "I think it's best if you come home as soon as you can."

I know he's just trying to look out for me, but I really don't want to come home right now. Still, I don't want to put the baby at risk either. I stand there, not sure what to say or do.

"Look, Penny, I'm sure everything is going to be fine," he says. "If it's just a little bit of spotting, it's nothing to be concerned about. It will probably go away overnight. If it continues for a few days or becomes heavier, or if you have any severe cramping, you need to get in to see a doctor right away."

Movement catches my eye outside and I see Mason walking toward the store.

"Thank you, Dr. Mallory," I say. "I've got to go."

"Please call me if you need help, okay?"

"I will," I say. "And Dr. Mallory? Please don't tell anyone I called, okay?"

He hesitates, but finally says yes.

I hang up and hand the phone to the clerk just as Mason walks through the door.

Chapter Forty-Seven

I barely sleep that night.

We stop at a campsite that has small cabins for rent and I convince Mason to splurge for the night. It's still modest, but there's a private bathroom. I keep getting up throughout the night to check for more spotting, but other than that little bit at the gas station, I don't see any more blood.

In the morning, I tell Mason I'm not feeling well and we decide to stay in the cabin for a few more days.

We take it easy, playing board games that were left in the cabin and taking turns reading from a few old romance novels with tattered pages. I laugh when Mason reads, because he adds some real theater to it, giving a different voice to each character. The sex scenes are the best part. Not because they're so sexy, but because he's so dramatic about it.

At night, he holds me in his arms and strokes my hair.

On our second night there, we're lying in bed when I notice a faded Polaroid sticking out of one corner of his open duffel bag on the floor. I recognize it from the first night he showed me his truck and told me he was leaving Fairhope.

I walk over and pick it up, studying the two blond children in the photo. I bring the picture back to bed and lay back against his chest. His body tenses as I hold it up.

"Tell me about her," I say.

He's quiet for a long moment, and at first I think he's not going to say anything.

Finally, he reaches up and takes the photo from my hand. His thumb moves along the bottom tenderly.

"Her name was Rachel," he says. "She was my sister."

I sit up so I can see his face. He's wearing a pained expression, sadness and regret in his eyes.

"I didn't know you had a sister."

He props the picture up against a lamp on the side table by the bed. "She died when I was seven."

I draw in a breath, my heart aching for him. I move closer to him on the bed and put my hand on his leg. "What happened to her?"

He clears his throat and when I look up, there are tears in his eyes. "She had leukemia," he says. "She was eight when she was diagnosed and six months later, she was gone. It was like one day she was fine and the next, she was too sick to stand. My parents didn't have much money back then and my dad was between jobs so we didn't have health insurance. They couldn't afford the treatments and by the time they were able to find a hospital that would help her, it was too late. When you told me you've given money to families like that—kids without insurance?—that really means a lot to me, Penny."

I don't know what to say. My chest tightens and my eyes sting with tears. I blink and they fall down my cheeks and drop onto the sheets. Mason swipes at his eyes and looks away. I move up next to him and put my arms around him. His shoulders are shaking slightly.

"I had no idea," I say in a whisper. "I'm so sorry."

"She was my best friend growing up," he says, his voice cracking. "Sometimes I still can't believe she's gone, you know?"

I have no words to comfort him. All I can do is hold him tight in my arms and let him talk.

"You're so lucky to have Preston," he says. "I watch you guys sometimes and think about what it would have been like if she hadn't died. What she would have been like. How my life might have been different."

So many thoughts swim through my brain. I can't believe I've known him for all this time—grown up beside him all these years—and never once heard anyone in his family mention Rachel. I always assumed he was an only child.

How could he have carried this pain around inside of him for so long and never shared it with anyone?

"Why don't you ever talk about her?" I ask.

He shrugs and wipes the rest of the tears from his eyes. "My parents don't like to be reminded of that time in our lives," he says. "It was a really hard time for all of us."

"Yeah, but isn't it hard to keep that inside?"

"I used to think it made things easier," he says. "Like, if we didn't talk about it or keep her pictures out where people could ask about her, then maybe it didn't happen. Maybe it was just a dream."

I hug him tighter, wishing I knew how to comfort him.

"I know it sounds stupid, but I think that's why I never really let myself love anyone completely," he says. "It hurts too damn much when you have to say goodbye."

He lets go, then, and the tears begin to flow. He clings to me, his shoulders shaking with sobs. I lean back against the headboard on the bed and pull him against my chest, our earlier roles reversed.

I realize, as I hold him, that the walls he's always put between us are higher and thicker than I ever imagined. All this time I thought he was putting those walls up to keep me out, but in this moment, I see that what he was really doing

The Moment We Began

was hiding his own broken heart.

Chapter Forty-Eight

In the morning, we pack up and continue on our way toward Texas.

Something has changed between us, though. It's a change that no one would ever see from the outside, but I know we both feel it. We trust each other in a way we never did before, and it gives my heart hope for the future.

On the drive, he tells me stories about his sister. Things they did growing up, like camping and fishing and playing games. He tells me how they used to sing together all the time and I mention again that I want to hear him sing. He just smiles and says no one ever gets to hear him sing these days.

Now I finally see why this trip was so important to him, though. I see why he needed to get away from the parties and the money. To get back to a life beyond those things when he may not have had money, but he had more than that.

When we finally get to Beaumont a few days later, it's well after midnight and both of us are exhausted.

"There's no way we're going to find a campsite this late at night," Mason says. "I think we should just splurge and get a hotel room. A nice one this time, with hot water and everything."

I nearly scream in excitement. "Oh, thank you, Jesus," I say, clapping my hands. The exhaustion is gone and now all I can think about is a comfortable bed and being able to take a shower in a room where I don't have to keep one eye open in case a spider decides to jump down and attack my face. "You are my favorite person on earth right now," I say, planting a huge kiss on his cheek.

Mason tries to hide a smile. He makes an exaggerated show of looking at his watch. "Let's see, you lasted almost three full weeks in the wild," he says. "I think you deserve one night of luxury."

"Hey, I didn't say we had to stay at the Ritz or anything," I say. "Not that I would complain about it if we did, though. I just want a bed comfortable enough to sleep in without waking up twelve times a night."

"If we have a comfortable bed, is that really what you want to be doing in it?"

I punch his shoulder. "Is that all you ever think about?"

324

The Moment We Began

"When you're around me, yes. Yes, it is," he says with a smile. "I can't help it if you're the sexiest woman alive. I'm the victim here."

I scoot back down in the seat, putting my feet up on the dashboard. "I guess after nearly three weeks straight of sleeping on the ground or in extreme budget hotels and cabins, we'd really be crazy not to at least take advantage of a nice, comfortable bed before we actually sleep in it," I say, a huge smile spreading across my face as he takes the next exit and pulls into the parking lot of a Hilton.

Chapter Forty-Nine

The next morning, we sleep in for the first time in weeks.

"I think we missed the free breakfast," Mason says, stretching.

We got a room with a king-size bed, but we're snuggled together tight on one side.

"Screw breakfast," I say. "I just want to stay in bed all day."

"Done," he says, pulling me into his arms and rolling over until he's on top of me.

He leans down and kisses me softly.

"I don't care how many days pass," he says. "I'll never get enough of seeing you like this."

"Like what?"

He smiles and twists a strand of my hair around his finger. "Your wild hair. Your slightly puffy and kissable lips." He runs the back of his hand across my cheek. "Not a drop of makeup on your gorgeous face."

I sink back into the pillow and scrunch my nose. "I hate the way I look in the mornings."

"You're so naturally beautiful," he says. "There's no one in the world I'd rather wake up next to."

I suck in a breath and meet his eyes. My heart aches at his words. They sound like the words of someone who is in love, but something is still holding him back. After all we've shared, what could still be standing between us?

I wish I could ask him. I wish I could ask him if he's falling in love with me. But I'm too scared.

So I let my eyes ask for me. And instead of getting up or running away from me like he used to, he stays. He caresses my hair, his eyes never wavering from mine.

And for now, it's enough.

Chapter Fifty

Mason and I spend the day in bed. We order room service for lunch, watch bad TV, and stay wrapped in each other's arms for the entire afternoon. Around six, I finally get out of bed and into the shower.

I stay in a long time, just letting the hot water run over my aching body.

Most of the campsites had showers, but depending on the time of day and how many campers there were, hot water was never a guarantee. I've never taken so many cold showers in my life.

It's amazing how fast you can get used to something, though. Even the most uncomfortable things like sleeping on the ground and taking cold showers can begin to feel normal. And really, as long as you've got a hot guy to snuggle up to at night, it's all worth it.

I've held up my end of the bargain by not complaining

along the way. Well, not too much, anyway. But damn, this shower feels amazing. I turn and lean my head back, letting the water run through my hair.

I think about the past few weeks of my life and how much things have changed for me. Not just because of Mason, but because of all the people we've met along the way. All the things I've tried that I never would have imagined myself doing before this trip.

I think about the baby that Mason and I created and wonder if it's a boy or a girl. I wonder if the little one is doing okay in there and how long it will be before I get to see his little heartbeat again. The scrape along my side is healing fast and there hasn't been any cramping or bleeding, so I think I'm in the clear. I have no idea how or when to tell Mason about the baby, though. Will he be mad at me for keeping it a secret all this time?

And I can't shake the feeling that he's still keeping some secret of his own. Something that holds the key to the last of the walls around his heart.

We're so close now, I know it. So close to a real commitment that would change both of our lives forever.

All three of our lives, really.

When I get out of the shower, Mason is gone, but there's a pink gift bag sitting on the bed, with a note.

My eyes grow wide and I rush over, pull the tissue

paper out and reach inside. My hand connects with soft fabric and as I hold it up, I realize it's a dress. I nearly collapse onto the bed in a fit of happy giggles. For someone who has a walk-in closet that's bigger than this room, it's been so hard for me to live out of a tiny little bag the past few weeks. A new dress—even one with no recognizable brand—is like heaven right now.

How did he possibly have time to go buy this? Was I really in the shower that long?

And where has he gone now?

I open the note he left for me and all it says is:

Get dressed, baby. I'm taking you out tonight.

I run my hand along the scrawled words. Baby. It makes my heart soar. And a real date? This is something we haven't done yet on our trip and it fills my stomach with butterflies. Why is he going to all this trouble to make tonight special?

We've been on such a strict budget this entire trip. This hotel stay alone is costing a fortune compared to the campsites, and now the dress? I hope this doesn't mean he's almost ready to go home and is spending what's left of the money so that we can have a fun last few days on the road.

I push the thoughts away. I don't want to think about what might happen to us when we go home. I know I can't go back to the way things were. I can't go back to being his piece on the side while he parades a new girl in my face every weekend. There are only two choices now.

Either we're together or we're not. There can be no in between for us. Not anymore.

Behind me, the door opens and Mason walks in. He's carrying a large brown paper bag.

"Thank you for the dress," I say, holding it up to my body again. "It's beautiful."

He laughs and touches my wet hair. "Did you just get out of the shower?"

I make a face. "Yes? Was I really in there that long?"

He laughs. "An hour? Maybe longer?"

"No way," I say. I bend to get a look at the clock beside the bed. It's ten after seven. "Holy crap."

"Yeah, hope no one else in the hotel needs to shower tonight or they're in for a rude awakening."

"Welcome to my life for the past three weeks," I say. I giggle and let my towel drop to the floor. "I'll get dressed."

His eyes travel over my naked body and he tightens his grip on the paper bag. "You better hurry," he says. "I'm not sure how much longer I can hold onto my self-control."

I throw the dress on the bed, then make a show of walking over to the chair where I left my bag last night. I find my bra and panties and take my time getting dressed, like the opposite of a strip tease.

The Moment We Began

Mason sets his bag down on the desk, then leans against the wall and watches, his eyes devouring me. I love it when he looks at me like that. It's raw and pure and real. There's no room for lies or deception or misunderstanding. There's just desire.

I finally end his agony by pulling the dress over my head. It's a simple off-the-shoulder white dress with lace around the bottom and a skirt that's gathered around the waist and poofs a little at the bottom. I adore it. After wearing nothing but the same dirty cutoffs and tank tops for nearly a month, it may as well be couture.

I pull my hair to the side and turn around in front of him. "Zip me up?"

He takes his time, slipping his warm hand inside and running his fingertips down my spine with one slow, deliberate movement that sends a fire through my body. When he gets to the bottom, he zips the dress up, then kisses my neck and pulls me close to him.

If I wasn't anxious to see what he has planned for the night, I'd just tell him to unzip me and get back into bed.

But this is the first time he's done something sneaky like this and made plans for us, so I want to know. I want to experience whatever it is that's coming next.

"What's in the other bag?" I ask.

He smiles and opens the brown bag. He pulls two

scratched up pairs of boots out and hands one to me. "I hope they fit," he says. "I thought we should at least try to look the part if we're going out."

I laugh and pull the brown leather boots on. They're a perfect fit. I have no idea how he knew my size, but when I look in the mirror, I'm so excited about our date I can hardly stand it.

"How did we afford all this?"

A twinge of worry eats at the corners of my happiness. If we still have weeks to go on the trip, he wouldn't be spending so much on the past couple of days.

"Don't worry about that," he says. "We saved so much in Little Lake that we can afford to live a little and have some fun while we're here. I didn't spend that much, really. I got all this stuff at a thrift shop around the corner. Besides, tonight is very special."

"Oh?" I say, my heart fluttering. "Why is that?"

One side of his mouth lifts in a smile that has mischief written all over it. "You'll see."

I watch as he pulls a white button-up shirt and a dusty black cowboy hat out of the bag. He dresses quickly, pulling on his boots and dusting off the hat before placing it perfectly on his head. Damn, he looks good as a cowboy, especially with that little bit of scruff on his face giving him a slightly rugged toughness.

The Moment We Began

I have never been so excited about a date in my life.
I just pray it's a beginning and not an ending.

Chapter Fifty-One

"Where are we going now?" I ask after dinner.

"You'll see," he says. "Wait here and I'll pull the truck around."

I stand in front of the restaurant. It's the first time we've eaten at a sit-down place that cost more than ten or fifteen bucks since we left Fairhope. The food was delicious, and it was fun to be dressed up again and feeling pretty.

As I'm waiting for him, I wonder at how quickly perspective can change. Three weeks ago, I would have complained about the food at a place like this. I would have said it was too crowded or too common. I think back to all the times my friends wanted to go out to grab fast food or sit down at a chain restaurant. Sometimes I went and complained about it, but sometimes I insisted on going to a nicer place, proclaiming that I would pay the check if we could go to the more expensive place.

Thinking about it, I'm amazed I have any friends at all.

Why didn't anyone ever just say no? Or tell me I was being a snotty bitch? Other than Jenna, none of my friends ever really said no to me or told me they thought I was acting selfish. That girl is one of the few friends I've made who doesn't seem to give a shit about my money or making me happy. But Jenna is a rarity.

Most of my friends have gotten used to just going along with whatever I want. I never really thought of myself as a bully, but that's sort of what I was. I insisted they all do what I wanted to do, thinking that if I paid for it, that made it okay to order them around. And what was worse, I made them feel bad about the places they liked, telling them that those places weren't good enough for a girl like me.

I'm feeling ashamed of myself and when Mason opens the door for me, he touches my arm.

"Is something wrong?" he asks. "You didn't like the restaurant?"

I shake my head. "It's not that," I say. "I'm having an amazing time."

He frowns as I climb into the truck. He closes the door and comes back around to the driver's side. "Do you want to talk about it?" he asks as he drives away from the restaurant. "I really want tonight to be fun. Did I say something that upset you?"

The Moment We Began

I'm touched that he noticed my mood without me having to say a word, but I don't want to destroy his plans.

"It's not you at all," I say. "I was just thinking about the way I used to be. Before this trip. I was kind of a bully, wasn't I?"

His eyebrow twitches a little. "I wouldn't call you a bully," he says. "You've just always liked things the way you like them."

"And anytime someone wanted to do something or go somewhere I didn't like, I offered them money to change their mind and do it my way."

He cringes. "You're making it sound a lot worse than it really was, Pen."

I shrug. "I don't know," I say. "I'm trying to think of one time when I didn't get my way and was happy about it. No complaining. No condescending remarks. Just a selfless acceptance of whatever the group decided."

He's quiet, and I wonder if he's trying to think of an example. He shouldn't waste his time. I already know the truth. I just don't know why I never saw it for myself.

"I was standing outside that restaurant thinking what a perfect night it's been so far and wondering how many perfect nights I've missed out on, or ruined, because I was focused on the wrong things," I say. "I should have been happy with the people I was lucky to spend time with instead of concentrating on the quality of the food or the prices on the menu."

He pulls the truck into an empty lot and turns to face me. "You aren't seeing the whole picture," he says. "There's nothing wrong with expecting excellence or wanting the best in terms of food or atmosphere or whatever. The problem isn't that you want those things or that you value those things. The problem is that you valued them above the people you were spending time with. I used to do the same thing. If I couldn't have a drink in my hand and there wasn't good music blasting out of the speakers, I wasn't there. I started to kind of hate myself."

I shake my head. "How is it possible that we've changed in such a short period of time? Do you think when we go back we'll be able to hold onto this feeling? This knowing? Or do you think we'll go right back to the way we used to be after a while?"

He smiles. "Maybe we'll have to plan a road trip like this once a year," he says. "Just to keep our feet planted firmly on the ground."

It's the first time he's talked about any plans for the future. Strange he mentioned keeping our feet on the ground, because I suddenly feel like I'm floating.

"Now, I have one last stop before we can head back to the hotel," he says. "Are you up for it?"

The Moment We Began

I wipe a tear from the corner of my eye and nod. "Absolutely," I say. "Let's do it."

He puts the truck in gear and drives us out of the empty parking lot and back onto the main road. We drive for a while before he finally pulls into the parking lot of a large building with these two huge neon boots on top of it.

My confusion only lasts a second, but then I read the name of the bar.

Knockin' Boots.

Chapter Fifty-Two

Inside, it's exactly how I would have imagined a Texas honky-tonk.

The floors are a beautiful wood that's scuffed and scratched on the dance floor from years of wear. There's a band on stage and country music blasts through the dance hall. Couples dressed just like us dance around the floor. I walk forward and find an empty space just off to the side so I can watch.

The only kinds of clubs I've ever been to have either been country clubs where mostly older couples dance cheek-to-cheek or nightclubs where everyone's bumping and grinding and sweating like pigs.

This, though, is something different entirely. On the floor, I see couples my age and couples older than my grandparents all dancing the same basic steps. A few fancy couples add in some extra swirls and whirls, but others seem more than happy sticking to the basics. There's a railing that goes in a circle all around the dance-floor, separating the watchers from the dancers. And on top of the railing is a ledge where people can set their drinks while they stand and chat and watch.

Mason leads me to a place along the railing, then tells me he's going to go grab a few drinks.

I can't take my eyes off the dancers. There's a strange beauty in the way they move. It's all variations on a theme. Everyone an individual, yet also part of the group.

When the song changes, the dance changes with it. This one's a slow song and couples come together. But it's not the kind of stand-in-one-place swaying back and forth kind of slow dance I'm used to seeing. These couples glide together across the floor, almost moving collectively in one big circle.

I stand watching until the slow song ends, then realize that Mason should have been back by now.

I lean over, trying to figure out where the actual bar is in this place. I search the crowd in the direction where he went, but don't see him anywhere. With their hats on, all the men in this place seem to blend together in the darkness outside the center.

I don't dare go looking for him. We might never find each other again in this crowd.

When Delores said her brother managed a bar in Texas,

The Moment We Began

I imagined some rinky-dink little place with sawdust on the floor and an outdated jukebox. Maybe four or five tables scattered about. Knockin' Boots is massive compared to what I pictured. And it's a Saturday night, so the place is totally packed.

Maybe the bar is just really backed up. Or maybe he went around asking about Delores' brother. I don't really have any choice but to stand here and wait, but I start to wish I'd just gone with him.

After the song ends, there's a break in the music. A tall man with graying hair steps out onto the stage and whispers something to the lead singer of the band. The crowd on the dance-floor stops and turns to see why the music has stopped.

"Good evenin' foks," the man says. "My name is Lester Jenkins and my wife Caroline and I would like to officially welcome y'all to Knockin' Boots."

The crowd cheers. A few people let out whoops and whistles.

"Now, I know this is a little unorthodox for us on a Saturday night, but I've had a special request that I just couldn't refuse. I hope you won't mind indulging us a little tonight. What do you say folks, do you want to hear a special song from a brand new friend of mine?"

I turn in the direction of the bar again, tempted to just

345

forget my decision to stay put and go look for him after all. There's no way it's taken him fifteen minutes to get a drink. Maybe he got lost.

The crowd dies down and from out of the silence, the music begins.

A single guitar, simple and soft. My eyes naturally drift back to the small stage.

That's when I see him.

Mason walks up to the microphone stand and takes it in his hands. The guitarist moves to the side and behind him, the rest of the band gradually joins in. A steel guitar. The drums. Keyboard.

I raise my hand to my heart and press it hard against my chest. Tears sting my eyes. I'm so surprised, I'm laughing and crying at the same time. I lean forward against the railing, wanting to be closer. Not wanting to miss a single detail of this moment.

His fingers grip the mic effortlessly, like he's not even nervous at all. I watch in awe, unable to believe this could be real. Did he do all this for me?

Seeing him there, my heart has never been so open or so fragile.

And when he begins to sing, the world around me quiets to nothing. In this moment, there's no one on earth but the two of us.

The Moment We Began

I recognize the song instantly. It's an older song by Garth Brooks. She's Every Woman. I used to listen to it on repeat when I was younger and going through a country music phase where I couldn't get enough. He used to tease me about it. How could he possibly remember that? It was years ago.

Something about this song always left me with a longing inside.

It's all about a woman who is everything to her man. She's complicated and beautiful and difficult, but to him, she's both his fantasy and his reality. Through the good and the bad, he's come to appreciate her for all that she is. Not just a woman up on a pedestal, but a real woman, flaws and all.

I have always wondered what it would feel like to be that to the man I love. To know that he loved me so much, I was the only one he could see. To know he didn't want anyone else.

Mason makes the song his own. It's slower, more deliberate. Each word is a direct line to my soul. And his voice. Oh, god, his voice is perfection. Smooth and effortless. Strong and true. And it makes it even more special because I know he's singing for me.

To me alone.

And for the first time in all the years I've loved him, I

know he loves me too.

Chapter Fifty-Three

When the song is over, the crowd is silent for several beats. No one moves, including me. The emotion Mason put into that song was raw and beautiful.

I've never seen him so vulnerable.

I've never loved him so much.

The applause that comes next startles me. I can't clap. It isn't enough for what he's just done. All I can do is watch him. Wait for him.

He stands and searches for me through the crowd. He lifts his hand against the lights, then jumps down off the stage and heads straight for me.

The crowd on the dance-floor parts as he walks through, even though the band is starting back up and the dancing has returned to normal.

My feet move on their own. I'm pulled toward him like a magnet and no one around us matters or exists.

I follow the railing around to where it opens and he meets me there.

We connect through our eyes, our souls, our hearts. And when he touches me, an electricity passes between us.

I fall into his arms and his mouth descends on mine.

And this first kiss of true love is different from any other we've shared. It's not all fire and lust and urgency. There's only strength and trust and total, glorious surrender.

When we part, the connection is still there. It binds us to each other.

He takes my hand and leads me onto the dance floor.

"I don't know how to dance like this," I say.

"I'll lead you."

He pulls me into his arms and guides me around the circle. I'm awkward at first, my feet unsure. But he's surprisingly good at this.

On the slow dances, he holds me close. We barely speak, but I don't need him to say a word. I just need him to never let me go.

We dance several dances, but then he slowly pulls me off to the side and kisses me again. He puts his cheek to mine and whispers, "There's something I want you to know," he says. "The reason I chose that song was because I wanted you to understand. You're every woman to me. All this time we've been together, there's been no one else,

Penny. Only you."

I touch his hand. "I know," I say. "I trust you."

He smiles and shakes his head. "No, I'm not talking about this trip," he says. "I'm talking about all the time since that first night on the boat a year ago. The night we first got drunk and made love. You have no idea how hard I'd been trying to resist you. How long I wanted you before that night."

I stop, pulling away to study his face in the dim lights of the bar. "What? What are you saying?"

I hear him, but he's not making any sense.

"I'm saying there's been no one else. Not since that night," he says. "There's only been you."

Tears well up in my eyes. "But I saw you with those other girls," I say. "I watched you flirt and tease and date and touch them. I saw you."

"I never brought a single one of those girls into my bed. I swear it."

I breathe in, still not believing this could be true. "Then why would you let me think you had?" I ask. "Why would you torture me like that?"

He leans down and presses his forehead to mine. "I'm so sorry," he says. His voice is so soft I can barely hear him over the music. "I never meant for any of this to happen between us. I wanted to keep my distance from you, because

351

I knew that if I let myself love you—if I admitted that to myself or to you—it would change my whole world. I thought that if I allowed myself to love you, I would lose you. The way I lost Rachel."

Tears fall silently down my cheeks. I don't know what to say. I don't know how this can be true.

"I tried to keep that first night from happening, but after it did, I couldn't stay away from you," he says. "It was all I could do to make you think I didn't care for you. I pushed you away so that you would hate me, but you never gave up on me. Then, after your accident, I knew I had to get away from you. I was so scared that I was the cause of everything bad in your life, and I couldn't face that."

He pulls me close so that my head is resting against his chest and his arms are tight around me.

"But when you showed up that morning with your tiny little bag and that look of hope in your eyes, I knew I was a goner," he says. "I knew I couldn't resist you anymore. And all I could do was hope that once we got away from Fairhope, I wouldn't be such poison to you."

"You've never been poison to me," I say, looking up into his eyes. "All those stupid things I did? I did them because I was crazy at the thought of losing you forever. If I had known you felt the same way about me, everything would have been different."

The Moment We Began

"I realize that now," he says. "It just took me a long time to understand that I'd rather have you now and lose you than to never know what it feels like to be in your arms."

I lift up on my toes and kiss him, my lips soft against his. "You aren't going to lose me," I say.

He stiffens and looks away. "I hope not, Penny," he says. "But there's something you need to know. Something I haven't been able to tell you about. It could change everything between us."

I place my hand on his lips. "Not tonight," I say. "Tonight, let's just be together. Let's just let these walls down and love each other. Tomorrow, we can share any secrets we have left."

I think about the baby and how I'm not quite ready to tell him. I'll tell him tomorrow.

He nods. "Okay," he says. "Let's go back to the room. I want to make love to you so bad I can't stand here one more minute."

We walk hand-in-hand off the dance floor and out the front door. The ride from the bar to the hotel lasts an eternity. I ride snuggled close to him, my head resting on his shoulder, his free hand entwined with mine.

There's a buzz between us. It's nothing anyone could see by looking at us. It's just something new that vibrates there between us. Something like hope.

In the parking lot, he lifts me into his arms and carries me through the lobby and down the hall to our room. When we're inside, he lowers my feet to the floor.

I lift up to kiss him, but he puts a finger to my lips, stopping me. He slips his hands around my face and stares into my eyes.

"I love you, Penny," he says, his eyes shining. "I know it took me a long time to get here, and I know I've hurt you in the past. I'm sure I don't deserve you, but I promise I'm going to love you with all that I am for the rest of my life."

"You have no idea how long I've wanted to hear those words from you," I say. I lift my hands to his and hold them tight in my own. "I love you, too, Mason. I've always loved you."

I lift up on my toes, pulling him down into my kiss.

He takes his time, exploring my mouth with his. There's no sense of urgency, but the passion is still there. It smolders between us like hot coals.

He undresses me one small piece at a time, letting his fingers trail a thousand paths across my skin. I shiver and moan under his touch as he explores me. When I'm naked beside him, I start to reach for the buttons on his shirt, but he moves my hand back to my side, a sly smile on his lips.

He bends down, tracing the same paths of his fingers, but this time with his lips. He moves with such tenderness, it takes my breath away. He kisses my neck, then travels down my chest to the peaks of my breast. He teases them with his tongue and I lift up, wanting more.

Below, his hands run like rivers down the valley between my legs. He slips his fingers inside of me. I moan and beg as he teases and kisses and moves above me, igniting a need so raw and deep that I ache for him.

His mouth weaves a trail of wet kisses downward and he places himself between my thighs, spreading me open. He lifts me up and my breath hitches in my chest as his mouth descends on me, his tongue teasing each fold and peak. I move against his mouth, my hands clutching the sheets as he brings me higher, then pulls away, and then goes back for more.

I bury one hand in his hair as he closes his mouth over me, dragging me to the edge of desire. I cry out as pleasure floods through me. My body bucks and trembles against him. He pulls away and kisses the inside of my thigh, his fingertips dragging across the skin on my legs. I lay there, breathless, my chest rising and falling and my heart pounding against my ribs.

When my breath has slowed and my body has melted into a pool of tingling warmth, he rises up and takes off his shirt. I come up on my knees and help him, one button at a time. He surrenders the job to me and I push the shirt from his shoulders and toss it to the floor. I lift his white undershirt up and over his head, then run my hands down along each ridge of his abs.

I slide my fingers around the edge of his waistband and look up into his eyes, wanting him to see just how much I want him. His lips are parted and I can feel his heart beating in time with my own.

I unbutton his jeans and push them down, then lay him back so I can pull them from his body. I crawl on top of him, leaving his boxers on so I can tease him the way he teased me. I straddle him, my heat centered above the length of him. He tries to lift his head and touch me, but a smile plays at my lips as I push his back flat against the bed.

I lower more of my weight onto him and he makes a low sound deep in his throat and throws his head back against the pillow. I take my time, running my fingertips along every inch of his arms and neck and chest. I use the lightest, feather-soft touch I can and his body trembles beneath me.

When my hands reach the waist of his boxers, his eyes fly open and he grabs my hips, lifting himself up so I can feel his hard length grinding against me.

I lick my lips and move to the side, slowly pulling that final barrier away from him so that we are fully naked together.

The Moment We Began

I run my hand up and down his legs, across his waist, making a circle around him. His breath is coming faster now and I know I've teased him long enough.

I watch his face as I finally close my hand around him, moving up and down slowly.

He closes his eyes and lets his mouth open as he draws in each tortured breath. His hips move against the bed as I caress him and his body shakes as I lower my mouth onto him.

There's a great release of his breath as I take him in, inch-by-inch. I taste him with my tongue, teasing the tip and moving my hand up and down, applying more and more pressure.

He moans and reaches his hand toward my back, running his palm against my spine, then tensing with need.

Before I can do more, he lifts up, taking control. There's fire in his eyes. Passion.

He moves on top of me and my legs part and lift around him. He hovers just at the opening, his hand on my face and in my hair. His eyes never leave mine.

"I love you," he says.

"I love you, too," I whisper.

Mason enters me, then. A slow, controlled movement at first as our bodies are joined together. I slide my arms around his neck and lift my hips to meet him. His rhythm grows faster. He moves deeper inside of me, filling me, completing me. We make love, and tonight I feel more than just our bodies connected. I feel his heart.

I feel his love.

The passion between us grows to a beautifully tense moment, then he releases into me.

I wrap my legs around him, holding him there as he shudders with one final thrust, never wanting this connection to falter.

Never wanting this moment to end.

Chapter Fifty-Four

In the morning, we wake up and make love again.

I am so used to seeing him open for only brief moments of time before he shuts himself off to me again. But this morning, he's still here and he's still in love with me. It wasn't a dream, and for the first time since we left Fairhope, I know he won't be walking away from me at the end of this.

As I lay here, I daydream about what it would be like to get our own place together. Or maybe even move away from Fairhope. We could build a house near Little Lake and raise our child there by the sea in Alabama.

I'm on the verge of falling asleep again, my body entwined happily with his, when someone knocks on the door of our room.

I lift up, yawning. "Did you order room service?"

Mason sits up slowly, his face tense and his jaw clenched. "No," he says. "Maybe they have the wrong room."

When they knock again, Mason gets out of bed and quickly pulls his jeans on. There's fear written across his face, but what does he have to be afraid of? My parents? Even if they've come looking for me, there's nothing they can do to us now. We don't need their money and we're free to make our own choices.

But I see his hand tremble as he reaches for the doorknob.

The second the door cracks open, Bernard Hunter, my father's bodyguard, pushes through.

I gasp and pull the sheets up to cover my naked body.

"Get the hell out," Mason yells, pushing Bernard backward. "You have no right to charge in here like this. Have some fucking decency."

Bernard rears back and punches Mason so hard, his head jerks to the side. I scream and draw up on my knees.

"Stop it," I shout. "Leave him alone."

Bernard ignores me and pushes past Mason. He leans down and snatches my dress off the floor. "Get dressed," he says, tossing it toward me on the bed. He never looks directly at me, but instead turns and stands between Mason and me, his legs parted and his arms clasped behind him. As if I somehow need protection from Mason.

Anger bolts through me.

The Moment We Began

How dare this guy push his way into our private hotel room. I'm not a child. I don't belong to anyone but myself.

"You have no legal right to be in this room," I say. I yank the dress over my head and reach back to try to zip it on my own. "What the hell is wrong with you?"

"As far as your parents are concerned, you're a missing person," he says. "They've been looking for you for weeks."

"I wasn't missing." I stand and come around the bed. I go to the door and open it. "I left on my own and told them not to follow me. I'm an adult, I have every right to go where I want to go without my parents' permission. I swear, if you don't leave now I'll call the police."

Mason stands beside me. He rubs his jaw and eyes Bernard with pure hatred. When Bernard doesn't make a move to leave, Mason steps toward him, but I put my arm out, stopping him.

The last thing we need is for him to punch Bernard and end up going to jail for assault or something stupid. My parents are very good at making legal matters turn in their favor.

"Your parents want you back in Fairhope tonight," Bernard says. "The jet is at the airport waiting for you."

I lift my chin. "I'm not going back."

"That's not something I'm being paid to debate with you," he says. "And I'm not leaving without you. I don't care if I have to drag you to the airport kicking and screaming."

Mason steps past me and gets in Bernard's face. "You lay a hand on her, and I swear to god I'll make you regret it."

"Tripp Wright has been searching for his daughter since the day she left. My job was to track her down and bring her home, and that's exactly what I plan to do. I'm not about to let some punk like you stand in my way."

Mason's hand closes into a tight fist, but I rush up and wrap my hands around it. "Don't," I say. "It'll only make things worse. They'll make it out like you assaulted him. You don't want to give them any more power than they already have."

He slowly releases his fist, but his eyes are still boring into Bernard. "She doesn't have to go with you," he says. "And you can't make her leave."

"I think Penny has a right to decide for herself," Bernard says.

"I've already made my decision," I say.

Bernard casually steps toward the window and opens the curtain a little, letting the light inside. "You don't have all the facts yet," he says. "Once you find out what's really been going on in Fairhope since you left, you might change your mind."

The Moment We Began

Fear bubbles up inside me. "What do you mean? Is everyone okay?"

Beside me, Mason's shoulders tense and he turns away.

Bernard stares at Mason, and I take a deep breath. What's going on here?

"About a week after you left, your father started to suspect that a close business associate had been stealing money from the company for years," he says. "Two days ago, he got proof and arrested that man."

But he's not looking at me when he says it. At first, I can't figure it out. Why is he looking at Mason when he says this?

I look to Mason to see if he has any idea what's going on, but instead of confusion, Mason's staring down at the floor, his shoulders hunched.

"Mason?" I suddenly feel sick to my stomach. "What the hell is he talking about?"

Mason runs his hand through his hair and when he looks up to meet my eyes, I understand with sudden clarity.

"Your father," I say.

My muscles nearly give way and it's hard to stand. This is the secret he's been keeping from me all this time.

"You knew about this all along?" I ask.

I want him to say no. That he's just as shocked to hear this news as I am. But I already know that's not true.

Mason takes a deep breath. "I knew," he says.

The words rip into my heart, and I can't speak. I move to sit on the edge of the bed, my vision blurring.

"Mr. Trent embezzled over five million dollars from your father's real estate and corporate deals over the course of the last ten years," he says. "Your father has suspected it for some time now, but it wasn't until recently that he was finally able to prove it. After your little accident with Mason's car, in fact. The title on that car led to some pretty conclusive evidence that was enough to get an indictment against Mr. Trent."

I have a death grip on the white sheet draped across the bed. I'm scared to move or react.

"How long have you known?" I ask Mason.

He doesn't answer at first. He paces the floor at my feet.

"How long?" I look up and his eyes flicker to mine, then away again.

"I figured it out over the course of a few years," he says. "I overheard a few conversations I shouldn't have, here and there. I saw a few papers lying around the house. It all started to add up."

"Dammit, how long, Mason?" I ask.

I'm scared to hear what he has to say. But I have to know. It's important.

"About six years."

The Moment We Began

His answer stuns me. Knocks me back. I stand up, anger and shock turning to rage. "You've got to be fucking kidding me," I shout. "Six years? Mason, how could you let it go on? Why didn't you tell me?"

"Tell you what?" he asks. "Hey, by the way, my father is stealing from your father and I want him arrested and put in jail, my family humiliated for the rest of our lives? How could I do that? Who could possibly make that kind of choice?"

I don't want to believe this could be true.

A wave of dizziness crashes over me. I collapse onto the edge of the bed, then slide down all the way to the floor. How could he have known about this for six years and never once mentioned it? How could he have continued to come to our house and eat with us and act like everything was okay?

"And that's really why you left town, isn't it? Because you knew after I wrecked the car that it was only a matter of time before they found out."

He looks down at me, his eyes haunted. His face pale.

"I was going to tell you," he says. "But I could never bring myself to do it. I was too scared you'd leave me, and once we got on the road, I knew I couldn't live without you."

I let my head fall into my hands. "Your car. Your money. That whole rich-boy act of paying for everyone's

365

drinks and leaving outrageous tips," I say, thinking back to the way things were before we left. "That wasn't even your money to spend, and you knew it."

He falls to his knees in front of me. "Penny, I'm so sorry," he says. "Can't you see that this is why I always kept you at arm's length? Why I wanted you to think I was bad for you? Because I am. The whole time you've known me, I've been a complete fraud who didn't deserve you. I still don't deserve you."

"You lied to me," I say, tears welling up in my eyes. "I don't care about the money. Regardless of what your father did, you lied to me about why you were even leaving. You weren't interested in getting back to basics and reconnecting with your past. I can't even believe I bought that fucking bullshit. You just wanted to get the hell out of town before everything came crumbling down on your family. You left because you were too chicken to stand and face it when everyone realized what your dad was doing."

He presses his lips together and they tremble slightly. "How can you say that to me after all we've been through? You know this trip has meant more to me than that," he says. "And you were the one who showed up begging me to bring you along," he says, standing. "It's not like I invited you to come with me."

"No, you were just going to walk away without an

explanation. You were going to let Preston and me find out the hard way while you skipped town on us. Why did you even agree to let me come if you knew it was going to end like this?"

"I tried to tell you no, but the truth is, I wanted you," he says. "God, Pen, I have wanted to be with you for so long. I mean, really be with you. Yes, I knew eventually someone was going to find out about my dad and you would probably hate me. After you totaled my car, I knew this whole thing was a ticking time bomb. I thought it would be best for everyone if I just disappeared. If I got out of your life once and for all so I couldn't hurt you any more than I already had. Then you showed up with your bags and your shiny eyes, looking at me with such hope and love. How was I supposed to resist you? How was I supposed to just walk away? And yet you were the one who said you'd let me walk if we could just have these few weeks together. If we weren't in love by the end of this, we could walk away. Well, I'm still here. And I love you."

I pull my legs tight against my chest, a terrible headache throbbing at my temples. Tears seem to come all the way from my throat, traveling some invisible line of tension and anger and sorrow from my neck to my eyes. They spill down my face like a waterfall.

"I never expected to fall this hard," he says. He kneels

down in front of me again and puts his hands on mine. "I never expected to love you so much that the thought of losing you would tear my insides out. I know it was wrong to keep this from you for all this time, but I was going to tell you, I swear. This is what I was talking about last night when I said there was something I still needed to tell you. Was I stupid to believe that you could love me enough to forgive me?"

Sobs shake my body and I can't catch my breath. I don't know what to say to him, and I don't think I could speak right now if I tried.

He waits for me to calm down, but before either of us speak, Bernard steps forward.

"There is already a warrant out for Mason's arrest," he says. "He's been named as an accessory to his father's embezzling scheme."

I lift my head and Mason stands, his face pale and scared.

"What are you talking about? I had nothing to do with that."

"You were a willing participant. You drove a car you knew was purchased with stolen funds," he says. "You spent money from an account after you knew the money was stolen. You might not have been the mastermind behind the scheme, but according to the law, you were an accessory to your father's crimes and Mr. Wright intends to prosecute your entire family to the full extent of the law."

Mason closes his eyes, his jaw tight.

I am teetering on the edge, unable to process all of this at once.

And that's when Bernard drives the stake into my heart.

"Penny, your father is waiting for my call." He makes a show of looking at his watch. "If he hasn't heard from me in the next fifteen minutes, he's also pressing charges against Mason for kidnapping."

"Kidnapping?" I stand up. "That's ridiculous."

"If the two of you try to run, he'll also issue formal charges against you, Penny," he says.

"Me? For what?"

Bernard raises one eyebrow. "A certain stolen diamond bracelet that turned up in a pawn shop in Savannah."

The room spins and my knees give out.

Mason runs to my side. "What's wrong?"

I bite down on my lips until my vision stops blurring. My head is spinning and nausea rolls through me.

"I know you wouldn't want Penny to be in jail in her condition," Bernard says.

Mason's head jerks up. "What condition?"

"Don't you know?" Bernard asks.

I suck in a breath as I look up at him.

No. Don't.

I say the words in my head, but can't do anything to stop him before he opens his mouth again and my entire world tilts sideways.

"Penny is pregnant."

Chapter Fifty-Five

Mason looks at me, confusion and wonder in his stormy green eyes.

He lets go of his hold on me and stands, backing away. His mouth is open and he clutches his chest.

"I was going to tell you," I say, my breath shallow and rough.

"How…" He shakes his head. "When?"

"I found out after the accident," I say. "When they took me to the hospital, they do routine blood tests to check. The doctor told me early that morning."

He swallows. "So you've known this whole time?"

I nod, my eyes never leaving his face.

How did this all become such a mess? Such an impossible, fucked-up mess?

"This isn't how I wanted you to find out," I say. "I wanted to tell you when the time was right. When I could say for sure that you loved me for me and not just for our baby."

"You have ten minutes to make a decision, Penny. After that, you're father files kidnapping charges," Bernard says. "I'm sure you don't want the father of your baby to spend several years in prison because of your choices."

My head snaps toward Bernard. I grind my teeth and stand. "He can't do that," I say. "It isn't true. I came on my own. All I have to do is tell them that and charges will be dropped."

Bernard chuckles. "You should know better than to think your father can't make something like this happen," he says. "If your father wants Mason to go down for this, he'll do whatever it takes and you know it."

I want to gouge his eyes out with my bare hands. I rush toward him, wanting to hit him. To make him pay for coming here and ruining what this could have been.

But Bernard grabs my wrists and holds me away from him.

"You're not in your right mind," he says. "I can testify to that if I have to. Besides, you're a thief and a liar. You're unstable."

"You son of a bitch," I say, twisting my arms until he releases me. My wrists sting.

"Seven minutes," he says. "You have a choice to make.

The Moment We Began

You can either come quietly and avoid sending your baby's father to prison on kidnapping charges for the rest of his life. Or you can stay here and wait for the police to arrive and force you both into custody. Either way, you're going to be home by nightfall. The question is whether you're going to let Mason walk out of here of his own free will or with handcuffs around his wrists."

It's an impossible choice. Either way, we both lose everything.

And I know Bernard is right. My father loves me, but he'll do whatever he has to in order to get what he wants. My whole life I've watched him bring people down with a single phone call to a friend. So many people owe him favors at this point, he can make anything happen. He can make anyone disappear.

And I'll never forgive myself if I let Mason go to prison because of me.

I turn and Mason's gaze meets mine.

He shakes his head. "Don't do it, Penny," he says. "We'll fight it. If you walk away now, you know they'll let never let us be together."

"They'll never let us be together anyway," I say. "Can't you see that? If I go with him, at least you're free."

"No, I'm not," he says. "They'll still press charges for my father's mistakes. I'll be on the run from this my whole life. Besides, without you, I might as well be in jail anyway. And knowing we're going to have a baby together? That changes everything. If you walk away now, then this trip hasn't taught you anything. You left so they couldn't control you. So that you could make your own choices and follow your heart. If you give them control over you—over us—they'll own you for the rest of your life."

"Three minutes," Bernard says. He pulls his phone from his pocket and my heart squeezes so hard in my chest I think it might explode.

Tears trickle down my face and my head throbs. "I'm sorry," I say to Mason. "I can't let you go to jail for this."

I turn to Bernard and nod.

Mason slams his fist into the wall as Bernard dials my father's number and tells him I'm on my way home.

"I don't know what else to do," I say to Mason. "I don't want to lose you."

He turns to me, anger hardening his face. His eyes are cold and hollow.

"You just did."

Chapter Fifty-Six

My father's jet is waiting for us at the airport in Houston. The flight home takes about five hours, and I stare out the window for most of the trip.

I have never felt so betrayed in my entire life.

By my father. By Mason.

By myself.

It doesn't seem real that he's gone. I was so happy out on the road with Mason. I was a better person just for being with him. He was right all along. I had always thought that if you stripped away the money and the jewelry and the expensive clothes and the fancy car, I would be nothing more than a hollow shell.

But on this trip, I realized that those other things are the shell. The money and the name doesn't make me who I am. It never has.

It took getting away from all of that to finally

understand it.

I was really beginning to love that version of me.

And to finally hear Mason tell me he loves me was the single happiest moment of my life.

When he made love to me, I felt transformed. I was ready for a life with him, even if we spent it in a tent on the beach without ever having more. All I wanted was him and this baby. We could have been a family.

But as real as it all seemed—as close as I thought we had gotten—there were still these lies that stood between us. Even if I could learn to forgive him for keeping the truth from me about his father, he might never be able to forgive me for walking away. But what choice did I have? My father is too strong. Too powerful. Without money and resources, we wouldn't have been able to fight him. We wouldn't have stood a chance.

And without complete honesty and trust, we didn't really have love. We may have had something that felt like love or looked like love, but without trust, it was all an illusion.

Mason called himself a fraud. And that's what he was. The whole time he was riding around town in his Porsche and spending money left and right, he knew that money was stolen from my family. And he still had the nerve to be a part of our lives. He still had the nerve to sleep with me and lead me on and to call himself Preston's best friend.

He knew he didn't deserve our friendship, but he took it anyway.

Mason betrayed us.

Still, no matter how much I damn him for his mistakes and his choices, inside I know I've made just as many bad choices. I've messed up just as many times. What right do I have to judge him?

How am I going to live without him?

I lie down on the white leather sofa in the main cabin of the plane and wrap a lush brown blanket around my body.

I don't even want to think about what my parents will say. I don't know if I will ever be able to forgive them for pushing me like this. For demanding I leave the one man I've ever loved—the father of my baby—to come home and be with them. I always knew my father was a shrewd man, willing to step on whoever he had to in order to get what he wanted. But I never dreamed that included me.

My heart is broken.

No, even the word broken does not come close to describing how I feel.

Devastated.

Ruined.

Obliterated.

There is no word strong enough.

I miss Mason so much already. I miss the feel of his arms around me. I miss his laughter and the way he'd tease me by lifting that one eyebrow, looking at me like I'd gone crazy. I miss everything about him.

By the time the plane touches down, I'm hit with the realization that I've made a terrible mistake. I've made the wrong choice.

And the thought of never being with him again destroys me.

Chapter Fifty-Seven

My parents meet me as I come off the jet.

Mom's eyes are ringed with red and she throws her arms around me and pulls me tight. "My sweet baby girl," she says. "I was so worried about you. I was so scared you were never going to come home to us."

I don't say anything. I hug her back, but I'm only going through the motions.

Dad stands to the side. He has no words for me, and I have nothing to say to him.

But Preston is the one who holds onto me. The moment his arms close around me, I burst into tears. He holds me and lets me sob into his shirt.

"I'm so sorry," he whispers to me. "I tried to talk to them and convince them to stop, but they wouldn't listen."

Preston takes my small bag and puts one arm around me as we all walk to the car and head home to Fairhope.

In the car, no one says a word. The tension is palpable.

It's still almost a fifteen minute drive from the small airport here to our house, and on the way, I can only hope my parents will have the decency to give me my space. I did what they asked. I played along even though it meant surrendering my own hope for the future. I hope they will at least give me time to deal with it in my own way.

I pull my legs up into the seat and lean my head against the window, watching the miles pass us by. I don't think about the future or about the things that happened on the trip. I clear my mind, concentrating on the trees along the side of the road. We're going so fast, they start to blur together. That's when I realize I'm crying again. Even if my mind has closed off, refusing to think of the things that will hurt me, my heart still knows.

My heart won't let me forget what I've done.

Preston puts a hand on my arm and when I look over, he motions for me to scoot closer. He opens his strong arms to me and I crawl inside, just like I've done a thousand times. Preston is my rock, and I'm so glad he's here with me.

He holds me as we cross the county line. He holds me as we pass the Solo gas station where Mason and I stopped before we left town. He holds me all the way until Dad pulls the car through the gate and our house appears.

Preston opens the door, but before he lets go of me, he

squeezes my shoulder and whispers in my ear. "No matter what, I'm here for you, sis," he says. "Everything is going to be okay. I promise."

I hug him back, then get out of the car. I stare up at the house where I grew up. It looks exactly the same as it always has, but it feels different. I guess because I'm different. For the first time, I'm seeing this all through the eyes of someone who didn't grow up in a place like this. I'm seeing it through the eyes of people like Delores and Walt and Buddy. People who take nothing for granted and who fight for everything they have and everything they love.

Before, this was always just my house. I didn't see anything special about it. It was just the house where we live.

But now, I see the ridiculousness of it. I can see why people think we act so high and mighty. After all, I just flew in on a private jet, drove home in a special edition Lexus, and came through a gated entrance to a house with over fifteen thousand square feet.

And none of those things could ever be enough to make me happy. None of it could ever replace what I had with Mason, sitting by the fire or holding each other inside a tent, our warm bodies pressed together in the darkness.

"Come inside, sweetheart," my mom says. "We'll get you something to eat."

I nod, but don't follow her inside right away. I stand there for another minute, staring up at the house, thinking about just how much I've changed since I left. How fast I would trade all of this for one more moment with him.

How I might never get the chance to make that choice again.

Chapter Fifty-Eight

I walk down the hall toward the stairs, but my mother's heels sound on the marble entryway and I pause.

"Penelope? Honey? Your father and I have a few things we need to talk through with you," she says.

I take a deep breath and push back the tears and frustration. I force them down so deep I can no longer feel them. I force myself to be numb. Heavy. I prepare myself to just take whatever they're going to dish out to me. I just need to survive it, then when I'm alone, I can feel whatever it is I'm feeling.

For now, I'm nothing.

The only thing that holds me to this life is the baby growing inside of me. As long as I have that, I can hold on to some hope that I can find Mason and that he will forgive me for what I've done. Hope that we can forgive each other and start again.

I turn and nod, then follow her into the living room. I'm still wearing my dirty cutoffs and boots. Ironically, it's very similar to the outfit I was wearing when I walked out of this house almost a month ago. I feel so out of place here with all the ornate decorations. I feel like this simply isn't where I belong anymore.

Out there, it didn't matter what I was wearing. I felt beautiful and sexy, because Mason made me feel that way.

But here, in this room with its pristine white couch and vases of fresh flowers, I feel wrong. I feel lesser.

My father stands behind the couch, his hand on the back. Mom sits down just under him and pats his hand for encouragement.

I sit in a straight-backed chair across from them.

Preston walks in with a tray full of ice waters. He sets them on the coffee table, then grabs one for himself and steps to the side.

I put my head down, playing with the fringe at the edge of my shorts. I wait. I already know what's coming. I already know what they're going to say and that no matter how they try to justify what they've done, I won't hear them. I won't listen.

I feel sick to my stomach and the room is hot. I swallow and take a deep breath. I want one of those ice waters, but when I start to reach for one, a sharp pain in my side stops me. I cry out and move my hands to the spot, doubling over.

Preston grabs a water, then rushes over to me. "You okay?" he asks.

For a second, it hurts to breathe. I wait for the pain to pass, then sit back in the chair. I take the water and lift it to my lips. The cold water is amazing in this heat. "Thanks," I say. But inside, I'm terrified. The doctor told me to watch for cramping, but the first time it happened, I thought maybe I had simply stood up too fast. My hands tremble and I clutch the glass tighter. "I'm fine. Just stressed out and tired."

Preston's eyes are clouded with worry. "Can't we do this some other time?" he asks, turning to them. "Penny's been through so much. She's in no condition to listen to this right now."

"Sit down, son," Dad says.

Preston doesn't move from my side.

"Penny." My dad says my name and I look up at him. I clutch the glass in my hand so hard, I'm surprised it doesn't break. He waits until I'm looking at him before he continues. "I cannot even begin to tell you how worried we've been. We had no idea if you were even alive. Do you understand how difficult these last few weeks have been for us?"

I'm not sure he really wants an answer, so I stay quiet. My role here is to listen. To take whatever punishment they choose to give. But what they don't realize is they can't hurt me anymore. They've already taken everything they can take from me.

"When the maid came to us with that note of yours, we didn't know what to think," he says. "We thought maybe you were just acting out after we took away your privileges and your spending money. We thought maybe you were just trying to make a point, so, as hard as it was, we decided to let you go. We thought you'd be gone for a few days. Maybe a week at most. We knew you were with Mason, and at the time, that made us feel some comfort."

He pauses. He makes it sound like I was only able to go because he allowed it. He let me go. In his mind, even after all this time, he still thinks he owns me. He still thinks he's in control of my destiny.

"After a week had passed without even a single phone call from you, we started to get worried," he says. He moves from behind the couch and takes one of the ice waters. He takes a sip, then sets it back on the tray and begins to pace the space between the couch and the window. "We made a simple call to the cell phone company, but I suppose you know what we found out when they searched for your cell signal."

I look down again. I pull my legs under me in the chair, wanting to curl into a little ball.

"How could you do something so reckless? So stupid?"

The Moment We Began

His voice is angry. Cold. "What if something horrible had happened to you while you were on the road? What if we had never found you?"

I can't even look at him.

"But I suppose that was the whole point, wasn't it? To make us worry? To punish us for what you thought was unfair?"

"This wasn't about you," I say, looking up. Making sure he sees my eyes.

Preston puts his hand on my shoulder. I know he's trying to tell me to be calm and to just be quiet and let Dad say what he needs to say. But I can't let this go on. I can't take it any longer.

"If you want to know why I left why don't you just ask me? Why do you have to assume that what you think is right? Why do you think you're the only ones with all the answers? I'm here now. Just ask me why I left."

"We know why," my mother says. Her voice is angry and her hands are shaking as she stands. "You left to be with that boy. Someone you've had a silly schoolgirl crush on since you were twelve years old and who never loved you back. Mason Trent will never love you, Penelope. What did you think? That if you got knocked up, he would suddenly have some kind of epiphany and realize you were meant to be together? He was using you. Why can't you see that? He was—"

"Stop it," I shout. I stand up, my hands by my ears. "I won't let you talk about him like that. If you think that's the kind of person Mason is, then you don't know him at all. And if you think I was trying to trap him into something, then you apparently don't know me at all either. I'm not going to sit here and let you talk to me this way after what you've just done."

I stand up and head toward the door, but my mother reaches for me, grabbing my arm and turning me toward her.

"Everything we did was for your own good," she says.

"See? That's exactly what I'm talking about." I look straight into her eyes. I want her to see that she doesn't control me. "You don't want to give me the freedom to figure anything out on my own. You want to fix it for me. It's been that way my whole life. I mess up and you guys swoop in and take care of the consequences. How am I ever supposed to learn about life if you never give me the freedom to live it? Yes, I have made some mistakes, but they are my mistakes. My choices. I should have every right to make those choices for myself without you forcing me to do what you want."

A wave of dizziness washes over me and my knees grow weak. I reach out and my mother throws her arms around me, holding me up.

The room is spinning and my entire body flushes with fever. A new pain stabs me low and I cry out. I can't hold on to my thoughts. Everything begins to blur together and I double over, clutching my stomach.

"Penny?"

Preston's hands are on my back. He and Mom try to lead me toward the couch, but I can't take another step. Another cramp seizes my stomach and I fall to my knees.

Then I feel a gush and something hot and wet and sticky trickles down my leg. I look down and see nothing but red. A river of red.

Please, don't let this be happening.

Voices around me are muffled, growing distant. Someone puts a soft pillow under my head, but I'm only half-aware of the movement around me. All I can feel is pain and absolute terror.

I close my eyes, darkness reaching for me. Someone yells my name and they flutter open again.

My mother is hovering over me, her eyes full of horror.

Then another wave of pain consumes me, and I give in, the darkness pulling me under.

Chapter Fifty-Nine

"Miss Wright, can you open your eyes for me, sweetheart?"

I hear the voice, but it's mixed with the sound of sirens. I try to open my eyes but can't. All I can see in my mind is blood.

"Penelope, I need you to try to open your eyes. Stay with me, okay?"

I don't recognize the woman's voice, but I concentrate on trying to force my eyes open.

They flutter and images go past like rapid pictures. A woman leaning over me. She's dressed in some kind of uniform.

An IV in my arm. My mother sitting next to me, her eyes filled with tears.

My eyes close again. They're so heavy, it's hard to keep them open. I feel like I'm going to throw up, but I can't find my voice to tell anyone, so I suffer in silence.

"My baby," I say, but my voice doesn't work.

We come to a stop and people rush all around me. I'm lifted up, then down again. Pushed down a bright white hallway.

I hear my mother saying she demands to be with me, but someone won't let her go wherever it is they're taking me. I reach up, forcing my eyes open again. I try to open my mouth, but I can't speak. I feel so weak, but somehow I manage to find my mother's hand and hold on tight. I see the doctor nod his head.

"Thank you," Mom says. "You're going to be okay, Penny. Everything's okay."

I'm cold and shivering. The pain is still there, but it's weaker now. More distant.

The terror, though, is close.

"Stand aside, please. We're going to move her over to the bed."

Hands slip under me, then move me from one bed to another.

I feel another gush between my legs and moan in fear. I thought my heart couldn't break any more, but this is life at its cruelest. My heart breaks in my chest with every second that ticks by.

"Penny, are you experiencing cramping?" the nurse

asks.

I nod and press one hand against my stomach. It hurts so bad, my head is spinning.

"What's happening?" I say, finally finding the strength to speak. "Is my baby going to be okay? Please."

I watch the nurse begin cleaning up the pad on top of the bed. It's covered in blood. I turn away as she removes it and places another pad down.

All I can think about is the bad choices I've made. This is all my fault. The drinking. The accident. The stress of carrying this secret.

"Miss Wright, I'm very sorry, but it seems you're having a miscarriage," she says. "We're going to give you some medication to ease your pain and something else to ease any nausea you might be experiencing."

I try to sit up, but the nurse puts her hand on my shoulder.

"Just try to relax," she says. "We're going to help you through this."

"No, don't give me any medicine that might hurt the baby," I say. "I don't want to hurt the baby."

Someone puts a pillow behind my head, lifting me up. I look over and see a kind-eyed nurse.

"Thank you," I say.

She nods and pats my hand. "We're going to do

everything we can to make you comfortable," she says.

I lay back against the pillow, tears falling down my cheeks and into my hair. Why are they talking like there's no hope? There has to be something they can do.

I need to be strong. I have to be strong for my baby.

"I'm here," my mom says. "I'm right here beside you."

I realize with a sudden force that the one person I want by my side right now is hundreds of miles away.

Mason is the only one I want here. He's the only one who would understand what this feels like.

"I need Mason," I say. I search my mother's eyes. "Please. Can you find him?"

My mother strokes my hair. "Penny, you've got to let him go," she says. "Maybe this is for the best. I know it doesn't seem like it right now, but you'll see. Everything's going to be okay."

Rage flares through me, white hot.

I release my mother's hand and pull my cheek away from her caress. "Don't ever say something like that to me again," I say. "Get out."

"Penny." She shakes her head. "Sweetheart—"

"Please, someone get her out of here," I say.

A nurse touches my mother's shoulder. "Maybe it would be better if you waited outside, Mrs. Wright," she says. "Penny's under a tremendous amount of stress right now and we need to do everything we can to keep her calm."

My mother protests, but the nurses usher her from the room.

For a moment, I'm alone in the room and everything is quiet except for the beating of my heart on the monitor.

I lay my hands against my belly and pray that there's another heart still beating somewhere deep inside.

Chapter Sixty

"There's someone here to see you," the nurse says. "If you're feeling up to it."

I sit up. "Who is it?"

I want her to say it's Mason and that he's come back for me.

"Leigh Anne Davis," she says. "She's been waiting out there for a little while and I thought maybe you might like some company."

I swallow, my throat dry and cracked from crying. "Yes, thank you."

Leigh Anne peers around the side of the door, her eyes wide and full of mixed emotions. Sorrow. Fear. Sympathy. She takes my hand and sits down by my side.

"I'm so sorry," she says. "What did the doctor say?"

I take a ragged breath. It feels like ages since I talked to the doctors, but I've lost track of time. "He said there isn't much hope," I say. My voice trembles and I have to take a moment before I can continue. "He did an ultrasound and for now, the baby seems to be fighting. I got to see his heartbeat, still strong and flickering away, but with that much blood loss, it doesn't look good."

"Isn't there something they can do?"

I nod and sniff, my nose running from crying so much. "They're giving me some progesterone, but he said that it might not be enough to prevent a miscarriage. All I can really do right now is wait and see. He said he'll be back in the morning to do another ultrasound. He said that since the bleeding has slowed down, if the baby can make it through the night, there's a good chance everything will be okay."

"That's good news, then," she says.

"I don't know how I'll survive if there's no heartbeat on that monitor tomorrow morning," I say, my face crumbling. "I don't know how I'll be able to walk out that door and keep living."

She squeezes my hand. "I know," she says. "But you will. You're strong."

I shake my head. "I'm a mess," I say. "I'm not strong like you are."

She smiles, her eyes filling with tears. "You've always been strong, Penny," she says. "And stubborn as hell. If that baby is anything like you, it's not giving up without a fight."

The Moment We Began

I laugh and hope she's right.
Maybe I'm stronger than I think I am.

Chapter Sixty-One

When the door opens and Dr. Mallory walks in, I hold my breath.

I close my eyes and pray for good news.

Fear and hope wrestle through me. There have been so many times lately when I wasn't sure if I was facing a beginning or an end. The path was unclear. The future was uncertain. None of those moments have been as difficult as this one.

I don't know what I'll do if he tells me my baby is gone.

I don't want this to be an end.

Leigh Anne stands up and moves around to the other side of my bed so the nurse can roll the ultrasound machine closer. I bite my lower lip, staring at the screen.

"How are you feeling this morning?" he asks.

"Better," I say.

"No more cramping?"

I shake my head. I don't want to answer questions. I only want to see that screen. To know which path I'm headed down.

Before he can get started, a commotion breaks out in the hallway. I sit up, my heart pounding in my chest.

There's shouting and something clangs against the wall. The doctor stands as two men push through the doorway.

As soon as green eyes meet mine, my heart leaps.

My world shifts and in that instant, strength flows through me.

Bernard tries to hold him back, but Mason can't be stopped. He punches Bernard in the face, knocking him backward. My father is close behind, shouting, but it's too late for them. Right now, there is only us.

"You can't be in here," Dad says, stepping forward.

"Like hell I can't," Mason says. He doesn't back down one inch. "This is my child's life on the line here, and I have every right to be here. You can threaten to lock me up all you want, but I'm in love with your daughter and I'm going to be here by her side through this whether you like it or not."

He turns to me, his expression full of worry and love. And forgiveness.

He crosses the room in three easy strides, then collapses at my side.

The Moment We Began

"Are you okay?" he asks. "Is the baby okay?"

I shake my head. "I don't know," I say, taking his hand in mine. "The doctor was about to do another ultrasound to see if the baby's heart is still beating. I'm so glad you're here."

Dr. Mallory walks to the door, waving everyone else out of the room. "I'll give you two some privacy," he says. "I'll be back in a few minutes."

"I didn't make it five miles from the hotel before I turned around," Mason says when we're alone. "When I got back to the room, you were already gone so I drove to the airport and caught the first flight home. I called Knox and when he told me you were in the hospital, I..."

He takes a breath, his eyes filled with tears.

"I made the biggest mistake of my life letting you walk out that door," he says. "I should have stood by you no matter what. I should have come back with you and faced whatever it was they wanted to do to me. Penny, you're the only thing in this world that matters to me. You and this baby. I love you with every ounce of my soul and I promise, if you give me another chance, I will never hurt you again."

My heart pieces itself back together again with every word from his mouth.

I pull him into my arms. I cling to him, my love for him overflowing. "I love you, too," I say. "I won't ever let anyone stand between us like that again. My future is with you, Mason. I want to start a family with you and I don't care if we have to live in a tent for the rest of our lives, I just want to be with you."

He laughs and puts his hands gently on my face. Tears spill onto my cheeks. He kisses my forehead, then wraps his arms around me. We hold each other like that for a long time, both of us feeling the gravity of this moment.

I have loved him for so long, but until now, there has always been something holding us back. Secrets. Doubt. Fear. Family.

But all that falls away as we surrender ourselves completely to love. A love so real, it reaches in to the deepest part of me and makes me whole again.

When the doctor comes back in, Mason takes my hand in his and holds tight. "Whatever happens from here, we'll face it together, okay?"

I nod and take a deep breath, gathering strength from him.

"Are you ready?" Dr. Mallory asks.

Mason leans forward and places his lips against my fingers. We both stare up at the black screen.

Neither of us can breathe as the doctor begins the ultrasound.

He moves the wand around and at first, there's nothing.

The Moment We Began

Only darkness.

Then, a flutter of movement.

I gasp, watching our baby's heartbeat flicker on the screen. The doctor flips a switch on the machine and the room fills with a whooshing sound, strong and steady. It's the most beautiful sound I've ever heard in my life. It's the sound of hope and strength and love.

Mason laughs, tears streaming down his face. He leans forward, pressing his soft lips against mine.

In that moment, nothing stands between us. No more lies. No more walls. All our past mistakes are erased.

We've been given a precious gift. A chance to start over. To make every choice count. To take nothing for granted.

And in that moment, we begin.

Epilogue

Two months later

"Are you sure you're feeling up to this, baby?"

Mason takes my hand and helps me out of bed. He puts his arm around me with such tenderness, walking me toward the closet.

I laugh. "I'm fine, hotlips."

He groans and rolls his eyes. "Are we back to that now?"

"Hey, I'm still searching for the perfect pet name for you," I say. I disappear into the closet of our brand new house and call back, "Eventually something's gonna stick."

"Please, just don't let it be hotlips or sugarbear or studmuffin," he says.

I start to suggest another, equally sugary name when he comes up behind me and wraps his arms around my waist, his hands resting on my belly. I'm just starting to really look pregnant, and I love it. Mason is always touching my little bump. He even sings to my belly every night before we go to sleep, which always makes me smile.

I never dreamed we could be so happy.

"I can tell them we need to wait another week or two if you're not feeling up to all the walking around," he says.

I turn and hook my arms around his neck, smiling. "I'm fine," I say. "The doctor says the baby is doing great. I still need to take it easy, but I'm not on bed rest anymore. Besides, it's just a walk around the garden."

"It's an entire afternoon of party planning," he says. "I don't see why you can't just let your mother handle the Christmas Memories event again this year. You can boss everyone around next year."

"Ha ha," I say. I turn and look through some of the maternity clothes Leigh Anne and Jenna picked out for me from the local thrift store. I choose a simple pair of black leggings and a long red tunic. "This is very important to me, and I don't want to put it off for another year. Besides, it's a big deal for my mom to step aside and let me take the lead on such a major charity event. I promise I won't let it put any stress on me or the baby. All my friends are pitching in. It'll be fun."

Mason kisses my forehead. "I'm going to get all the

packages together and put them in the car," he says. "I'll see you in a few."

As I dress for the day, I think of how far we've come in such a short time.

My parents released their hold on the trust fund I received from my grandparents, and Mason and I used some of the money to purchase this little house on the edge of town. It's small, but there's a cute bedroom for our little one and it's going to be plenty of room for the three of us.

We put some money away in savings for a rainy day, but used the bulk of it to start a new charity called Rachel's Kids in honor of Mason's sister. The money we raise will go toward helping families without insurance coverage pay for their kids' medical treatments. As a way to heal our relationship, my mother offered to let me plan the annual Christmas Memories dance this year. And instead of sending the money we raise to a larger international charity, we'll be donating all the money to Rachel's Kids.

There's still a lot of healing to do between me and my parents, but it's a start and I'm glad they're trying.

When I'm dressed, I walk into the living room to help Mason with the packages. We've spent the last few days putting together care packages of food and other supplies to take to the local homeless shelter.

I look at my watch and realize we're running late.

"We've got to get going," I say as I come around the corner. "Delores and Buddy are probably already at Mom's. I'm so excited about having them cater the event this year."

Mason is standing in the living room, a small square box in his hand. It's wrapped in red paper with a big white bow.

"What's that?" I ask.

"An early Christmas present," he says.

I turn my head and narrow my eyes at him. "It's only November," I say. "You shouldn't be buying me early Christmas presents."

"It's not for you," he says, a grin spreading across his face. "It's for the baby."

I take the package from him and tear the paper off. I open the box, wondering what in the world he's got up his sleeve.

"For her first camping trip," he says.

I giggle and throw my arms around him, drawing him into a kiss.

Inside the box, wrapped in tissue paper, is a teeny little pink sleeping bag.

Read all the books in the Fairhope series:

The Trouble With Goodbye
The Moment We Began
A Season For Hope
The Fear of Letting Go

About the Author

Sarra Cannon writes contemporary and paranormal fiction with both teen and college age characters. Her novels often stem from her own experiences growing up in the small town of Hawkinsville, Georgia, where she learned that being popular always comes at a price and relationships are rarely as simple as they seem.

Her best selling Young Adult paranormal series, Peachville High Demons, has sold over 125,000 copies and been featured on Amazon's Top 100 eBooks for Children & Teens. The first book in the series, Beautiful Demons, will be adapted into a graphic novel by Sea Lion Books later this year, and a spin-off series will begin in 2014.

She is a devoted (obsessed) fan of Hello Kitty and has an extensive collection that decorates her desk as she writes. She currently lives in North Carolina with her amazingly supportive husband and her adorable son.

Made in the USA
Middletown, DE
12 November 2019